Books by Joanne Pence

Something's Cooking

Too Many Cooks

Cooking Up Trouble

Cooking Most Deadly

Cook's Night Out

Published by HarperPaperbacks

SOMETHING'S COOKING

JOANNE PENCE

HarperPaperbacks
A Division of HarperCollins*Publishers*

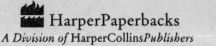

HarperPaperbacks

A Division of HarperCollins*Publishers*

10 East 53rd Street, New York, N.Y. 10022-5299

This is a work of fiction. The characters, incidents, and dialogues are products of the author's imagination and are not to be construed as real. Any resemblance to actual events or persons, living or dead, is entirely coincidental.

ISBN 0-06-108096-9

HarperCollins®, 🔥 ®, and HarperPrism® are trademarks of HarperCollins*Publishers*, Inc.

Cover illustration © 1997 by Moline Kramer

First printing: April 1993

Printed in the United States of America

Visit HarperPrism on the World Wide Web at
http://www.harpercollins.com

❖ 10 9 8 7 6 5 4

This book is dedicated to Rose and Pancho, and to the whole, wonderful Italian side of my own family—with much love.

1

Wine Eggs Mornay. Poached Eggs on Canapés with Cheese Fondue Sauce. Soufflé Aux Blancs D'Oeufs.

Angelina Amalfi tossed the recipes aside. They'd never do. They were simply too common.

She sat cross-legged on the floor of the den in her Russian Hill penthouse apartment. Stacks of recipes sent to her by readers of her food column—as well as those she'd clipped over the years from other newspapers, magazines, and fund-raiser cookbooks—lay scattered around her. It was Sunday. She had barely one hour left to fax Monday's column to the newspaper, but even so, she was being choosy. She needed a recipe that was eye-catching and appealing, perhaps with some particularly interesting ingredient.

She ran her fingers through her hair in frustration, then let herself slump, her elbows on her knees and her head in her hands.

How could a sweet, little old man like Sam have failed her this way? He frequently contributed to her column. Her readers loved his unique recipes, as did her editor. And Sam enjoyed seeing his words in print, even if they were only recipes. When he had called that morning and said he had a recipe for her next column, she had offered to meet him at a nearby park to pick it up. Nice though Sam was, she felt uneasy about inviting him to her home. Besides, he dyed his hair black, and something about a man in his late sixties with hair the color of Count Dracula's was just plain weird.

They should have met two hours ago, but he hadn't shown up. She had waited for him for over an hour, enjoying the warm October sun, and then hurried back to her apartment to meet her deadline.

She frowned as she glanced at the unrelenting clock.

Chocolate Meringue. Almond Mocha Torte. Italian Rum Cake. Yes, these recipes were much more her style than the ones for breakfast foods Sam usually gave her.

There was a knock on the door to her apartment. Now what? she wondered. She didn't have time for interruptions.

The knocking grew louder.

Irritated, she stood up and stuffed her silk blouse back into her slacks as she hurried through the elegant, antique-laden living room. She reached the front door and swung it open.

No one was there.

Puzzled, she stepped onto the plush carpeting of the hallway. The well-polished doors of the elevator were closed, as was the door to the stairwell.

All was quiet.

As she turned back, she saw a small, brown package, about the size of a pound of butter, propped up against the doorframe. She looked around again, puzzled, and then picked it up and walked back inside, kicking the door shut as she searched for the sender's name and address. There was none.

Who would hand-deliver a package to Occupant?

Occupant! She'd been interrupted, her deadline upon her, for nothing but a lousy sales pitch? These advertising companies were getting pushier every day.

She stomped into the kitchen to toss the package into the trashbag under the sink, then hesitated. Today was Sunday. Would a sales delivery be made on a Sunday?

The package was heavy for its size. Quite heavy. She gave it a little shake.

Nothing seemed to move inside. She raised it to her ear and shook it again. A soft *tick-tick-tick* filled the cold silence of the kitchen.

She shuddered. This was silly. She reached for the string binding the package, but her hand shook. She clenched her hand a moment, then relaxed and tried to touch the string again. She pulled her hand back as if burned.

This was nothing short of foolish, she told herself. Still, it might be even more foolish to take chances.

The police. She'd ask them what to do. She laid the package on the counter above the dishwasher and tiptoed backward out of the kitchen. Once in the living room, she looked up the special phone number her father had given her from his friend, the police commissioner. She avoided relying on her father's money or influence under normal circumstances, but a mysteriously ticking package was definitely not normal.

"Police," a youthful sounding voice answered.

"My name is Angelina Amalfi. Commissioner Barcelli told me to use this number if I ever needed special assistance."

"Yes, ma'am. This is Officer Crossen. What can I do for you?"

"I've got a strange package here."

"Yes?"

"It's wrapped in brown paper and it ticks."

"Someone sent the package to you?"

"It was left at my door. It's marked Occupant."

"Occupant? Are you sure it's not some advertising campaign? A sample from Timex or something?"

That gave her pause. "Are you suggesting I open it and find out?"

"No, ma'am. Please don't do that. I'll send someone out right away. He'll take care of everything. What's your address?"

"1010 Green, apartment 1201. What should I do in the meantime?"

"It's probably nothing dangerous, but to be safe, don't touch it."

"But it's in my kitchen!"

"That sounds like a good place for it, ma'am." She hung up.

She went back to the kitchen and stood in the doorway, looking at the package. Her kitchen was a food columnist's dream. She loved her over-sized, fire engine red stove imported from France, her Cuisinart, espresso machine, Belgian waffler, pasta maker, her Magnalite pots and pans, Henckels knives, cast-iron bakeware, microwave, and even her electric wok. These things filled her shelves, walls, and snowy white Corian countertops. Was the ticking louder, or was it her imagination? She should leave the package alone, as the policeman said, but then he didn't seem to think it was a bomb. No one would send a bomb to Occupant, for pity's sake. But if it did go off. . . .

She hurried across the kitchen, opened the door of her dishwasher—a Maytag, advertised as indestructible—gingerly placed the package inside, locked the door, and spun the dial to start the water flowing. Whatever the wretched thing was, she'd just defused it, she hoped.

She returned to the living room and sat down, one hand against her chest, breathing deeply to still the rapid pounding of her heart.

A loud blast from the kitchen shook the walls and rattled the windows. Angie clutched the arm of the sofa as a Dali lithograph fell off the wall, shattering its glass facing.

A puff of smoke and plaster dust billowed out of the kitchen doorway. Over the ringing in her ears, Angie heard the hiss of a stream of water.

No need for panic, she told herself.

Reaching for the phone, she fought to keep her hand steady as she punched the number. "Officer Crossen, please." She couldn't quite control the quiver in her voice.

"Officer Crossen, this is Angelina Amalfi. Don't bother to send a bomb expert. Send a plumber."

2

Sunday afternoons during football season were quiet times in Homicide. On this day, the 49ers were on T.V., the fog over San Francisco Bay had lifted, and the October sun shone bright and warm.

The city was lazy, enjoying the mellow warmth of Indian summer before the chilling winter rains began. The Hall of Justice, a massive, gray, granite structure, cold and intimidating, stood quiet without the chaos that routine police business brought during the week.

The few inspectors on duty spent their time catching up with reports and other paperwork or, more likely, with the Sunday crossword puzzle. They relaxed in the certainty that nobody would get killed until the postgame brawls began.

All except one. San Francisco Police Inspector Paavo Smith rubbed his chin as he looked over the office. It was too quiet, too peaceful. They had a name for it out here: earthquake weather.

Paavo leaned his long, angular frame back in his chair, propped his feet up on his desk, and skimmed through the stacks of papers in front of him. Ten-plus years on the force had taught him not to expect anything of particular interest in all the official memos. He wasn't disappointed.

Had the vending machines offered anything better than cold coffee, warm Coke, or brittle candy bars with stale nuts, he would have considered battling one for a snack—anything to block out this disturbing sense that something was going to happen.

He glanced over at his partner. As usual for a Sunday afternoon, Matt Kowalski was fast asleep, his head cradled on his arms on the desk top. The fluorescent light twinkled off the bald spot on his crown. Paavo sometimes referred to Kowalski as Sleeping Beauty, all six-foot-five, two hundred fifty pounds of him. Yet he envied this man who was able to sleep with such ease throughout their years on the force as rookies, as beat patrolmen, and now, as partners in Homicide.

Over the years Paavo had come to trust Matt's laid-back competence and professionalism and appreciate the way he never intruded into Paavo's life. He accepted Paavo's silent, intense ways. Paavo was a self-contained man who believed for many years that loneliness was preferable to loss. But Matt's easygoing nature, along with the thoughtfulness and warmth of Matt's wife, Katie, had worn down Paavo's resistance. A strong friendship had gradually grown between them.

Paavo stood and stretched. If Chief Hollins could see Matt now, he'd keelhaul him without the benefit of a boat. But then, Hollins never showed up on Sundays.

He walked to the window. This part of town was far from the tourist areas. It was bleak and dingy with soot from the freeway that ran too close by. With his back to the others, he rested his forearms against the center rail of the double-hung windows and gazed at the broad street below, feeling wistful at the quiet passage of the warm afternoon.

At two P.M., the telephone rang. Paavo lunged for it as Matt jumped up like a punch-drunk fighter hearing the bell for round ten.

Less than fifteen minutes later, the two of them were standing beside a body. The man had been killed, it appeared, by a single bullet in the chest, then shoved under bushes in the small, hillside park one block below the crest of Russian Hill.

Matt held back the bushes as Paavo made a careful search of the body. The victim carried no identification. He was a thin, white male, in his late sixties or so, with hair the color of black Grecian Formula at the ends and white at the roots. Old, clean, but ill-fitting clothes, the kind bought at thrift shops, made the man look like a harmless pensioner—except for one small detail. Using his handkerchief, Paavo plucked a six-inch switchblade from the victim's jacket pocket and held it up for his partner to see.

Their eyes met. Silence communicated their years of shared experience with sudden, violent death. Old men with switchblades, children with guns, and quiet women with deadly rages were a part of the landscape of destruction so familiar to them.

Paavo laid the knife and handkerchief on the ground, stepped back, and stared at the body. Death brought no serenity to the faces he had gazed upon at murder scenes over the years. Pathetic vulnerability, terror, and fragility were the characteristics he discerned. Old men should die in bed, and Paavo was commissioned to find those who had deprived their victims of that final dignity. Even after more than ten years, he still believed in that duty.

When the deputy coroner took over, Paavo watched a moment, then thrust his hands into his pockets and walked to the uppermost part of the park, where the views were broad and the air didn't hold the stench of death.

He was about to leave the murder scene when a report of an explosion in a nearby luxury apartment came over his radio. He was told to get over there to see what was going on and that the bomb squad would be right behind him.

"Was someone killed?"

"Not clear," the dispatcher said. "A rookie took the call. Said the woman, who's friends with the Commissioner, was kind of hysterical. He thought she said to send a plumber. Must have said 'coroner.' Guess the woman wasn't the only hysterical one. The Chief says Homicide needs to take a look."

As Matt headed downtown to begin working on the identity of the body, Paavo got into his car and drove the short distance to the apartment.

By the time Angie put down the receiver, the pounding on her front door had already begun. Her next-door neighbor, Stan, called out her name, as did Edith, the widow who lived on the floor below. A loud thud shook the door.

"I'm okay!" She sprang from her chair and crossed the room. "Don't break the door down."

As she opened the door, Stan lunged toward her and grabbed her arms, his brown eyes owlish. "What was that noise? It sounded like a bomb."

Already the hall was filling up with people trying to see what had happened.

Angie's gaze snapped back to Stan's boyish face. "The kitchen."

He dropped his hands and rushed into the apartment. Smoke had billowed into the living room and was hovering against the ceiling.

"Oh my God!" Stan cried as he stood in the doorway to the kitchen. "Oh my God!"

Edith and the others from the lower floors could contain their curiosity no longer and rushed inside.

Angie pushed her way past them to see for herself. Despite the explosion, she had not expected the sight before her. Squinting against the smoke and dust, she saw that the dishwasher door had blown off its hinges and made a hole in the plaster on the far wall. The inside of the dishwasher looked like the inside of a barbecue pit, and water was everywhere. While Edith opened windows, a man from a ninth floor apartment, with whom she'd never even spoken, crawled under the sink and shut off the valve.

Stan pressed his hands against his lips. "Oh, Angie, it's so horrible. I didn't know a dishwasher could do that!" He looked faint.

"Be brave, Stanfield." She took his arm and pulled him into the living room. "They're really no more dangerous than refrigerators."

"But if you'd been loading it you could have been . . ." He shivered noticeably.

His unspoken words rocked her with greater force than the blast, and her carefully structured world began to spin. Images of her parents and sisters flashed before her, and how they would have felt if . . .

She groped for the back of a mahogany dining chair, trying to block out what he had said, the stricken way he looked. Her fingers clutched the chair and she leaned forward, willing her head to clear.

A while passed before she looked up again. When she did, she saw a dark-haired man standing in the doorway to her apartment, surveying the scene. Tall and broad shouldered, his stance was aloof and forceful as he made a cold assessment of all that he saw.

If you're going to gawk, she thought, come in with the rest of the busybodies.

He looked directly at her, and her grip tightened on the chair. His expression was hard, his pale blue eyes icy. He was a stranger, of that she was certain. His wasn't the type of face or demeanor she'd easily forget. And someone, it seemed, had just sent her a bomb. Who? Why? What if this stranger . . .

As he approached with bold strides, her nerves tightened. Since she was without her high heels, the top of her head barely reached his chin.

The man appeared to be in his mid-thirties. His face was fairly thin, with high cheekbones and a pronounced, aquiline nose with a jog in the middle that made it look as if it had been broken at least once. Thick, dark brown hair spanned his high forehead, and his penetrating, deep-set eyes and dark eyebrows gave him a cold, no-nonsense appearance. His gaze didn't leave hers, and yet he seemed aware of everything around them.

"Your apartment?" he asked.

"The tour's that way." She did her best to give a nonchalant wave of her thumb toward the kitchen.

She froze as he reached into his breast pocket. "Police." He pulled out a billfold and dropped open one flap to reveal his identification: Inspector Paavo Smith, Homicide.

The relief that filled her upon hearing he was with the police department vanished when she saw the word *Homicide* on his badge. A little premature, she thought.

"I'm Angelina Amalfi. This is my apartment."
Her voice shook. She took a deep breath.

He glanced around the room. "Was anyone
hurt here, Miss Amalfi?"

"Only in spirit."

"You didn't call for the coroner?"

"The coroner? Of course not."

He regarded her for a moment, without expression. "Excuse me, please," he said as he
turned toward the crowd. "All right, everyone,
show's over. Police. Clear the premises."

At that moment, a uniformed policeman entered the room, followed by four men in blue
jumpsuits. One was carrying a black metal box.
Angie folded her arms. The bomb squad, a half-
hour too late.

She watched as Inspector Smith's merest
glance caused people to scurry away, even Stan.
She understood why. He had the harshest glare
she'd ever seen, and he used it as a weapon. The
bomb squad went into the kitchen. Inspector
Smith and the uniformed policeman glanced at
each other, then the inspector went into the
kitchen and the other stepped outside the apartment.

Angie pulled the chair she had used for support away from the dining table and sat in it,
willing her heartbeat to slow down. She was
grateful for this moment alone, this moment of
silence to get her feelings in order.

Before long, the inspector returned to the living room.

She stood up to face him again, hoping he

would tell her what was going on and that this was all just a big mistake.

He said nothing but studied her with a professional, detached air. His gaze moved over her from head to toe, ticking off her attributes—or flaws, judging from his expression. She suddenly felt self-conscious in her fluffy pink bedroom slippers.

As his gaze rose again, his eyes fixed on her hands. She'd recently had her long nails silk-wrapped and painted a deep mauve. Now she was reminded of the time Sister Mary Ignatius had given her ten demerits for wearing polish in the eighth grade.

Men usually found her attractive, but the way the inspector looked at her, she might as well have been one of Homicide's corpses. She slid her hands into the pockets of her slacks and gave a slight *ahem*. His eyes met hers, but still he said nothing. It was as if he was calculating all he saw here, her included, but the numbers weren't adding up.

Angie couldn't remember the last time she had met anyone so infuriatingly close-mouthed. He clearly wasn't a man to give false assurances, to placate her with softness or warmth. She walked to the window.

"Was it a bomb, Inspector?" She clasped her hands behind her back, her head held high as she gazed out at the bay.

"It looks like it was. We'll know exactly in a day or two."

She bowed her head. "I see. I had hoped . . ."

"Would you tell me what happened?"

She folded her arms and shrugged, looking out the window again. "There's nothing to tell. I received a package marked Occupant and threw it in the dishwasher. I always wash my mail, doesn't everyone? This time, though, it blew up. Must have been one dynamite detergent. . . ."

He waited until she had finished babbling. "I have a few questions."

"Sure, so do I. Like what's going on?" she whispered as tears welled up in her. She turned to face him, to implore, but he stood rigid and frowning. At a loss, she looked around her familiar surroundings, trying to get something to make sense to her. She touched her forehead. "Would you like some coffee?" The question struck her as so inappropriate she nearly laughed. I sound like my mother, she thought. Whenever anything went wrong, Serefina Amalfi brought out the coffee. Supposedly, it made the world a little more tolerable. Angie was ready to try anything.

"Coffee?" he asked in surprise.

"As long as my coffee maker wasn't damaged, that is."

His same impassive stare gripped her a moment. "All right. Thank you." His reply was polite and controlled, yet his acquiescence gave Angie a welcome chance to do something other than stand around and listen to questions to which she had no answers.

"Please be seated, Inspector Smith," she said, gesturing toward the small armchair beside her. She squared her shoulders and went to make a pot of Italian roast. At least I can still do that, she thought. She went into the bathroom to fill the coffee pot with water, since the kitchen water was off, then stood in the corner of the kitchen while it brewed, watching the bomb team collect the fragmented remains of her package. When the coffee was ready, she served them each a cup, and even brought one to the patrolman outside her door.

When she returned to the living room, she saw the tall, intense-looking detective folded into her delicate, yellow, nineteenth-century Hepplewhite armchair. She tried to suppress a smile. Poor man hadn't even complained. The chair squeaked in an ominous way as he turned to take the coffee she offered.

"Thanks," he said with a grateful look. It was the first glimmer of humanity she had seen from the Great Stoneface.

She sat on the sofa, her hands clasped, and waited.

He took a sip, then glanced at her as he pulled out his notebook and a pen. His hands weren't particularly large, but she saw power and strength in them. "Good coffee," he said. "Full name?"

"Angelina Rosaria Maria Amalfi."

He seemed to take forever to write it down. She smiled, wondering how badly he'd mangled the spelling. "Age?" he asked.

"Twenty-four."

"Marital status?"

"Single."

"Engaged?"

"No."

"Boyfriend?"

"Which one?"

He glanced up. "Anyone special?"

She shook her head. "Not at the moment." A slight smile played on her lips as she glanced at the dusty mess around her. "My luck's been bad in a lot of areas lately."

His eyebrows rose ever so slightly. "Do you live here alone?"

"Of course."

He pierced her with a harsh blue gaze.

"Occupation?"

"I do free-lance writing for magazines now and then, I'm working on a history of late-Victorian San Francisco, and I have a newspaper column."

"You're a columnist?"

"Yes. The *Bay Area Shopper*. It's an advertiser, published three times a week. I write a kind of offbeat food column called 'Eggs and Egg-onomics.' " She smiled. "The name was my idea. Readers send me recipes. The column has a very loyal following."

His gaze deliberately traveled over the spacious apartment with its lavish furnishings, paintings, sculptures, and million-dollar view that stretched all the way from the Golden Gate Bridge to the Bay Bridge. Her back stiffened at the skeptical expression on his face. "This is a pretty expensive apartment," he mused, as if to himself.

"Perhaps."

He swallowed more coffee and then remarked,

"I didn't know magazine articles and food columns paid so well."

"They don't."

He leaned back in the chair and stretched his long legs in front of him. "Someone, I assume, helps you out here, so to speak."

She couldn't believe his audacity. Her temper flared, but she managed to keep her voice low. "I am not a . . . a 'kept woman,' Inspector Smith. I don't see that it matters where I get the money for my apartment."

He gave her a sidelong glance and hooked his thumbs in the side pockets of his slacks. "Maybe where you get the money has something to do with what happened here today."

He looked so cocksure of himself, she would have liked nothing better than to give the chair a little shove and watch him land on the smuggest part of all. "I pay my own rent. To my father."

He pulled himself up straight. "Your father owns this building?"

She lifted her chin. "He also owns several shoe stores."

One dark brow arched. "I see." His voice was quiet, pensive.

She shrugged. "He helps keep a roof over my head and shoes on my feet. I take care of the in-between."

He glanced over her "in-between," but not so quickly that she didn't feel the force of his perusal. Then he directed his gaze at hers again.

Her mouth felt dry. "I have investments."

While appearing to ponder her words, he finished his coffee and then stood and began to pace. "Now, Miss Amalfi, would you explain to me how you came to have this bomb in your dishwasher?"

She leaned forward and rubbed her forehead, again overwhelmed by the unreality of what had happened. She wanted to scream, but instead she relayed the story in detail. She explained that she had put the package in the dishwasher because the appliance was made of heavy metal, was well sealed, and she thought the water would destroy whatever was ticking. In fact, she told him, she considered it pretty clever to have put the package in there.

"Miss Amalfi, are you aware of any enemies or people who dislike you for any reason whatsoever?"

Faces of people she knew whirled through her mind. She had dozens of acquaintances but few close friends. Her college friends were scattered all over the world, her best girlfriends from high school were married now and had little in common with her, and boyfriends drifted into and out of her life without much impact. For confidences, she turned to her family, especially her oldest sister, Bianca. She knew a lot of people from work and through her parents, and she attended most big social functions in the city, but who, out of everyone, could have reason to hate her? "There's no one," she finally said.

"Are there any connections you might have reason to worry about? Enemies of close friends, or of your family, perhaps?"

Feeling suddenly tired and frustrated, she leaned forward. She slid her fingers against her scalp, rubbing her head, as if by mere concentration she could make this nonsense go away. She felt the inspector's gaze upon her and raised her eyes to meet his. "It's impossible, Inspector."

His voice was soft when he said, "I see the impossible every day." He walked to the window and looked out toward San Francisco Bay and Alcatraz.

Perplexed, she allowed her gaze to follow him. Something about his words, his tone, set off an unnerving resonance within her. What was it about his simple words that made her, for the first time this afternoon, fear seriously that there might be a plan at work here, that she might have actually been targeted by someone? The last thing she wanted was to believe him.

He's wrong, she thought. He's insensitive, indifferent, and hateful. She studied his profile as he stood by the window. His brow was wrinkled with concentration, his lips pursed tight, and the corners of his eyes were lined with the weariness of a man who'd seen too much suffering and sorrow.

She looked away a moment. The bomb blast must have made her truly loopy to imagine any compassion in those glacial eyes.

He turned to face her. "Okay, Miss Amalfi." He tossed his notebook on the coffee table in front of her, then smacked his pen on top of it. "Write down the names of your family and your employer while I go check on my men. Then we'll get out of here for now."

She reached for the notebook, then pulled back her hand. "I'm sorry, but this is a waste of time. The more I think about it, the more I know a terrible mistake was made. There's no one after me or my family. The package must have been delivered to the wrong address."

He stood directly in front of her, forcing her to tilt her head back to keep eye contact. "People who send bombs don't make mistakes like that," he said. "That kind of thinking could be dangerous. Someone doesn't like you, Miss Amalfi. It would be best to keep that in mind."

She felt a rush of fear, and then doubt. "You're just trying to scare me."

"If that's what it takes to keep you alive, yes."

"Maybe it was a random attack by some kind of terrorist group."

"Going all over San Francisco leaving little packages in doorways?"

She hated his sarcastic tone. "Exactly. A sort of Welcome Wagon in reverse."

His eyes narrowed. "Are you afraid to give me the names of your family?"

She glared right back at him. It was plenty clear, she thought, that Paavo Smith was used to intimidating people by his stern looks and height as well as his profession.

"I can't remember the last time I was afraid of anything, Inspector Smith. For you to investigate all those names would be a waste of time."

"Look, Miss Amalfi," he said, his voice a low

growl, "if someone's out there who's interested in blowing people up, it's my job to find him. And I never waste my time on anything. So write those names down. After I check everything out, I'll think about whether it's a waste. Not before."

He walked out of the room.

Cold, arrogant S.O.B., she thought. Who does he think he is, Dirty Harry?

3

Early the next morning, Paavo eyed the thick report waiting for him on his desk. Matt must have been up all night pulling information out of the computer. Paavo took a gulp of coffee then began to go through the printouts.

The murder victim was Samuel Jerome Kinsley, a.k.a. Sammy Blade, so called because of his penchant for carving people just enough to get them to cooperate with his employers. The rap sheet on him was a foot long: burglaries, bookmaking, and plenty of assault charges. Still, Sammy was strictly small time, not the sort of guy who attracted bullets.

By the time Paavo finished looking at the early returns on Sammy Blade, Officer Rebecca Mayfield dropped another file under his nose. She was tall and had fluffy, shoulder-length blond hair and the kind of well-toned and well-developed body that resulted only from months of workouts at a gym.

"What's this, Rebecca?" Paavo stared at the title, then held up the few pages as if they were contaminated. "A bomb-squad report?"

"It's all about your exploding dishwasher," Rebecca said, struggling to keep her voice serious.

"Real funny."

She leaned against the low bookcase beside his desk. "So, what's she like?"

"Who?"

"The Amalfi woman."

"What do you mean?"

"I guess you don't read the society pages," she said with a grin.

"Sure I do. Every word."

"In that case, you know all about the Amalfis. You know they've got money, prestige, and lots of friends in City Hall, among other places. Chief Hollins wants to be sure the attack on the youngest Amalfi daughter gets top-notch attention. That is, your attention."

She's joking, Paavo thought. Why were the women around him turning into comedians all of a sudden? "My job's Homicide, remember?"

"Sorry, Paavo. You were on the scene, you got her statement. Hollins doesn't want someone else to start over. He says it'd look bad to the Amalfis."

"I don't believe this."

Rebecca placed her hand heavily on his shoulder. "Listen, if you get the feeling she's twisting you around her well-manicured pinky—the way it's said she does with men—you let me know. I'll set her straight, hear?"

He looked from the hand on his shoulder to her eyes. "There's no need, Rebecca."

"But I've heard—"

"I'll handle it."

She pulled her hand back and folded her arms. "Fine, then. You're such an expert on women, I'm sure the rest of the men should just sit back and take notes!"

He picked up the bomb-squad report, put it on the top of his stack of papers, and turned to page one.

"Just wait!" She turned and stomped down the corridor.

Trying to ignore her, he gave his full attention to the report. The bomb, he read, was a simple one, fast and easy to assemble, cheap to buy if you knew the right people, but powerful enough to kill a person standing nearby—like a person opening the box that contained it. At the very least, the bomb would maim and probably blind.

He rubbed his chin as he remembered the big, wide-set brown eyes of the Amalfi woman. They had looked like they could melt stone if she set her mind to it. She was little—"petite" he guessed was the right term for her slim, trim figure. Her short, feathery brown hair had some of those glittery "highlights" women seemed to like to put in their hair. Still, he had to admit she was an attractive woman, although his preference leaned toward tall, buxom, and blond—women like Rebecca Mayfield, in fact. But he'd never mix business and pleasure. Business was important and long lasting, while pleasure tended to be illusory and fleeting.

He glanced back at the report. By all rights, Angelina Amalfi should have opened the package, and it would have blown up in her face. Why didn't she? The women he knew would have torn the wrapping off as soon as they got their hands on it. Maybe that's what comes of being a rich girl and having so much. You don't care about little surprises, little gifts, in life. What's a freebie in the mail to a woman like her?

Angelina Amalfi was obviously pampered, arrogant, and mouthy. Women were supposed to be the salt of the earth, not stardust. Her tongue was too sharp, her chin too proud, and she wore the damnedest silly pink bedroom slippers he'd ever seen.

A homicide inspector has no business handling a case like this, he decided, suddenly irritated. Maybe that was why he'd treated her the way he had. He felt bad about it, he had to admit. He'd always been easy on victims, tried to comfort and reassure them even while his mind was already analyzing motivation, suspects, even signs of guilt. And she clearly was a victim. She could have made things a lot simpler, by just answering his questions, listening to his advice, and locking her doors. But instead she had kept up this dangerous insistence that the bomb was a mistake, as if such ugliness couldn't possibly enter the charmed, unsullied life she led.

It had, though, and now it was his job to do

something about it. He had no business letting her behavior get to him. He forced his concentration back to the report.

In addition to being rigged to go off when opened, the bomb had a timer on it. Why? To be sure it went off while Angelina Amalfi was in the apartment alone?

Whoever delivered it must have been someone who knew her habits. Or, someone who had been just plain lucky to catch her alone.

No, Paavo thought as he considered how powerful the bomb was. Angelina Amalfi was the one who was lucky. She might not be so lucky next time.

Angie clutched the sides of her head. It felt ready to explode, throbbing mercilessly every time the plumber banged on the kitchen pipes. She stared at the words reflected on the screen of her computer, trying to concentrate, but they seemed to jump and grow blurry.

That damn newspaper article about the bomb blast had caused this trouble. Her phone had rung off the hook all morning. All four of her older sisters had come by to see her, but none of them had brought their husbands or kids. She figured they were afraid more mad bombers might be lurking around her apartment. Her sisters' visits were "duty," but they must have thought it foolhardy to expose their families to danger.

She thanked God her parents were in Palm

Springs. It had been difficult enough to tell them by telephone that some stranger had left a bomb outside her apartment. Face to face, it would have been impossible. Her mother had sounded half hysterical at the news. Eventually, Angie had gotten her parents to see it in the same light as poison placed in an aspirin bottle—a random, one-in-a-million bit of bad luck. Still, it was all she could do to convince them to stay in Palm Springs and not worry about her unnecessarily.

Everyone who called was given the same story, that the bomb was a random attack. The package was sent to Occupant, after all, and she'd never done anything interesting enough to make anyone want to kill her. She really hadn't ever done *anything*, interesting or otherwise. She wasn't even married at age twenty-four, which her family considered a more serious failing with every passing day. Her mother was convinced none of this with the bomb would have happened if Angie were married. Angie had asked if that meant the bomb had been sent by a frustrated wedding caterer, but her mother had found no humor in her words.

The attack was random. It had to have been. No one had meant to harm her.

Still, the night before, she hadn't been able to sleep. At the slightest sound she'd bolt upright in bed, listening, her heart pounding, and when she did doze off, her dreams were bizarre and nightmarish. Never before had she worried about being alone in her apartment. Suddenly, she did.

The plumbing noises, constant callers, and lack

of sleep made her head pound. Finally, she gave up and pushed her chair away from the computer. She was working on her history book, a light but historically accurate study of the bawdy bowery of San Francisco in the 1890s. It was a task she could usually continue for hours, but not today. On top of everything else, the *Shopper* editor, George Meyers, was irritated that she had missed her last column. She promised to give him a headline story for his next issue: "Food Columnist's Kitchen Blows Up—Recipe On Page 7."

Her apartment made her nervous. Every time someone came to the door, she flashed back to the previous day. Even the ringing of the phone made her jump. She considered going shopping to lift her spirits, but the thought of the downtown crowds made her stomach knot.

Maybe just a short walk around the block or over to the park? That sounded good. It was just a matter of getting over the initial shock, she decided. That's all. She grabbed a red suede jacket, walked to the front door, and then paused and stared at the door, unable to touch it.

She steeled herself a moment, then swung the door open. No problem. It was just as she'd told the inspector yesterday when he kept trying to frighten her. Her getting the bomb had been a mistake. She pulled the door shut behind her. Just a mistake.

She stepped onto the sidewalk. The day was warm and placid, the October sun bright upon the cars parked bumper to bumper along the quiet residential streets. Sparsely leafed trees stood in tubs, every fifty feet or so, along the sidewalk. Only one or two vehicles drove past her, and no pedestrians were around.

How could there be any danger here? Still, she found herself looking over her shoulder as she walked, unable to shake the eerie feeling that someone was watching her.

She walked toward the hillside park, two blocks away, where she usually met her friend Sam. It was strange that he hadn't called her about missing their meeting yesterday. In the aftermath of the bomb, she had forgotten all about him.

She loved the view from the top of Russian Hill, of Chinatown to the right and North Beach to the left, of lofty churches and low neighborhood shops, all framing the white column called Coit Tower. Beyond were the blue waters of the bay.

She walked down the steps on Vallejo Street. The top of Russian Hill was so steep that the sidewalk had a cement stairway paved into it.

The park was just ahead of her, across an intersection. It was a place of peace and beauty, a place, she knew, where there couldn't be anything amiss.

As she stepped into the intersection, a large, blue American car pulled out from its parking space down the street. She continued forward across the street.

The engine roared as the car sped up and headed straight toward her. She stopped, shocked, and then ran. The sidewalk seemed immeasurably far away. Each step, each lifting of her leg and meeting of the pavement with her foot, took an eternity as the car gained on her.

She reached the sidewalk, but the car swerved in her direction, bounding up onto the curb. She screamed and then lunged toward the first tree she saw. She clutched the tree and scooted around to the far side of it, hugging the trunk, trying to breathe even though her lungs didn't seem to want to work and her heart was beating so fast she thought she'd faint. The squeal of brakes rent the air.

A half-block away, Paavo was methodically going door to door to question people who lived in the vicinity of Sammy Blade's murder. Other than the ID of the victim, he and Matt were having no luck with the investigation.

He had been at it for over an hour when a call came over his car radio that another attempt had been made on Angelina Amalfi's life. He dropped the microphone back onto the hook. He didn't relish facing Saks Fifth Avenue's pinup girl again. Still, after what he had learned about the bomb, he'd half expected to hear about another attempt. He slammed the transmission into drive and left the murder investigation to go to her apartment.

Meanwhile, at Angie's apartment, the plumber had finished his work and all was quiet. After her narrow escape, she'd hidden in the park until she saw a police car drive by. She had chased after it, yelling and waving her arms until the policemen noticed her. They had escorted her to her apartment, then called in the report.

Now, shaking and close to hysteria, she telephoned her father's lawyer, Marty Galquist. She asked him to recommend a bodyguard but made him swear he wouldn't tell her parents. Her father had a heart condition, and she didn't want to cause him any more worry than the bomb blast had already.

The frightening words of the inspector came back to her. "Someone doesn't like you, Miss Amalfi." She almost laughed at how understated the words seemed now.

She thought about leaving the city. She could buy an airplane ticket for some far-off place, or simply go to her parents' home in Hillsborough. Since they were in Palm Springs, the house was empty. But how long would she have to hide? How long before whoever was after her would find her again?

Her father was friends with the mayor and the police commissioner. The police wouldn't dare let anything happen to her. This was her home, in her father's building. Surely she'd be safe if she just stayed put. She had to believe that.

She heard a knock on the door and froze. "It's me," her neighbor Stan called. Don't scare me like that, she wanted to shriek, but she admitted him and even managed some enthusiasm. It was one of the few times she was genuinely happy to see him.

Stan was more of a pest than a companion, she had to admit. He was twenty-nine, thin and wiry, with brown hair and eyes. He considered himself an up-and-coming young bank executive. At least he did when he bothered to go to work, which wasn't nearly often enough to suit Angie, or, apparently, his bosses, who hadn't given him a Christmas bonus. He suffered from numerous mysterious ailments—laziness, mostly—and called in sick whenever he thought he could get away with it. On such days, he'd stop by Angie's place for tea and sympathy. She'd give him a cup of the former and a thimbleful of the latter and make it clear that even though she was home, she had work to do. Stan, impervious to subtlety, would stay until Angie kicked him out.

He didn't even sit down now. He took one look at how upset she was and, making himself at home as usual, walked into the kitchen to fix them each a brandy and soda. While he did that, Angie called the bodyguard service, Hallston and Sons.

Stan placed their drinks on the coffee table and sat on the yellow Hepplewhite chair. He looked comfortable in it. She'd never realized before how very slight he was.

"What's with the bodyguard, Angie?" Stan leaned forward and took her hand in his, his slim fingers wrapped lightly around hers. "Is there anything I can do to help? You know I'd do anything for you. Just name it."

"Stan, I'm scared. I don't understand what's happening, but I just—"

In one quick motion he slid to her side on the sofa and put his arm around her. She told him about the car trying to run her down. While one part of her registered that he was taking advantage of the situation, another part appreciated the comfort too much to resist.

They hadn't yet finished their drinks when there was a loud knock at the door.

"That must be my bodyguard. He wasn't kidding when he said he'd get here fast." Angie started to get up when Stan lightly touched her shoulder to stop her.

"Let me get it. You never know." He tried to sound macho, but she noticed his Adam's apple bob a couple of times.

She curled up on the sofa, wondering if she'd feel this frightened every time someone came to her door. She led a busy life. She didn't have *time* to be a shrinking violet. She wanted to get back to the way things were two days ago.

Stan peered through the peephole in the door. Angie realized she had never bothered to use it before. She would now, for sure.

Stan pulled the door open all the way, nearly flattening himself against the wall.

Inspector Paavo Smith strode slowly into the room, his brow knitted, taking in everything before him. He wore a gray sportscoat, gray slacks, and a white shirt. A Sherlock Holmes trench coat and deerstalker hat would have been more appropriate, Angie thought.

"You here again?" the inspector asked as he passed by Stan. He glanced at the brandy glasses side by side on the coffee table and at Angie huddled on the sofa. He turned back to Stan. "Stanfield Bonnet, right?"

"That's, um, Bonnette." Stan emphasized the second syllable.

Despite feeling suddenly safer with the inspector in the room, Angie was annoyed at the way he had marched in there as if he owned the place. "I suppose you were in the neighborhood again, Inspector."

"As a matter of fact, I was. I'm trying to work on a murder case that's getting colder by the minute. Nonetheless, Miss Amalfi, I do have a few questions about today's incident."

He was going to upset her again, she thought, bracing herself. He was probably thinking how stupid it had been for her to go out that day. She folded her arms. "I thought you worked in Homicide. No one's dead here."

"Not yet."

"Thanks for the small comfort."

"Speaking of which." His gaze fell on Stan. "Were you with Miss Amalfi this afternoon?"

Stan cleared his throat. "No."

The inspector looked at Angie. "Was anyone with you?"

"No!"

"Any witnesses at all?"

"Sorry. I was too busy hiding to ask for references."

He glanced at Stan again. "You don't need to remain here, Mr. Bonnet, thank you." It was a statement of dismissal, not choice.

"That's Bonnette," Stan muttered. He hurried out the door and slammed it shut.

Angie stiffened her back. She really didn't need this. "You do get your way, don't you, Inspector?"

His eyes narrowed. "Always."

"You make it sound like a challenge."

"It's a fact."

Her gaze traveled from the tall detective to the small antique chair. "Since you're staying," she said, gesturing toward it, "you may as well sit."

Instead, he took a step toward her. She fought the urge to step back. "Your cheek is scratched," he said. "Did that happen today?"

Surprised, she touched her face and felt a small, raised welt just below her left cheekbone. "It must have."

He nodded, then proceeded past the small chair to the sofa and sat squarely in the center of it.

She turned, her gaze following his steps, her fingers still on her cheek, surprised both that he'd noticed such an insignificant thing and that Stan hadn't.

He spread his arms across the back of the couch. "All right, Miss Amalfi, tell me about it."

She dropped her hand. "I already told the policeman on the phone."

"And now you get to tell me."

Maddeningly, tears filled her eyes. She fought to hold them back, unwilling to let him see any weakness in her. "I don't need you to scare me, Inspector. I'm afraid now. You can feel relieved, you've done a fine job." She lifted her chin, daring him to criticize her again, daring him to exclaim that he'd been right and she wrong about the danger.

Surprise flickered in his eyes, then his mouth tightened. He dropped his gaze and began fishing through his pockets, finally pulling out a pen and the same small notebook he'd used yesterday.

"When are you going to say 'I told you so,' Inspector?"

"It's not my job to criticize or frighten you, Miss Amalfi."

"What a pity when you do both so well!"

"It wasn't my intention—"

"What is then? What is your intention around here?"

"I intend to keep you alive."

His simple words caused her stomach to clench.

"And then," he continued, "I intend to find whoever's behind this."

Her chin trembled. Her embarrassment at the things she'd said warred with her anger over this whole situation. "I'm sorry, I didn't mean . . ." She couldn't go on.

His expression softened ever so slightly at her apology. Slowly his gaze drifted over her face and held her eyes for the briefest moment. Then he abruptly flipped open the notebook and clicked the push-cap on his pen. His voice, as he spoke, was firm and matter-of-fact. "I need to know what happened this afternoon."

"If only I knew!" She squeezed her eyes shut

for a moment, then opened them and gazed at the Cézanne hanging over her stereo system, the brilliant blues and yellows of the carefree, pastoral scene.

"Can . . . can I get you some coffee, Inspector?" Her voice shook. "My oldest sister, Bianca, brought some *biscotti* over this morning. They're fresh, and . . ." She rubbed her forehead, then dropped her hand and looked at him, waiting for his answer.

"I'd like that," he replied.

She fled to the kitchen to make some coffee and compose herself.

She set a mug before him and a small plate of cookies and then sat on the Hepplewhite and began her tale.

As she was telling him how she had hid under some bushes in the park until she was sure the car that had chased her was gone, a tap at the door interrupted her. She jumped at the sound and spun toward the detective.

She caught his gaze and clung to it. Without a word, he stood and walked to the door. Angie followed close behind. He glanced through the peephole, then stepped back, inviting her to take a look.

Her mouth dropped open. Before her stood the biggest man she had ever seen. She looked at Paavo and shook her head.

He gestured for her to step to the wall behind him. "Who is it?" he called through the door.

"The name's Joey." The man sounded as if he

had a terminal sinus condition. "Nicky Hallston
sent me to work for Miss Amalfi."

"My bodyguard!" she whispered to Paavo.

"Bodyguard?" he mouthed, looking as if he
couldn't decide whether to laugh or sneer.

He opened the door to let the large man enter.

Angie's gaze traveled over six and a half feet
from the man's buzzed haircut to his round face,
no neck, bulging biceps under gray gym clothes,
to surprisingly small running shoes. "I'm glad
Nicky's a friend," she murmured with awe.

Joey carried a shopping bag. "My dinner," he
said. "Me and Rico'll take this one. Twelve hours
on, twelve off. Okay?"

She blinked in astonishment. So there really
were people who talked like 1930s Warner Broth-
ers movies. "I won't argue."

"Huh?"

"Fine!"

She introduced him to Inspector Smith.

"Don't worry about her," Joey said. "I done
this a long time. Ain't lost nobody yet."

"Sounds good. She's all yours then."

"Now, just a minute, Inspector—" Angie
began.

He gazed at her, his eyes heavy-lidded.

"I don't plan to have a bodyguard the rest of
my life, you know. I expect you to get this settled."

"Right."

"Soon."

He arched one eyebrow.

"I mean, I don't want you to forget about me here, just because I'm safe now."

"Miss Amalfi," he said with a sigh, "I couldn't possibly."

She gasped and put her hands on her hips, daring him to say more.

He crossed the room and settled back against the sofa, with what she could have sworn was a hint of smugness in his cold expression. She couldn't remember the last time she'd encountered such a completely irritating man.

As Joey put his dinner away in the kitchen, Angie continued to tell the inspector the conclusion of her story.

She was describing running down a police car to get an escort back to her apartment when the telephone rang. It was an old boyfriend of hers, an actor with the San Francisco Conservatory Theater. "Lewis! It's so good to hear from you! . . . I'm fine, thank you . . . Yes . . . Yes . . . Oh, that sounds wonderful . . . No, I'm afraid it's no better. The police haven't turned up one single thing yet . . ."

She looked up to see the inspector scowling at her.

"Well, it's true, you know!" she said to him and then went back to the phone call. "I'm sorry, Lewis. I was talking to a detective here with me. . . . Oh sure, they'll investigate family, friends, you know. . . . What? You have to go right now? But . . . Wait! . . . Lewis? Lewis?"

She glanced at Paavo. "He hung up." Her shoulders sagged as she stared at the phone, the hum of the broken connection filling the quiet of the room.

Paavo tucked his notebook in the breast pocket of his jacket. "You've given me enough information for now, Miss Amalfi. I suggest that, for a time, you refrain from too much socializing and stick close to home."

"That was almost an invitation to the theater, Inspector. I've always loved the theater . . ."

"Remember Abe Lincoln, Miss Amalfi. Good day."

4

The next morning, Paavo pondered the paucity of information he and Matt had turned up so far on Sammy Blade. They had located the small studio apartment where Blade had lived for the past six months, but his landlady knew nothing about him except that he paid his rent in cash and that he was very "sweet." Sure, Paavo thought, as sweet as cyanide.

The kind of man Blade was and the way he was killed were signs that this case would become another unsolved homicide. Blade wasn't the kind of man anyone cared about when he was alive, and it was the same way in death. A smart cop would mark the death a suicide; a bad cop would toss it in a dead file. Paavo figured he was neither. He wanted to find Blade's killer.

It was time to hit the streets. Men like Sammy Blade were known in certain parts of every big city. The trick was to find someone who'd admit to having known a loser like Blade.

Paavo would make some contacts in the rough, gang-infested area south of Market Street where Blade's apartment was located. It was an area Paavo knew too well.

Matt was also going out tonight. He'd take the Tenderloin, a red-light district in the heart of the city, adjacent to the theater district and just blocks from the civic center and the high-priced hotels of Union Square.

Right now, Matt was home sleeping. The Tenderloin didn't come alive with the people he needed to see until long past midnight.

Paavo decided to finish writing his report on the Amalfi bombing before hitting the streets.

"It's Rico," Joey called out to Angie, as he looked out the peephole before pulling the door open. "His shift now."

Rico stepped into the room. He looked like a slightly older version of Joey: big and muscular, with short, gray hair, brown eyes, and the same cork-shaped head sitting on an oil-drum body. He held his shopping-bag lunch with one hand and, with the other, a shoebox with a white handkerchief in it.

"What you got in the box?" Joey asked.

"Look." Rico put down his lunch. "I found it in the hall."

Angie stepped out of the den holding her next *Shopper* column. She was going to ask Joey to fax

it to the paper on his way home. Just four blocks
down, on Polk Street, there was an office supply
store with a fax machine, but she was in such a
state these days she didn't want to go herself.
Even reams of paper, pens, and rolodexes
seemed threatening.

As Joey hovered nearby, Rico moved to lift the
handkerchief that covered the box. It took a second for her mind to register the scene before her.

"Don't!" she cried, a sense of *deja vu* striking
her.

The two men started. Joey blanched, and Rico
lowered the handkerchief. Both tried not to meet
her eyes.

"What is it?" she asked.

"Nothing to worry about, Miss Angelina. We'll
take care of it."

"Let me see."

Rico and Joey exchanged glances, and then
Rico slowly lifted the edge of the hankie. "Oh,
God!" She spun away, her stomach turning over.

The remains of a gray pigeon were in the box,
its head split open and its body smashed.

Fifteen minutes later, Inspector Smith was at
Angie's apartment. A patrolman came with him,
picked up the "evidence," and left. Paavo would
quiz Joey and Rico about their finding, but most
important, he had to work carefully with Angie.
He knew she'd be upset, but he needed to solicit
any hint of what the image of a pigeon might
mean to her. This case so far was nothing but

frustrating, with no clues or apparent motive for any of these threats.

Angie sat at the dining table, her hands folded on the table top.

He took a step toward her. She was pale, her face the sallow-alabaster shade of so many Mediterranean women, devoid of the pink ruddiness of the north. Her lips were colorless as well, and her almond-shaped eyes were puffy from crying. Their eyes met, and for the first time he felt as if he could see past her sophisticated facade and straight to her heart. His insides twisted at her look of fear, at the realization that the bold, carefree woman he had met two days ago was being systematically beaten down. He put his hands on the back of the chair across from her. He wished for a moment that he were the type who could lie to her, tell her not to be frightened, assure her that he'd take care of everything. But he couldn't do that, couldn't find any comforting words to say, so he said nothing.

His fists clenched as he stood there far too long, watching her, sensing her disappointment, yet feeling awkward and tongue-tied, not knowing how to ease her distress. He didn't even know why he thought he should ease her distress. To be fearful and therefore careful was what he wanted of her, wasn't it?

Two days ago, when he first saw the "exploding dishwasher," he couldn't believe anyone meant to harm her seriously. A nasty reminder sent by a jealous boyfriend, he had suspected. The report on the bomb had changed his opinion, and now the case was taking on a sick cast.

He couldn't find any rationale for what was happening here. It wasn't logical, which made it all the more dangerous. There could be some maniac behind it all. He ran his fingers through his hair.

Angelina Amalfi was just a little thing, as easy to crush as that bird. He thought of what could happen to her, recalling what he'd seen happen to other women who'd been hunted this way, stalked, tormented, and then captured. . . . He forced away the images as he looked at the woman before him. Somehow, he had to protect her. He was thankful that she hadn't had his experiences, that she didn't really know, the way he did, what it was she should fear.

He walked around the table toward her and tentatively placed his hand on her shoulder. He lifted it away quickly, but not before he had felt the fuzzy warmth of her sweater, noticed the fragile delicacy of her bones, and smelled the light, tantalizing scent of roses that always lingered in the air around her. His fingers tingled from the feel of her as he continued toward the windows to look out at the bay and to try to make sense out of all that was happening here.

5

Not again, Angie thought as she heard the light rapping on her front door the next morning. She felt like she had more callers these days than the White House. She pushed herself back groggily from her computer and walked to the living room. Rico was quizzing her visitor in the hallway outside the apartment.

"Miss Angelina," he said as he shut the door, "it's some weird guy calls himself Edward G. Crane. Says he's your biggest fan."

"I don't know anyone by that name."

"You want I should get rid of him?"

"Wait. Did he say what he wanted?"

"Says he got some recipes. Sounds fishy."

Crane must have found her because of the newspaper article the day after the explosion, which had given her address. Now she would have recipe peddlers and well-wishers adding to her stream of visitors. She sighed. "Have him give you the recipes and thank him."

Angie watched as Rico opened the door.

"Sir, I must see Miss Amalfi," whined a man with a high-pitched, nasal voice.

"The recipes first. Take them out of that envelope. I don't take no chances with Miss Angelina."

"Oh? Oh, certainly! But tell her I must see her."

Rico shut the door again and brought her three sheets of paper. On each was a recipe: *Marshmallow and Bean Sprouts Blintzes, Liver Pâté Waffles,* and *Peanut Butter Omelet.* Her stomach flip-flopped, as it did whenever she read Sam's recipes.

These recipes were quite similar to Sam's, in fact. They were most unusual, sometimes interesting, and always nauseating. What was going on?

"Stay nearby, Rico."

She opened the door herself. Before her stood a short, plump man, his shaved head covered with blue-tinged stubble. He looked at her through round, rimless spectacles, his eyes gray pinpricks and his nose red and bulbous. He was of indeterminate age, the pudginess of his face filling in any wrinkles.

"I'm E. G. Crane," he announced.

"Mr. Crane. To what do I owe this honor?"

"Sammy won't be coming to see you anymore."

Angie glanced at Rico. He stepped closer to

her. "What do you mean?" she asked, trying to keep her voice calm, though her heart began to race.

Crane's tiny eyes darted from Angie to the massive figure beside her. "Don't worry," he said hurriedly, "Sammy is fine. He's gone back to work in Carmel. I'll be sending you recipes now."

"You'll be sending me Sam's recipes?"

"No, no, no. My recipes." His already high nasal voice screeched. "They've always been my recipes, my own little delicacies. Sammy just delivered them for me."

Delicacies? The little man not only made her nervous, he was tasteless besides. "If you wish to supply any recipes to my column, Mr. Crane, you can send them to the *Bay Area Shopper*. I'll be sure to give them my personal attention." She used her most gracious brush-off manner as she moved to swing the door shut.

"You used to meet Sammy," Crane cried, holding out his hand to stop the door.

She frowned. "I like Sam!"

"Oh." He looked abashed. Angie didn't care.

"Good-day, Mr. Crane."

"But—"

She shut the door.

She returned to the computer and whipped out a short column all about persimmons.

"Grab your jacket, Rico, we're going to the *Shopper*."

"But the inspector said don't go nowhere."

"I'm not a prisoner!" She put on her coat and picked up her purse and the recipes. "This is weird, and I want to talk to my editor about it."

Rico followed reluctantly. They rode the elevator down to the basement garage, where her white Ferrari Testarossa was parked. As Rico rode shotgun, Angie tore out of the garage and across town to the *Shopper* office.

Paavo read the report on the pigeon found outside Angelina Amalfi's door. The "autopsy" caused more than a few snickers from the other homicide detectives. He ignored them.

A band-tailed pigeon, *Columba fasciata,* a species found throughout San Francisco. Bludgeoned to death. End of report.

Paavo rubbed his chin. Why would anyone sneak up to the door of an apartment and leave a dead pigeon?

Why not, when at the apartment, try to get past Joey or Rico? If this was the same person who had sent the bomb and tried to run Angie down with the car, why this grotesque stunt with the bird? Was the man, or woman, trying to kill Angie or just scare her off? Did the perpetrator change his or her mind midstream? Or was there more than one person involved?

City Hall had a lot of pigeons around it. Chief Hollins said Angie's parents had friends in City Hall. Maybe they weren't all friends?

He glanced at the report on the incident again. At least he knew she was safely inside her apartment. He'd checked out Joey and Rico. They were no intellectual giants, but as bodyguards, they were given high marks.

The *Bay Area Shopper* offices were located in a two-story converted warehouse on Folsom Street, just south of downtown San Francisco. The city room, a glass-partitioned office for the editor, and a private office for the publisher were on the second floor. The ground level held the presses.

Angie rode the elevator to the second floor, crossed the short hall, and pushed open the glass double doors to the city room. A hush fell over the room as salesmen, typists, and messengers stopped what they were doing to look at her. She strode toward the bosses' offices.

"You okay, Angie?" asked Mrs. Cruz, secretary to Jon Preston. "We heard about the bomb."

"Yes, thank you." Angie spoke loud enough for the curious to hear. "It was just some random thing, it seems. No one was after me in particular."

A deep voice boomed out. "Really? What a relief that must be to you, Miss Amalfi!" Jon Preston stood at the door of his office. The owner and publisher of the *Shopper*, he was a man in his fifties, tall and blond, impeccably dressed in a navy blue double-breasted blazer, white slacks, and a yachting cap. He looked like an ad for Cunard Lines.

"It was quite a relief, Mr. Preston."

That Jon Preston came from a wealthy family

was immediately evident to anyone who looked at the man. His chief work consisted of studying tide tables for his yacht and experimenting with high-tech metal woods and irons for his golf game. His sole business, the *Shopper,* was a shoe-string operation whose main purpose, if not its only purpose, was as a tax write-off.

Preston was pleasant in a pompous, bumbling way, despite his trim, spit-and-polish naval image, and Angie had always assumed he was a bit slow—or more appropriately, didn't have all his oars in the water. She imagined that Papa Preston, who was said to be a financial genius, realized this sad fact and gave his boy Jonny a business and a boat to play with as a way to keep him out of trouble.

Preston said, "I had feared my best little columnist would have to take some time off after such a frightening experience. What a yeoman you are, Miss Amalfi."

Best columnist? "Thank you, Mr. Preston."

"And you've still got those marvelous 'spoof' recipes, I trust." Angie had first printed one of Sam's recipes as a put-on and showed his name as "Waffles." She was shocked when readers wrote in and said they liked it. "The spoof is in the pudding," Preston had announced and had referred to Angie's popular "spoof" recipes ever since. Sam liked the name "Waffles," and it stuck.

"I've got some odd recipes," Angie replied, "but my regular source didn't make it. These are probably a fair substitute."

"No need. If not the real thing, the *Bay Area*

Shopper offers no cheap imitations. Well, ship ahoy, mates." At that, he walked toward the elevator, waving *bon voyage* to the staff. Before he stepped into it, he turned back to Angie.

"You know, you don't look well, Miss Amalfi. If you'd like a vacation, take it. We'll get along fine for a few weeks. Take a cruise. I'd recommend it, in fact."

"I'll give it some thought, Mr. Preston."

He got on the elevator and gave her a snappy salute as the doors slid shut.

Angie rolled her eyes. It was a wonder the man didn't demand to be addressed as "Captain Preston." She hurried towards George Meyers's office. She could see him through the glass partitions, hunched over his desk. George Meyers was always hunched, even when he stood upright. He was a thin, nervous man, about forty-five, with bushy salt and pepper hair that looked like crinkled wire and black-framed eyeglasses.

She'd known George for fourteen months, ever since the day she'd walked into the *Shopper* office, asked to meet the editor, and proceeded to tell him why he needed a food column in his paper and why she was just the person to write it. She was willing to work for peanuts, or less, because the experience and name recognition were far more important to her than a salary.

Less than peanuts was what he had offered, but he had been willing to give her a chance. As she had predicted, the lure of good recipes and a snappy column caused women shoppers to thumb through the paper more faithfully than they might have otherwise. As George saw the stack of recipes from contributors grow, he realized Angie's column was a hit and hired her.

Angie had quickly come to like George Meyers. She learned from Mrs. Cruz, the *Shopper's* own Louella Parsons, otherwise known as Preston's secretary, that George had once been a "real" newspaper man in Seattle, a crime reporter whose beat included the central station at night. One night, following a lead about a drug raid, he walked right into a set-up. The three policemen with him, all friends, were killed. For seven hours, until the dealers were all killed or wounded, George had crouched in a corner of a back alley, afraid that if he moved he'd be caught in the cross fire between the drug dealers and the police. After that, his nerves wouldn't let him return to his old job. He didn't have the skill or wit to write a column, and he had too much pride to take anything less prestigious than reporting. After about five years of living on disability compensation and odd jobs, he left Seattle to become the editor of the *Shopper*, a newspaper job in name only.

"Hello, there." Angie stuck her head into George's office and he jumped up.

"Angelina!" He tugged off his glasses. "You startled me."

She explained that she was safe from mad bombers and that she had brought her food column. She gave him the persimmon write-up and Crane's recipes.

George read them over. "More recipes from your friend, I see." Sam never used the mail but always dropped his recipes off at the *Shopper* office or met Angie at a park or coffee shop to deliver them in person. He had lots of time on his hands, he had said. She'd quickly been charmed by the man. He was one of the sweetest people she'd ever met.

"They aren't from Sam," Angie replied. "It's the oddest thing. These are from a man named Edward G. Crane. He said all Sam's recipes had really been *his*. He was a creepy little man. I didn't know what to think. It strikes me as very strange, so I came to see you. What do you think?"

"Think? Does it matter who gives you the spoof recipes, Angie?"

"I guess not, but Preston doesn't think we should run these."

"Not run them? But Preston always insisted . . ." George took them from her. "We're getting attention because of your offbeat column. Other editors look down their noses and sneer, but advertising is up."

George ran a handkerchief over his brow as he leaned back in his chair with a sigh.

"Are you all right, George?" She thought George was pale, but then, everything seemed to make George ill.

"Yes. Just a little tired. Now, let's see these recipes." He looked them over quickly. "I don't see what Preston's worried about, Angie. Or you. I think we should run these just like the others. I don't see that anything else matters, as long as they're from your readers. Let's run *Liver Pâté Waffles* in tomorrow's column with the persimmons, the omelet next Monday, and the marshmallow sprout blintzes the Monday after that."

"Clearly the *crème de la crème*," she said with a sigh as she took back the remaining two recipes. She didn't see how he could care so much about them, but then, he was the editor, not her. "Maybe I do need a vacation," she added.

The flesh between his earlobes and jawbones twitched nervously. "It's up to you, but your column is hot now, Angie. One of the local T.V. shows is even thinking of doing a five- or ten-minute spot about it—cooking up some of your 'Waffles' recipes and seeing what they taste like and everything. You know how this town is—it's got a very short memory. All this attention could disappear in a couple of weeks. Then we'll be back where we started." His jaw tightened. "And that's nowhere."

The bitterness in his voice came as no surprise. She had long suspected George's disenchantment with his work, and his words revealed the full extent of that unhappiness. "I guess you're right, George," she said. Under normal circumstances, the news about the television show would be exciting, even fantastic, but now, she just didn't know. It made her uneasy.

As she left the office, George called out, "Be careful, Angelina. Keep your door locked."

That's an odd thing for George to say, she

thought as she waited for the elevator. She had told him the bomb was just a random attack.

After impatiently waiting a couple of minutes, she decided the elevator must not be working. It was only one floor down to ground level, and the stairs led to a side alley a half block from the parking lot where Rico would be waiting.

The staircase felt unnaturally cold, and she hurried down it. A strange echo made it sound as if someone was following her.

She reached the warm, sunny street and pulled the door shut behind her just as Rico drove the Ferrari around the corner toward her. She smiled, realizing that Rico, like most men she knew, had taken the opportunity to drive her Ferrari, even if only around the block a few times.

He pulled the car to her side and she jumped in.

She wasn't sure why she turned around just then, but she looked back at the *Shopper* building and saw the side door slowly closing. She could have sworn she'd shut it as she had left. She must have been mistaken.

6

"*I just read* your lady friend's food column, Paavo," Matt said with a chuckle two days later. "The things she can do with persimmons! And those recipes—she's a regular Lucrezia Borgia. I think you should turn this case over to Vice."

Paavo gave the big, blond detective a cold stare. "When did you turn into Milton Berle, Kowalski?"

"Skin a little thin, there, Paavo?"

"Tough as ever, Matt."

"Good. I'd hate my partner going soft on me. Guess that means the boys are wrong when they say you've enrolled in a French cooking class."

Paavo shut his eyes as Matt, still chuckling, walked off to get coffee. Between revolting recipes, dynamited dishwashers, and bashed birds, he had been the brunt of Homicide's jokesters for almost a week, and he was sick of it.

The most sickening part was that he wasn't any further along in solving the case than when he had started. He had gotten a jolt when one of the top chefs in the city was murdered. But hours after the murder, the chef's jealous male lover confessed. So much for the murder theory Paavo was developing about a crazed food-fanatic.

In the meantime, Matt was doing most of the legwork on Sammy Blade's death, and also getting nowhere. As expected, they found that Sammy had frequented the seamier parts of the city. The investigation came down to walking around neighborhoods, finding his cronies, and trying to find out something useful—anything. They spent a lot of time sifting through the meager reports and the few leads they had, hoping that something new would strike them, but nothing did.

Each afternoon since the bird incident, Paavo had found himself in Angie's neighborhood with a legitimate reason to stop at her apartment for a few minutes. But there were no more leads, and no more threats. Chief Hollins began to question the car episode. Was someone trying to run her down, or was she just overly nervous? Was the pigeon sent by someone who meant her harm, or just some sicko who read the newspaper article?

Paavo had checked everything from her bank balance to the schools she had attended to her friends, relatives, colleagues, boyfriends—there had been plenty of them—and neighbors. He even knew when she had last been to the dentist.

Angie was the youngest of five daughters of

Salvatore Amalfi, an Italian immigrant who had started out with nothing but had worked hard and amassed a fortune from shoe stores and San Francisco real estate. Seven years ago, the Amalfis bought a twelve-room estate in Hillsborough.

The story was a Horatio Alger dream come true. Despite Paavo's skepticism, he found no hint of falseness anywhere. Neither could he find anything in Salvatore's wheeling and dealing that might have led to a death threat against the youngest daughter.

Angie was liked by most of her acquaintances and coworkers and was considered cheerful and easygoing, though some saw her as a bit of a dilettante, taking nothing very seriously. Her father, one friend told Paavo, would have given her the world had she asked, but she had never figured out what to ask for.

She expected a lot from friends, but she was also generous and, everyone conceded, gave as much or more than she received. In short, she wasn't involved with drugs, drink, or porn; had no burning desire for money, fame, or success; was neither megalomaniac, schizophrenic, nor manic-depressive; had only a passing interest in politics and oddball causes; and was not into deviant anything.

So why in the hell did someone want to kill her?

Paavo hoped Hollins was right —that this case was more nerves and imagination than danger— but as Paavo reviewed the evidence, he knew that if he overlooked anything, his error might make it easier for someone to get at Angie, and he couldn't let that happen.

Still, he had other, bigger cases. Finally, Hollins said he didn't want Paavo spending any more time on the Amalfi case unless he had a good reason to.

On this day, he ran out of reasons. She had Joey and Rico to protect her, nothing new had happened, and there were no new questions he needed answered. So he stayed away.

If she needed him, she'd call.

She didn't.

He should have been glad.

He wasn't.

He stormed around the office all morning and spent the afternoon apprising anyone who wandered too near of their many shortcomings.

When his shift ended at six, the other detectives breathed a sigh of relief.

He got into his car and revved the engine. Home seemed too quiet. If he went to Angie's place, though, he'd probably just stand around, first on one foot, then the other, feeling like a damn fool and not knowing what to say or how to explain why he'd shown up. He should go home.

He pulled his car out of the parking space, made a U-turn, and headed north toward Russian Hill.

Angie glanced once more at the clock on the desk as she sat at the computer. It was 6:03.

Inspector Smith had come by every day up to now. Where was he?

She frowned. Truly, she'd been cooped up too long if she cared where the human ice chest might be. He was so cold and bossy. He never smiled, and the temperature in the apartment dropped at least ten degrees whenever he walked in the door. If he stayed away, she should shout *Hallelujah*.

She was weary from working on the book she felt obligated to write. What else could she do with B.A.'s in both English and history? She stretched and rubbed the back of her neck, and then went into the living room to see Rico. He lay on the sofa, feet up, watching highlights of last weekend's football games on a cable station.

"Any word from Joey?" she asked.

"Uh-uh."

"I expect he'll be here any minute."

"Yeah."

She joined Rico watching the T.V., hoping America's favorite sedative would numb the aching frustration of not knowing who was after her or why. She'd gone over, again and again, all the bad things she'd done in her life, like breaking theater dates after the tickets had been purchased, or accepting a date with a man she knew another woman had her heart set on. But these weren't exactly heinous crimes. She couldn't think of any weird or scary character interested in her. Once her father had to tell a love-struck high school classmate to stop hanging around their house or he'd break the kid's legs, but other than that, she hadn't attracted any troubles. Surely no one could object to her food column or her San Francisco history. Her last three magazine articles had been guides to restaurants, and she had only mentioned places she *liked.* Upon reflection, she realized her life had been pitifully dull.

The police were no closer to finding out who had sent the bomb, or the pigeon, or who had chased her with the car, than they were right after these incidents first happened. Maybe it was time to let Rico and Joey go and return to her normal way of life. Did she dare?

A half hour later, there was a knock on the door. She knew that brisk, no-nonsense knock—Inspector Paavo Smith coming to call. "It's the Inspector," she said, her voice lilting as she hurried towards the door.

"Maybe he found Joey," Rico said as he struggled to raise his bulk off the sofa.

Angie opened the door and looked up at Paavo. "He's alone."

"Expecting someone?" He brushed past her into the living room, as she leaned out the door to peer down the hallway, toward the elevator.

She shut the door and turned to face him. He was dressed as conservatively as usual, his frown as deep as ever, and his eyes sharp, questioning, and analytical. Yet she had to admit that she did feel a whisper of pleasure at seeing him again. Maybe even more than a whisper. "We were hoping Joey was with you."

Paavo's gaze grew wary as he looked from

Angie to Rico, who now stood beside the petit point sofa. "What's wrong?" His voice was low.

"Nothing, Inspector," Rico answered.

"I'm so sorry," Angie said softly, twisting her hands together.

"About what?" Paavo's gaze leaped from one to the other.

"Everything! It's Rico's daughter's birthday. He should be home now. With his family. Instead, he's stuck here because of me! Joey was supposed to come by early instead of his usual ten o'clock, so Rico could leave." She sighed. "I guess Joey forgot."

"The wife'll understand," Rico said. "She knows Joey ain't got too much on the noodle. And I can't leave Miss Angelina here alone."

Angie sighed. "I'd just be alone a few hours. Nothing has happened in three days. Nothing's likely to now, is it?"

"I don't know," Paavo said.

Some detective, she thought.

Paavo regarded them both, his mouth a thin line, downturned at the edges. "Get out of here, Rico. I'll stay."

Angie felt herself blanch at the thought, and at his expression. He looked like he had just volunteered for *kamikaze* duty. "I'm sure you're too busy. I'll be just fine alone."

"I'll stay," he repeated, even more crisply.

Angie spun toward Rico with a glare. He caught her eye and her meaning, then turned to the inspector. "You don't have to, Inspector. It's my job."

Paavo glanced at his watch. "I'm off duty. I stopped here on the way home."

Her mind was in a whirl. If Joey didn't arrive until ten o'clock, whatever would she do with the man? He was cold and aloof and seemed to be constantly analyzing her motives and her words. They had nothing in common, nothing to talk about. The idea of having him there with her for hours made her stomach knot. "I can stay alone, really."

"No."

She gaped at him, not believing his bossiness. She wasn't used to hearing the word "no" like that. But before she could respond, Rico jumped up and put his jacket on. "Okay, Inspector, if you say so. Thanks." He lumbered out the door.

Angie stared after him. She had never seen Rico move so fast.

She followed him to the door and locked the dead bolt after him. The click of the lock was like an explosion. Slowly she turned around, then swallowed hard. Inspector Smith's presence seemed to fill the entire room.

7

The inspector walked over to the sofa. "May I?" His fingertips lightly touched his gray sports jacket.

"Please!" She was surprised that he asked. Did the man have manners after all?

He removed the jacket and laid it across the arm of the couch. He tugged at the knees of his slacks as he sat, then loosened his gray-and-blue-striped tie. With the jacket off, the conservative pale blue shirt and charcoal slacks would have appeared quite undetectivelike . . . except for the shoulder holster and gun.

Her eyes fixated on them. Trying to make small talk while glancing continually at Smith and Wesson just wasn't going to work.

She took a couple of sideways steps toward her telephone. "I could call my neighbor. You remember Stan Bonnette? Oh, of course, he told me you questioned him one day. If he's home from work he can stay with me until Joey arrives. Or I can stay at his place."

Paavo leaned back against the sofa, his hands folded on his stomach. He stretched out his long legs in front of him, then crossed them at the ankles. He didn't say no. In fact, he didn't say a word as Angie babbled on and on, but the look he gave her said it all.

She left the phone and plopped down on the chair. The inspector was staying.

The clock in the VCR showed 6:55. Only three hours and five minutes to go.

He gazed at her expectantly but said nothing.

He's doing this to torment me, she thought.

"Since you're here," she began, soliciting a look of interest, "would you like some dinner? I haven't eaten yet myself."

"It's not necessary."

So he could talk! "I'm an excellent cook." Why in the world did she say that? The words were barely out of her mouth when she regretted them.

He hesitated. "Well—"

"Right, forget it. I'm sure you aren't supposed to fraternize with clients."

"You're not a client, Miss Amalfi," he said.

"I'm not?"

Suddenly he grinned, an honest, eyes-crinkling-at-the-corners kind of grin. If she hadn't been sitting, she was sure she'd have fallen over. She didn't think the muscles in the man's face could even *move* that way but were stuck in a perpetual scowl. Now she found that not only could he smile, but she liked what a smile did to his face. Liked it a lot. She felt her cheeks grow a little warm at the thought, which was silly. No woman blushes just because a man smiles at her! It was embarrassing.

She cleared her throat. "Call me Angie."

His eyebrows lifted slightly.

Her mouth formed into a silent "Oh" and she put her hand to her forehead. "God, where's my head! You've probably got a wife and kids and a dinner waiting for you at home. I'm sorry!" She felt her blush worsening. "You just seem so single—I mean, I guess because you come here alone, but—"

"I am single."

"—I should have realized that your off-duty life . . . You are?"

He nodded.

She jumped to her feet. "In that case, you've got to eat here. I know all about single men's diets, and I know you simply do not eat properly." His eyes widened with bemusement, but she ignored his look and continued. "Let's cook something Italian, okay?"

His brow knitted. "Opening a can of Chef Boyardee's about my limit."

"Is that a joke, Inspector?"

"I'm afraid not."

She laughed. "With a name like Paavo Smith, I guess I should have expected that answer. What kind of a name is Paavo, anyway?"

"Finnish, the equivalent of Paul."

"Hmm." She studied his face, the high cheekbones, piercing light-blue eyes, strong nose, nicely shaped mouth. Paavo. "I rather like it."

He shifted uneasily, and the tone of his voice turned formal and businesslike again. "What were you thinking about cooking?"

"No third degree tonight, Inspector." Angie grinned. "Come on, let's see what I've got."

Paavo followed her into the kitchen and rolled back his shirt sleeves as he sat on a stool at the counter. Angie handed him a beer before she took out flour and eggs to make linguine and plugged in her pasta machine.

As she began to add the ingredients, he wanted to learn all about the machine, and she explained how it worked. By the time the first inch of linguine noodles oozed from the opening, Angie saw that the stern lines of his expression had eased and the stiff set of his shoulders had relaxed.

Angie, too, found that for the first time in days she was able to put her anxiety aside. As the machine spewed out the noodles, she found herself telling Paavo about growing up in San Francisco, about her large family with four older sisters, going to Vassar to get away, spending a year at the Sorbonne, another year in Rome, and yet another year in New York City.

"Then, last year," she said, "I came home."

"Why was that?"

"I found I missed my family, this area, the way of life here. I wanted independence, but once I had it, it wasn't enough."

"What is enough, Angie?"

His elbows were on the counter, and he leaned forward, watching her every move. She glanced at him a moment, then shook her head, embarrassed to admit her lack of ambition, her drifting through life this way. "I wish I knew," she whispered.

"Your writing?"

"Perhaps. Someday, I'm going to tackle a project that's really close to my heart. But I'm not ready for such a task yet. I'm afraid I'd just botch it up. Right now, my food column gives me discipline and responsibility, and the magazine articles keep me involved in current events and interests, and the history gives me a sense of time, place and scope. I need to learn all that."

He studied her. "That's very wise."

She shrugged and gave him a half-smile. "Or maybe it's a nifty justification for fooling around, Inspector Smith."

His gaze softened. "I don't think so, Miss Amalfi."

"Lots of others do, though."

"It's what you believe that's important."

She felt her face grow warm from his words and the way he looked at her, and she quickly spun around to the stove to check on the large pot of water. She couldn't understand it. She hadn't blushed since she was fourteen, and now it'd happened twice in one evening. This was no time to take on that hideous trait again.

"Ah," she cried, "water's boiling." She put in the noodles. "The linguine can cook while I make a nice mixture to pour over it."

She began rummaging through her cupboard. "I could do a plain old cheese sauce, but I thought . . . Ah! Here they are." She pulled out a small tin of anchovies.

"Cheese is fine, Angie. Don't go to any trouble."

"What's the matter, Inspector? Doesn't anchovy in your pasta appeal to you?" The man looked a little pale. "Hmm, I bet you even pick it off pizza."

"No. I never put it *on* pizza."

"Trust me."

She opened the tin, minced two anchovies, and then put a coat of olive oil in a big frying pan. Over low heat, she sauteed them with a couple of cloves of garlic and a few sprigs of parsley, then added a pinch of crushed red pepper and basil. Last, she added a half of a can of pitted black olives. Paavo watched her every move.

As she chopped and stirred, she tried to get Paavo to talk a little about himself. All she learned, though, was that he, too, had grown up in the city. But he had lived in the Mission District—an old, tough neighborhood, far different from the stylish Marina District of her childhood. She listened closely to everything he said, every intonation and nuance, trying to glean insight from the few words he spoke. The man was a mystery to her. One of the biggest parts of the mystery was why she was so curious about him.

She liked mannered, genteel men who were worldly and polished—men who could toss out a *bon mot* or devastating put-down in the cleverest of ways, men who lived in a world of elegance and took it as their due. A number of doctors, CEOs, and even a judge were among her coterie of suitors, and she thought them all just fine. Inspector Paavo Smith was completely different, and she didn't understand him at all.

While she drained the cooked linguine, she gave Paavo the job of stirring the olive-and-anchovy mixture and making sure it didn't burn. Angie chuckled inwardly seeing him there, the wooden spoon dwarfed in his hand, his eyes never leaving the pot. He was clearly a man who took his duty seriously. She was sure he gave no less attention to his stickiest cases.

Dinner was almost ready. Angie added the linguine to the pan, along with more olive oil, red pepper, and a quarter cup of grated Parmesan. As she tossed the mixture, Paavo stood behind her, leaning over her shoulder, watching intently.

"It actually smells good, and looks even better."

"I can cook, you know," she said, turning her head toward him. His face was only inches away. The sparkling blue of his eyes, the thick, rich waves of his hair, the clean, spicy scent of his aftershave reached her senses. Her breath caught at his nearness, and his eyes seemed to darken as they moved over her face. Flustered, she turned her attention to the linguine again.

He stepped away from her quickly, too quickly, she thought. He too had felt whatever it was that had passed between them, and he wanted no part of it.

◆ ◆ ◆

The three hours they spent together went by quickly. Although Paavo was quiet, the few words he said were straightforward and honest, and he seemed to value her words, which she appreciated, because she loved to talk. As she warmed up a bit to his personality, so, too, did she come to appreciate his looks. She could have drowned in the blue lagoon of his eyes, and the couple of times she coaxed a smile out of him were well worth the trouble.

Paavo helped her clean up the kitchen after the leisurely dinner. For dessert, she took some tortoni out of the freezer. They hadn't even finished their espresso when Joey arrived. Angie smiled at him, feigning relief, while hoping her disappointment didn't show.

Paavo's presence, to her surprise, had made her feel warm and safe. Even after he had left, when she lay in bed, she thought about the man, not the inspector, and was comforted.

8

The next afternoon, the telephone rang.

"You're going to die, pigeon." It was a man's voice, very deep and slurred.

Shock raced through her. "What?"

"Thought you had the brains to understand a clear message. Guess I was wrong. You're dumb. Keep it up and you'll be dead."

Her hands shook as she clutched the receiver tightly. "Who is this?" she screamed. "What did I do? Tell me, please! Don't do this to me!"

There was a *click* as the caller hung up.

An hour later, Paavo entered the apartment. "Did you receive any more phone calls, Miss Amalfi?" She had called him immediately to report the threatening call, and she was puzzled at how formal and businesslike he sounded on the phone. He remained so now, and a sense of disappointment settled over her.

Last night, for a little while, she had allowed herself to forget he was a detective—Mike Hammer and Dick Tracy rolled into one—and had enjoyed his company until he had turned back into that pumpkin otherwise known as a homicide inspector.

Facing Paavo now, though, she realized that he clearly regretted the lapse in their strictly professional relationship. She had believed that he, too, had enjoyed the evening before, but obviously she had been wrong.

She tried to shake off her feeling of loss and lifted her gaze to his, inwardly vowing to never again forget that he was a cop just doing his job. But his eyes were so beautifully blue. . . .

Her lips tightened. This reaction to him did nothing but irritate her. She felt like a schoolgirl, a real sucker for a uniform—even if it was a plainclothes one.

Rico had replaced Joey on the sofa in front of the T.V., so she gestured toward the large wingback chairs nestled in a corner of the room.

"No other calls," she replied finally, when they were seated. He quizzed her about the one she'd received—the exact words used, the voice, accent, anything special she could remember. The caller had used the term *pigeon,* and Paavo questioned her over and over about birds, stool pigeons, chickens, turkeys, fowls, fouls, foes, even badminton, until she was ready to scream, if not chirp or caw.

"All right," he said, backing off. "Tell me again about any visitors you've had."

"I told you. I've stopped everyone from coming by except my sisters, my neighbor Stan, and you. That's it. Others came by, but I didn't let them in."

"What others?"

"Delivery men, Edith from downstairs, the paper boy, people asking for money, a contributor to my food column—"

"You never mentioned that before."

"The contributor? I told you I went to the *Shopper* to drop off recipes. You were too busy yelling about me going there to even ask me where I got the recipes."

"I never yell. But anyway, you're saying this 'contributor' dropped off the recipes in person?"

"Right."

"Isn't that unusual?"

"Everything's unusual about my food column. But since that newspaper article gave out my address, I guess anyone can find me the way he did."

"He?"

"A fair number of men contribute recipes."

"Oh? So, why didn't *he* just mail the recipes to the paper?"

"I think he wanted to explain. This man, his name is Edward Crane, said he's friends with another contributor named Sam Martin. Sam brings me 'spoof' recipes for breakfast foods, and signs his name as 'Waffles' for use in my column. If you'd ever seen my column, you'd know what I mean. Anyway, Waffles, or Sam, has gone to

Carmel to work, and now Crane will be giving me the 'spoof' recipes."

Paavo just looked at her for a long time as if trying to sort out what she had just said. "A number of people mentioned your column and that sometimes it can be pretty . . . funny. Tell me more about these 'spoof' recipes."

"Well, for me, they started out as a joke, I mean, they're really weird recipes—things like Chocolate Oyster Pancakes, or Peppermint Brains Soufflé. But Jon Preston, my publisher, liked them, and claimed a lot of readers wrote in and said they liked them as well. He insisted I publish the 'Waffles' recipes whenever I got them. As long as they're popular, we've kept them up."

Angie caught his head shaking. She should feel insulted, but instead she laughed, imagining this whole recipe thing must sound like science fiction for all he understood about women's food columns or male contributors to them. But he wrote down the names Edward Crane and Sam Martin, and said he'd have them checked out.

"Are you working on anything else?"

"I was given the go-ahead for an article on the mayor for a Los Angeles–based magazine. I haven't been able to start it yet."

"The mayor?"

"He's a friend of the family. I've done several human interest stories on him already. It's no big deal, but I guess he's good copy."

Paavo leaned back in the chair, his expression thoughtful.

"That's not what's behind all this, Inspector."

He shrugged. "I'll keep it in mind, though."

She shook her head, then looked at him a moment before speaking. "Did you have lunch?"

He jerked his head toward her. "I never eat—"

"I am a food columnist, after all," she said as if that were an explanation as she disappeared into the kitchen. She returned almost immediately with a mug of hot coffee. While he sipped it, she made him an enormous cold cuts and cheese sandwich.

"You'll be less difficult on a full stomach," she said in response to his questioning look as she handed him the sandwich.

He paused, as if contemplating how anyone could call him difficult, then began to demolish his lunch.

There was a knock at the door. Now what? Paavo stepped toward the door as Angie and Rico stood clear of the entry.

The detective peered through the peephole, glanced back at Angie, then with an oddly amused expression on his face, swung the door open all the way.

Rico took a step backwards into Angie, who nearly lost her balance. Scrambling to see what was going on, she peered around Rico's arm toward the doorway.

There, filling the lower half of it, stood her mother, Serefina Teresa Maria Giuseppina Amalfi, all five-foot-one, one hundred fifty pounds of her. She entered the room like the HMS *Queen Mary* lumbering from its berth.

"Mamma," Angie whispered, her hand going to her throat.

Serefina slowly took in Angie and the two men beside her, and clearly found them all wanting.

"I'll be outside," Rico muttered as he slipped out the door.

Coward, Angie thought. "Mamma," she said, "what are you doing here? I thought you were in Palm Springs."

Serefina stared at her a long moment, then crossed the room and dropped her handbag on the coffee table with a thud. She took off her neckscarf, then her overcoat, revealing an expanse of white polka dots against a navy blue background and hefty, black walking shoes. Her black hair was pulled straight back into a bun.

"Che pasticcio!" she said, reproach emanating from every outraged inch of her.

"Mamma, what did I do?"

"Dimmi! I ask you that!" She looked at Paavo. "Who's this?"

Paavo cleared his throat.

Angie came to his aid. "This is Paavo Smith, Mamma. Paavo, my mother."

"Mrs. Amalfi," he held out his hand, "nice to meet you."

"Hah!" came the response. He pulled back his hand.

"Angelina! You don't talk to your mother or your sisters. I came myself to find out what's going on."

"I telephone you, Mamma!"

"Hello, good-bye. That's a phone call?"

Paavo tried to interrupt. "I think I'll be going—"

"*Aspetti!*" Serefina ordered. She studied Paavo, top to bottom, then looked back at Angie. "What does he do?"

"He . . . he's a homicide inspector."

Serefina's eyes widened as her gaze jumped from one to the other. "Homicide? So you are in danger, Angelina!"

"No, Mamma. There's nothing to worry about, believe me. Don't worry."

"How can I not worry when my baby has strange things blowing up under her very nose? Living alone here this way. It's not good, Angelina!"

"Please, Mamma! It's all right. Just go back home."

"Go home? *Dio!* You're talking to your mother this way!"

"Ladies," Paavo began again as the two stood wringing their hands and looking at each other, both on the verge of tears. "If you'll excuse me—"

Angie spun toward him. "How can you think of leaving when my mother is so upset?"

"Well—" he began.

"Angelina, *poverina!*" her mother wailed. "Does he always want to run out on you like this?"

Paavo's face tightened.

"He's assigned my case, Mamma. That's all."

"That's all?" Serefina cast her gaze, full force, on him.

Paavo loosened his tie. Poor man, Angie thought. He had to face Serefina when he could be out chasing a simple murderer.

"Something's strange here," Serefina said, "but he's got good eyes. He's quiet. I like that in a man."

Paavo raised his eyebrows.

"I know more is going on than you're telling me, Angelina. What can I do? Right, young man?" She finally addressed Paavo.

Angie chuckled inwardly as she realized he had no idea how to respond.

"There, now I've embarrassed him! *Mi dispiace!*" She reached up and grabbed his cheek between her thumb and forefinger and gave it a little squeeze.

"It's all right," Serefina continued. "You take Angie to her cousin's wedding tomorrow, and you watch her good, you hear? Meet the family, too, except Salvatore, he couldn't come. His heart, you know. But Gina's father is only his second cousin, so it's okay."

"God, Mamma," Angie lay her palms against her forehead. "I forgot about the wedding."

"*Dio!* How could you forget your own cousin?" Serefina raised her hands upward with desperation.

Paavo stepped back.

"She's only my third cousin, Mamma."

"She's family." Serefina turned to Paavo. "You come to my house at three tomorrow. It's formal. Angelina, give him the address."

"I'm sorry . . ." His voice had a slight quiver to

it. Angie recognized the symptom shared by many who ran headlong into Serefina. She hadn't realized even hard-nosed police detectives were susceptible. She feared Paavo would find himself at a wedding tomorrow with no idea how he got there.

"Mamma, he's a detective. He's got to work."

Serefina shrugged. "So? Watching you isn't important work? I'll call Commissioner Barcelli."

Paavo cleared his throat. "I have tomorrow off."

"Maybe Rico should take me," Angie quickly suggested.

"Rico?"

"He was the man who was just here who ran out the door."

Serefina's eyes drilled her daughter.

Angie sighed and looked beseechingly at Paavo. "It's all right for you to come with me, isn't it? I'm not a suspect or anything."

"It's not against procedure, but—"

"*Va bene.*" Serefina interrupted. "Enough talk. You know how to keep my Angelina safe. I know it's hard. She makes my hair gray the way she won't listen. And she never phones her mother."

Serefina turned Angie toward her bedroom. "Get your things for tomorrow, Angelina. You come home with me now. We have a lot to do. I have a taxi waiting. I came here straight from the airport."

"Walk us to the cab?" Angie looked back over her shoulder at Paavo.

"Sure." His eye caught hers as if to tell her not to worry, she'd be watched.

Serefina looked from one to the other, then nodded.

9

Angie felt like a bird released from its cage as she waited for Paavo in the library of her parents' Hillsborough mansion. Her apartment had become a prison cell. Now, for a little while at least, she could forget about all that madness.

She had summoned her hairdresser to her parents' home that morning, saying she was too busy to get to his shop, but paid him well enough to cover any lost business. The back of her hair was pinned up, while the front and sides were softly curled, framing her face and making her eyes seem even larger, darker, and more dramatically almond shaped than usual.

The late afternoon wedding was to have a formal reception. Angie wanted to wear something particularly beautiful and had chosen an ice-blue silk Celine that skimmed her waist and hips to a short, sexy puff of a skirt. With it she wore matching pumps and a simply mounted diamond necklace, earrings, and bracelet.

She knew, at her cousin's wedding, with Paavo, she could feel safe. She also wanted to feel glamorous and alive, once more. Not that it would matter to him. He had made it clear that to him she was just another case.

Now, standing in the library with bright sunshine streaming in through the windows, her freedom was heady. She felt good for the first time in days. She shut her eyes and tilted her head back, soaking up the warmth.

"Miss Angie?" the housekeeper called. Angie turned to see Paavo standing in the doorway of the library watching her. Their eyes met, and for a moment the way he looked at her made her head spin. But then his expression closed, becoming shuttered, as always, and she wondered if she had just imagined that there was ever anything more. Still, the sensation lingered.

She fluffed out her skirt, feigning nonchalance. The housekeeper nodded and walked away.

"I see why you told me not to bring a corsage," Paavo said as he slowly approached her, eyeing her bare shoulders. "You look . . . beautiful."

"Thank you," she murmured, her eyes sweeping over his tall, powerful figure. He wore a black tuxedo with a black bow tie. Rather than making him appear awkward, it accentuated his underlying strength. His hair had been carefully brushed into place, and only one wayward lock had sprung loose onto his forehead. "You, too, look very nice today."

"I feel like a maitre d'," he said, looking down at the tuxedo.

She smiled. "I have something for you!" From the desk she picked up the white silk handkerchief she had ordered for him. She moved close to him, close enough to smell the spicy musk of his after-shave, and tucked the handkerchief into his breast pocket. She rubbed her hand against the material to smooth it, feeling the hardness of his chest beneath her fingers.

"Perfect," she whispered. As her fingers stilled, he covered her hand with his own in what began, she realized, as a defensive gesture by a man not used to being touched. As their hands met, though, instead of brushing hers aside, his lingered, creating a confusion of feelings within her. She pulled her hand away and stepped back.

He quickly turned, forcing his attention toward the room. He put his hands in his pockets in a gesture that reminded her of a little boy told not to touch anything. "This house is beautiful," he said.

She followed his gaze to the vaulted ceilings, the tapestries, and the mahogany furnishings of the library.

"It's nice," she said in a flat voice.

Just then, Serefina entered the room. She was wearing a floor-length gold dress with an overblouse of yellow chiffon that billowed wildly as she walked.

"*Buon giorno,* Paavo," she said, taking both hands and kissing his cheek. "You are so handsome today! *Bellissimo!*"

"Thank you. You look lovely, Mrs. Amalfi," he responded.

She turned, grabbed her handbag, and headed out the door. "*Andiamo*. We'll take my car."

Paavo took Angie's arm and followed Serefina. Angie wished she had a picture of Paavo's face as the chauffeur, Grayson, drove up with Serefina's silver Rolls Royce.

"Hurry." Serefina shooed Angie into the car. "You can be late to your own wedding, but not to your cousin's."

Serefina sat between Paavo and Angie. Serefina talked the whole way to the church.

When they arrived, the church was already filled with people. Angie felt herself grow tense as she looked at the crowd. Whoever was after her couldn't be at her cousin's wedding. Too many people were here. She was safe. Her hands felt suddenly cold and clammy. She was perfectly safe.

She didn't do more than wave at family and friends as she proceeded straight to an usher who led her and Paavo through the crowd to a place to sit. She breathed a heavy sigh and settled back in the pew.

"There are enough people here," Paavo said, turning one way, then the other, finally unfastening the button on his jacket so he could move more easily.

"No one special. Mostly cousins."

He gave her a disbelieving look and continued to eye the crowd.

The bridal march began, and the wedding

guests rose as the entourage marched down the aisle. Cousin Gina looked resplendent in a full, white gown and veil.

The guests sat, stood, and kneeled through the nuptial mass. As a soprano sang "Ave Maria," Angie found herself watching Paavo out of the corner of her eye, surprised to see how wistful and soft the expression on his face had become. She decided she must be misreading him. He couldn't possibly be touched by a wedding.

After the recessional, Paavo led Angie out of the church. "Nice," he said.

Before she could say anything, a cousin grabbed her arm and pulled her over to a group of relatives.

"Look, it's little Angelina!" an old family friend shouted. Angie particularly hated that name—it made her feel akin to Tom Thumb. "How have you been?"

"It's the baby!" one of her father's cousins said. "Look at how she's grown! I remember when she played on my knee."

Someone else grabbed her. She stiffened. Where was Paavo? She turned her head to find him, but the crowd was too thick. She tried to pull back, even though she knew everyone around her must be finding her behavior strange. She usually joined right in with the whoops, shrieks, and hugs that accompanied greetings in these big family get-togethers, but instead she found herself unable to say anything. People laughed as they hugged and kissed her, all saying they had heard about the bomb and were so relieved she was safe, and wasn't it terrible that the random act of some madman could touch their own family that way? She grew confused and dizzy as they spun her from one person to the next, and her anxiety mounted.

Then Paavo was there, right in front of her, capturing her with both arms. He drew her toward him and tucked her against his side. "Thank you," he said to the family group, "for bringing her back to me."

"Ooooh," the crowd murmured approval at his words, then "Aaaah" as Angie, without thinking about what she was doing, wrapped her arms around him.

She felt Paavo stiffen and she pulled back.

"Let's go," he said, his arm around her shoulders as he led her to the Rolls.

They climbed into the back seat. "I'm sorry," she began, "but the crowd, even though it was my own family—"

"It's all right."

"I hate this, Paavo! I hate it and I don't know what—"

The chauffeur opened the car door for Serefina. "Ready to go?"

Angie nodded to Paavo that she would be all right and took a deep breath before she turned to Serefina and found the strength to act as though nothing had upset her.

They soon arrived at a modern redwood-and-glass building on a bluff, with the ocean on one side and a lake on the other. The late afternoon sun was warm, and there was a light breeze.

Angie stopped at the ladies' lounge to comb her hair, freshen up, and get over her anxiety. Her cousin Pia slinked to her side. Leaning against the vanity countertop, she eyed Angie for a second before speaking.

"That's some guy you showed up with. Good-looking."

"I guess." Especially when he's not reading you your rights, she was tempted to add.

"Hi, girls," Angie's second oldest sister, Caterina, called out as she walked in.

"Love your hair," Angie said, despite being appalled at seeing her sister as a platinum blond.

"Thanks. Actually, your blond highlights gave me the idea."

Angie's mouth dropped. She'd definitely have to reconsider her hair color.

"I'm sure glad I got to see the mystery man you've been hanging out with," her sister said in between quick swipes at her mouth with a tube of lipstick.

"Mystery man?" Pia stepped closer.

"Mamma told me about it," Caterina replied. "He's a detective, and Angie met him when that bomb went off. I can see why she's spending so much time with him."

"That bomb!" Pia smoothed one eyebrow. "God, I heard about it so many times I feel like it went off in *my* kitchen!"

She glanced at Angie and then tugged at the hips of her dress. "A police detective, huh? If you're not serious about him, let me know."

"Hey, Angie," her sixteen-year-old cousin

Loretta stuck her head in the lounge, "your sexy friend is pacing around waiting for you. And about six women are closing in on him."

Without a word, Angie left, walked straight to Paavo, hooked her arm in his, and led him to the other side of the room, near the buffet table.

"What's wrong?" he asked, his eyes intense on her flushed face.

She glanced quickly at him. He was definitely *not* Pia's type. "Nothing, nothing at all," she replied and lifted two glasses of champagne from the tray as a waiter walked by. She handed him one.

Serefina joined them. "Paavo, *caro mio*," she said, turning *Paavo* into an Italian word, "come with me. I want to introduce you."

"Mamma, I don't think—" Angie began.

"No, you don't. But that's all right, Angelina. Come along if you wish."

At that, Serefina dived into the crowd, pulling Paavo in with her. One hour, two more glasses of champagne, and untold numbers of hors d'oeuvres later, they came up for air on the far side of the room. Somewhere along the line, "Mrs. Amalfi" had become "Serefina" to Paavo, and they talked together like long-time friends. Angie tagged along, wondering why she bothered.

When Serefina finally became distracted while talking to Bianca, Angie's oldest sister, Angie took Paavo aside to whisper, "Sorry about that."

"Sorry?" He frowned. "Your mother's a warm, affectionate person, able to make a stranger, even a cop, feel welcome. It doesn't happen often. A lot of people could learn quite a bit from her."

She wondered if he'd include her in that group.

During dinner, Paavo sat between Angie and Serefina. He hardly said a word as Serefina kept everyone near her entertained with her stories, and Angie filled Paavo in on who the numerous relatives were that Serefina was talking about.

"You know, Paavo," Serefina turned to him abruptly, "when I met my Salvatore, after only three days I knew I wanted to marry him. We were in Calabria, right after the war. The country was poor, and he found a job on a small freighter that would take him to America. He left only three weeks after we met. But I waited. And two years later, he spent his savings on boat fare for me to come to him." She smiled knowingly at the two of them.

Angie glanced at Paavo. His expression was suitably blank, but the look he cast toward Angie was one that should be inflicted only on mass murderers or child molesters. She wished she could dive under the table.

After the meal, the guests milled about with coffee and liqueurs until the band started up. The bride and groom danced the first dance, then others began to join them.

As the band finished its third rendering of "Volare" and began "Arrivederci, Roma," Paavo held out his hand. "Angie?"

She looked at him in astonishment. Surely, police inspectors didn't dance!

"I don't think so," she said, vigorously shaking her head.

He turned to her mother. "Serefina?"

She beamed. "*Caro,* I love to dance. But I'm such an old lady!"

"You'll show us all how it's done, Serefina." He lightly touched her back and escorted her to the dance floor.

Angie folded her arms, her lips pursed, as she watched her mother and Casanova doing a fancy waltz step.

"Pretty good, huh?" Bianca nudged her arm.

Angie made no comment.

When the song ended, Paavo helped Serefina, laughing and puffing, to a chair. He got her some champagne before she sent him back to Angie.

As the band played, "That's Amore," Angie's third sister, Maria, asked Paavo if he'd talk to her husband, Dominic, because his business had been burglarized three times recently and he wanted better police protection.

"Well . . ." he glanced at Angie.

"Go ahead, I'm fine." She waved them away.

"I'll waltz him back to you," Caterina leaned toward Angie and whispered. "Pia's making a beeline for him right now."

"Super." Angie sniffed and then folded her arms and watched her platinum blond sister disappear into the crowd.

Bianca, still standing beside her, chuckled.

"So where's Francesca?" Angie asked, looking around for her fourth, and final, sister. "She should be next in line with Mr. Bojangles."

"Fran's at the bar, sloshed. She's having trouble with Seth again. American men are so difficult!"

Angie rolled her eyes. Then she turned down a dance with her cousin Vince, who had sweaty palms and used to sock her when they were kids.

Bianca gave Angie a scathing look. She felt obligated to accept Vince's request to dance. Angie watched the two of them waltz off to "Non Dimenticar."

Suddenly, she realized she was alone in a room full of people. It was the strangest sensation. She looked from one person to the next, realizing any one of them, stranger or friend, could . . . *No!* Her heart began to pound, as dizziness swept over her. She hadn't felt this way before, when Paavo was near. With him she was secure, protected.

She shut her eyes, swaying, and then rushed blindly to the exit, needing to get away from the closeness of the room, away from the music, away from her horrible thoughts. . . .

She stepped onto the well-lit deck, gripped the railing, and gulped the fresh ocean air. As her head cleared, she felt foolish and disgusted with herself. She wondered if she could ever again be as carefree as she had been in the days before the threats had begun and her life had turned upside down.

The sea breeze was cool against her skin, and she tossed her head back, savoring it.

"Excuse me."

Startled, she looked down to see a pretty little

girl holding out a champagne glass. "The man said you'd enjoy this."

"He did?" Angie took the glass. She looked around to see where the child had come from or if anyone was near. They were alone.

"Tell me, was he a tall man who is very handsome?"

The girl giggled and nodded to both questions.

Angie smiled, relieved. "Tell him thank you, then."

After the girl turned and ran off, Angie put the champagne glass on the rail, cupping it and running her thumbs over the condensation that had formed on it. Paavo Smith could be a surprisingly thoughtful man.

"Is anything wrong?" The subject of her thoughts appeared beside her. He put his hand out as if to touch her shoulder but then seemed to think better of it.

"I needed some air," she said softly, feeling flushed and more than a little foolish over her behavior. "Boring in there, wasn't it?"

The white of his teeth flashed in a wry smile. "You're lucky to have a fine family." She nodded and leaned against the railing, looking down toward the beach.

He bent forward with his forearms on top of the railing. A full moon cast a corridor of light on the water, but the rest of the ocean and the night sky was lost in darkness. Just beyond the deck, the hillside dropped away to the beach far below.

"My, uh, father used to take me bass fishing on

the beach down there when I was a kid," Paavo said softly.

"Really?" Angie looked at Paavo's proud profile. "My grandfather and I used to come fishing out here, too."

Paavo's eyebrows rose as he turned to her. "Bet you never touched the bait."

"I did, too! My hands aren't so delicate." She reached out and placed her hand on top of his, gripping it as if to show the strength of her fingers. He rolled his hand over so that it was palm up. She placed her hand in his. "My grandfather used to take me duck hunting, too. I didn't like it, but I'm good at skeet shooting. He didn't have any grandsons, you see, so he taught me to fish and hunt instead. Fishing was my favorite, though. I'd like to again, someday."

"Oh?" His thumb lightly ran over her soft skin.

"Yes, I would!" Her tone was defiant, but she left her hand in his a moment longer before she pulled it back.

"Do you feel any better?" he asked gently.

"A little."

He straightened. "Would you like me to take you home?"

"I ought to stay a while longer. I guess we should go back in. I'm afraid you'll have to listen to 'Volare' a few more times."

He grinned. "It could be worse."

"Right. It could be 'O Sole Mio.' Oh, my champagne." She reached for it and lifted it toward her lips. "Thank you for sending it to me."

"Wait." He grabbed her wrist. She jumped

back as some champagne sloshed over the side of the glass. "What did you say?" he asked. "I didn't send you any champagne."

She froze. "But the little girl said . . ."

"That I sent it?"

"No. A man . . . I assumed . . ."

He lifted the glass from her hand and sniffed the champagne. "Do you carry perfume?"

"Perfume?" She opened her handbag, dug around in it, and then held up a tiny vial.

He put the champagne glass on the rail, unscrewed the top of the vial, and dumped the perfume over the deck.

"But—" she cried. He glanced up at her. "That was three hundred dollars an ounce," she whispered.

He poured a little champagne into the vial, swished it around, poured it out, then refilled it with more champagne. He put the vial in his pocket.

"You can't believe . . ." she began, her voice quivering slightly now. She shivered at the hard, calculating look in his eyes.

"I don't know what to believe. We'll find out for sure."

They found the little girl and Paavo quietly and gently questioned her and her upset parents. But the child was only four and could only say a tall, black-haired man had given her a dollar to carry the champagne to Angie. They walked around, trying to find the man again, but he was probably miles away.

"Even here," Angie cried when she and Paavo

were alone again, "even here, with my family.
. . . It can't be any one of them. It simply can't."
The thought appalled her.

"A clever stunt." Paavo ran his fingers through
his hair as he looked over the crowd. "Who would
question one more guest at a party this large?"

Angie shook her head. "I give up, Paavo. I can't
bear it any longer!" To her dismay, her voice
broke.

She lifted her gaze to his. Their eyes met and
locked as the band began the slow ballad "Al Di
Là."

Without asking, he took her hand and led her
to the dance floor. Her stomach clenched as he
stepped toward her, his face serious and shuttered as always. His arm circled her waist, draw-
ing her closer, and she lifted her free hand to his
shoulder, without will, without hesitation. Up
close she could see that his eyes were even lighter
in the center and sky blue on the edges, that his
lashes were thick and dark. She could see the
funny bend in his nose, the sensuous, well-
defined shape of his lips. Similarly, his gaze
slowly slid over her, his expression harsh as if
against his will his arm tightened and the space
between them closed to nothing. She shut her
eyes as a tremor rippled through her, and she let
herself lean against him, willing, for this moment
at least, to lose herself in the arms of this quiet,
puzzling man. She felt his cheek touch her hair as
he, too, seemed to relax a bit. He tucked her hand
against his chest and their steps grew slower and
smaller until the music ended.

10

Paavo's hand lightly touched Angie's back as they walked down the hall to her apartment. Now she knew what a prisoner whose bail had been revoked felt like, and she sighed as she pulled out her keys. Still, in a prison cell, there was safety, just as there was safety in her apartment. If Paavo's suspicions about the champagne were correct, it would do her no good to stay at her parents' home, because the killer would have already found her there. Staying there would only bring danger to the rest of her family.

At least her apartment was defensible.

"It's me, Rico," she called as she placed the key in the lock. No answer. And no sound coming from the T.V. Odd.

"He's asleep, I guess," she said, but Paavo pulled her away from the door and reached for the snub-nosed revolver hidden under his tuxedo jacket. She gasped and then leaned against the wall, her mind reeling with fear.

Not here, she prayed. Not at my home. Please be all right, Rico. Please!

Paavo turned the key in the latch, then twisted the doorknob until the latch clicked. The door slowly swung open, revealing a well-lit but too quiet apartment.

Cold perspiration formed on her upper lip, and her pulse quickened.

Paavo peered into the doorway and then entered. Angie inched closer, bolstering her courage. As much as she was afraid of what she might find inside, she wouldn't stay in the hall alone. Only with Paavo did she feel safe. She entered the apartment. On the floor lay Rico, tied up. Paavo was kneeling beside him, removing the gag from his mouth.

"Oh my God!" she exclaimed, rushing to help unravel the ties from his legs, while Paavo moved to the bindings that held Rico's hands together.

"It wasn't my fault, Miss Angelina," Rico protested as soon as the gag was off. "I called for a pizza. Some delivery man. He gave it to me and when I put it down to pay him, he bashed my noggin."

"It's all right," Paavo said.

"I'm sure sorry, Inspector. Nothing like this never happened to me before. I thought it was okay, you off with Miss Angelina, so I eased up. I'm sure sorry."

"Nobody's blaming you," Angie said, working alongside Paavo to free Rico. "How do you feel?"

"Like a jerk."

She smiled wanly as she and Paavo helped Rico stumble to the sofa. He muttered more than a few choice words as blood began circulating again through his limbs. Angie handed him some straight scotch and then surveyed the room. There wasn't much damage, only papers pushed around, drawers opened, and the T.V. pulled out from the wall. It's not so bad, she told herself. She wouldn't admit that the break-in had anything to do with that other business. It was a simple robbery by a poverty-stricken pizzaman who saw her fancy apartment and decided to steal some money.

She shuddered and rubbed her arms as the image flashed through her mind of some stranger touching her things, violating her home, her haven. She struggled to control the anger and hysteria building up within her.

Rico raised his face somewhat sheepishly to the tall policeman. "He come in with the pizza. Then he don't even leave it. Sonafabitch."

"You get a good look at him?"

"Not much. He wore a Giants' baseball cap and he kept his head down, looking at my pizza. I guess he wanted it, even then."

Paavo turned to Angie. "I'll take him to Emergency to get him checked over. Then we'll go to the station. I'll need a description of the man, ask a few more questions, and have Rico check out some mug shots. Some men will come over to dust for prints. You'd better call Joey."

She nodded, then pressed Rico's hands. "Are you sure you're feeling okay?"

"I'm sure, Miss. . . . Wait, I just remembered." Both pairs of eyes turned to him. "I think I heard him in the room with the computer. Looking for something, by the sound."

"Oh, no." Angie ran to her den. Papers and disks were strewn all over the floor. Her eyes filled with tears.

"My work!" she cried. "He's destroyed everything!" Her emotions had been on a roller coaster ride all day, and she felt like the track had just ended in midair.

Paavo came up behind her and gently placed his hands on her shoulders.

"It'll be all right," he said. "You can put it right again."

"No! It's gone. All of it."

"Angie," he whispered, turning her around with a light pressure on her shoulders. She guessed he wanted her to pull herself together, hold her chin up, and not fall apart, but she was beyond that. She hurled herself at him, her arms circling his back and clutching him tight against her. His nearness and strength were the only real, secure things in a world suddenly hostile and frightening. She buried her face against his shoulder and sobbed. It wasn't just her papers, it was days and days of fear and madness all come together.

His hands remained properly at her shoulders a long while, and then she felt his body soften. Slowly, he moved his hands across and down her back, gathering her to him, his cheek resting against her hair. "It's okay, Angel," he whispered, stroking her hair, her face. "Don't cry." Perversely, as much as she had hoped he'd understand, when he did, she cried even harder.

When her tears eased a bit, he straightened, his hands found her shoulders again and he stepped back, breaking her hold, yet calming her still with his gaze. How could she ever have thought his eyes cold?

"We'll stop the person who's doing this, Angie. We'll protect you."

"He's been here in my apartment. He's followed me to my family. No one can even find him, how can anyone stop him? He's like some kind of monster out of childhood nightmares, and I just don't—" Her voice choked.

"He's human, and human beings make mistakes. I won't let him hurt you."

She needed to believe him, to trust him.

Slowly he lifted his hands to her face, then rested his fingertips lightly against her jawline. As she gazed up at him, he gently brushed the teardrops from her cheeks with his thumbs. His eyes darkened as one thumb passed slowly over her top lip, then under the fullness of the bottom one. Her breath grew shallow at his touch, and she lay her hands against his waist to steady herself and to bring her closer to him. Suddenly, though, he lowered his hands, his mouth forming a grim line.

Angie stepped back, wondering bleakly how it was possible for him to be so gentle in one moment, then turn away so completely the next, as if he regretted allowing himself and her that momentary lapse, as if he regretted even touching her.

"I'll call Joey for you," he said briskly, again the police inspector as he walked to the telephone on her desk.

She rubbed her arms, suddenly cold.

He also called the police department to send some lab people, so that by the time he left to take Rico to the station, Angie's apartment was crowded with Joey and numerous other policemen, more than one of whom looked with astonishment at Angie's elegant dress and the inspector's tuxedo. No one dared ask why they were dressed that way, though.

Angie tried to stay out of the way and was sitting in a corner of her kitchen when a youthful-looking policeman, tall and lanky, came up to her. He shifted from one foot to the other before he spoke.

"I'd like to apologize," he said finally.

"Apologize?"

"Yes, ma'am. I'm Officer Crossen. I got the call from you about the bomb at your place."

"I remember."

"Oh. Then you probably remember that I didn't take your call very seriously."

"That's right."

He blushed. "I'm sorry. I'm just glad, well, you know. . . ."

Angie studied him a while. He seemed too young to have so much responsibility for other people's lives and to be so willing to put his own on the line. "It's okay."

"At least Inspector Smith's on the case. He's the best."

"The best?" Angie said, hoping to draw out more information about Paavo.

Crossen needed little coaxing. He sat on a counter stool. "Do you remember the big Aquarius case?"

She nodded. It had been in the paper for months.

"He cracked it. And the nut who was systematically killing insurance executives? Smith figured out that one too. Plus lots of other cases that weren't famous because he nailed the killers before they got much play in the papers."

"I see." She had no idea Paavo was in that kind of a position. She tried to remember what she had read in the papers about those cases. "Didn't the Aquarius case end in some kind of a shoot-out?"

"Oh, yes. Just Smith, his partner, Kowalski, and two patrol cops. They brought in the whole 'family'—twenty people. It was a fine action."

She stared at Crossen as his words penetrated. Killings, shoot-outs—and getting misty-eyed at weddings. Would she ever understand Paavo Smith?

"Holy sh——! I mean, excuse me." Crossen's exclamation jarred Angie out of her reverie.

"What is it?"

"This." He waved a recipe she had hanging on the refrigerator door. "My Mom's a great cook, and I know a little about it myself. I heard you had some crazy recipes, but I never thought they'd be *this* goofy. 'Mix together one package chocolate cake mix, half a cup of butter, three eggs, one cup of water, and two thirds of a cup of sauerkraut drained and chopped!' Can you imagine? Kee-rist! 'Bake at three hundred and fifty degrees for thirty minutes.' Ha! My Mom would bust a gut laughing at this."

Angie's face went rigid. "That's *my* recipe." She sniffed. "It's really quite tasty."

Crossen put down the recipe, his eyes wide as he backed out of the room.

11

Paavo reread the lab report on the champagne: a quality bubbly with a lethal dose of arsenic.

He ran his fingers through his hair. It didn't make any sense. The more he got to know Angie, the more he saw that her life revolved around her family and a few friends. She didn't seem to know anything that could make a person particularly angry at her, let alone want to kill her. She was slowly driving him crazy.

She was friendly and warm, devoted to her family, and fearless in protecting her loved ones.

On the other hand, she knew how to bat her eyes and get a man to jump through hoops for her.

She was trusting; she was mouthy.

She was thoughtful; she was stubborn.

Most of all, thoughts of her kept him awake at night.

He wished he had never heard of her. Yet, around her, he felt more alive than he had in years.

Paavo stood up from his desk, slipped his fingers into his back pockets, and walked to the window that overlooked the gray, concrete freeway. He'd find out who wanted to harm her, arrest him, and then close the file and go back to his life, just as it had been before Ms. Society Belle made it all into a big muddle. Go back to the world he belonged in, where he faced no temptation of anything so far beyond his reach. Such temptation was the true road to Hell.

He'd thoroughly checked out her family. If he were the IRS, he might see a problem, but as a cop, he didn't.

He'd checked out her job. The *Shopper*'s sole purpose was to serve as an excuse to publish advertisements. Jon Preston was a name-dropping snob who seemed to think being a small-time publisher made him important. George Meyers looked as if he was just this side of a nervous breakdown. There were a couple of other columnists, one who did travel and one for finances. They worked the way Angie did: they faxed in their columns, showed up at the paper once in a while, and held the jobs strictly for the pleasure of seeing their words and names in print, not for the tiny remuneration received. The other employees were typists or telephone salespeople who seemed to know Angie by sight, but no more. He saw nothing crooked in the operation.

Angie's last three magazine articles had all consisted of complimentary reviews of restaurants in San Francisco. And she hadn't started her next one yet.

Her historical research? So far, original research was nonexistent.

This case was slowly driving him as batty as George Meyers.

"You must be thinking about her again, Paavo," Matt said with a wink as he walked to his desk and dropped a load of papers on it.

Paavo looked up. "Who?"

Matt folded his arms and sat on the corner of his desk facing Paavo. "Who, he asks! Who you think you're kidding? I know lovesick when I see it."

Paavo began to leaf through a memo. "I don't know what the hell you're yapping about now, Kowalski."

Matt chuckled. "What else? I'm talking about the girl of Ptomaine Tommy's dreams. The queen of the greasy spoon. Your girlfriend, the one, the only—"

"Stuff it!"

Matt lifted an eyebrow. "You care about her that much, do you?"

Paavo frowned. "Hell, I'm not even sure I *like* her."

Matt gave him a long look. "We should talk, pal. This sounds serious."

Paavo shook his head, a wry smile on his lips. Matt could always read him like a book.

"Come over Wednesday night. Katie's going out with the girls, and you can help me with

Micky. That'll let you know what you're in for if this gets *really* serious."

The phone on Paavo's desk buzzed, and he lunged for it, glad for the distraction. "Come in to my office, please. And bring Inspector Kowalski with you."

Paavo and Matt looked at each other with raised eyebrows. It *sounded* like Chief Hollins, but it couldn't have been. That man was never so polite to his own mother.

Paavo and Matt put on their jackets and went into Hollins's office.

"Ralph Sanchez and Don Klee, Treasury. Inspectors Smith and Kowalski," Hollins said. The four shook hands.

"These gentlemen," Hollins told Paavo and Matt, "work for Alcohol, Tobacco, and Firearms. They've been watching a man called Samuel Greenberg, but Mr. Greenberg disappeared. A week ago, they ran a routine fingerprint search and learned their suspect had been murdered. His name is Samuel Jerome Kinsley. You know him as Sammy Blade."

"What were you watching him for?" Matt asked.

"Gun smuggling," Klee said. "Automatics."

Paavo looked from one man to the other. "Sammy Blade was no gun smuggler."

"True," Sanchez replied. "But there are a few groups the FBI's been watching in this area— white supremacists to black brotherhoods and every nut case in between. A lot of Uzis and AK-47's have been showing up lately, and it's got the FBI real worried. A few of the trails of these groups cross with those of Samuel Greenberg, or Blade. Too many for coincidence. We'd like to see your files on the Blade case."

"Miss Amalfi?" The thin, older woman rapped against the open door of the den.

Angie turned around in her chair. "All finished, Mrs. Clark?"

"Good as new."

Angie searched for her purse then paid the housekeeper. She thanked her for coming to clean up on such short notice. While Mrs. Clark was putting the apartment back in order, Angie had done the same with her papers and disks. Paavo had been right; it wasn't as difficult to put back together as she had feared. She'd spent the morning concentrating on her disks and papers, without letting any other thoughts intrude upon her work.

Mrs. Clark stepped toward Joey, supine on the sofa. "It was so nice to meet you, too, Mr. Butz. A widow, like myself, quickly learns to recognize quality in a man. . . . I do hope we meet again."

Joey opened one eye. "Charmed, I'm sure."

Mrs. Clark beamed as she turned toward the door. "Such a nice man! Do call me any time, Miss Amalfi. I can always find time for you."

Angie held open the door as Mrs. Clark left and then fastened the deadbolt once again. She looked at Joey, undershirt tight over bulging stomach, wrinkled brown slacks held up by suspenders, shoes off. She shook her head in amazement.

"Nice lady," she said as she sat on the Hepplewhite.

"Reminds me of Olive Oyl," he mumbled.

She turned her attention to the T.V., but in no time her thoughts wandered to Paavo, and her mind replayed again how good it had felt to be held by him, the gentle touch of his hands, his words of comfort . . . and the way he had abruptly turned away from her.

She sighed and went into the kitchen to make some *rispedi* for Rico and Joey—a good old Italian recipe from Serefina—but with a new twist. Instead of working for hours making dough, watching the yeast rise, kneading it down, and so on, she had bought frozen bread dough and thawed it. It had grown to about double its original size, so she pulled off a piece, twisted it around a dried red chili pepper, then deep fried the whole thing to a golden, bar-shaped puff. She could see her diet-conscious friends swooning at the mere thought of these little gems.

She'd just brought a plate of fresh-made *rispedi* to Joey and sat down to eat a couple with him when someone knocked on the door.

Angie stood.

Joey went to the door. "Who's there?"

"My name is Bill, sir," a youthful voice answered. "I need to see Miss Amalfi."

Angie looked at Joey and shook her head. She knew no one named Bill with that voice.

"What's your business?" Joey asked.

"Messenger, sir, *Bay Area Shopper.* I've come for Miss Amalfi's column."

"Oh my God!" Angie cried. " 'Eggs and Egg-onomics.' George threatened to send someone after it if he didn't get a column from me. But I still forgot to send it. Let him in, please."

The young fellow seemed to be nothing but a pair of eyes as he entered the apartment, staring first at Joey and then at Joey's gun, exposed in his shoulder holster.

"What a surprise," Angie said to Joey. "I didn't think the editor would care if my column never appeared again. Then, to actually send someone to save me the trouble of faxing it! I can hardly believe it!"

She rummaged through her papers. She had an extra column that she had written some time ago, in case of emergency. This qualified. There it was, an ode to squash and sensitivity, plus the interpersonal meaning of asparagus. She needed only to include one of Edward Crane's recipes, as George had asked her to do, and the column would be ready for publication. But where were the recipes?

She had tossed the large manila envelope Crane had given her on her desk top, but with the break-in last night, everything had been moved. She looked all through the desk. The envelope wasn't there.

Tapping her fingertip against her chin, she looked around the room. Where had she put it? She looked on shelves and in the closet. Nothing.

The recipes couldn't have disappeared.

She walked slowly back to the living room, trying to imagine where else she might have put them.

"Is anything wrong, ma'am?" asked Bill.

"No . . . no, not really. Joey, did you see a large manila envelope laying about?"

"A large what?" His eyes squinted slightly.

"Nothing."

She looked in the kitchen and bedroom with no luck. Mrs. Clark wouldn't have left it there anyway, but she might have brought it into the den.

She returned to the den for one last search, but to no avail. The envelope was gone. In fact, the only thing that seemed to be missing since the burglary were Edward Crane's recipes.

She had to call Paavo, but first she needed to get rid of Bill.

She started up her computer.

Place in blender:
    1 can sardines (deboned)
    3 oz. maraschino cherries
    1/2 cup soy sauce
    5 boiled brussels sprouts

(Wonderful! Now what?)
Blend thoroughly, then stir in 8 oz. warm chocolate syrup.

(Now for the coup de grace.)
Spoon over one dozen soft-boiled eggs.

(Yech!)

She picked up the recipe, entitled it "The P.S. Special" *(take that, Inspector Smith!)*, stapled it to her column, and brought them to the patiently waiting messenger, who was standing transfixed in the presence of Joey's gun.

"Here you go, Bill." Angie handed him the papers.

"Thank you, Miss Amalfi." He held them tightly in both hands and bolted out the door.

As soon as he had left, Angie ran to the phone and dialed the number Paavo had left her. He was no longer at the station. It was supposed to be his day off, though she couldn't imagine him taking two days off in a row. Being an inspector seemed to be his whole life.

She hung up, sulking and feeling abandoned. How could he take a day off the day after she had been burglarized? She had expected him to be down at the lab, looking for fingerprints or something.

The ring of the telephone made her jump. She picked it up.

"This is Smith," was his stern answer to her friendly hello.

"I thought you had the day off," she replied. Two could play at this icicle game.

"What's wrong?"

"You're not busy?"

"I thought you were in trouble."

Suddenly, she wasn't sure. "Well, yes. I mean, no, not at the moment."

"Do you want to tell me about it?"

"I don't know."

"Want to call back when you do?"

"So you are busy. I should have guessed."

"It's just the laundry."

"Laundry! Terrific! I'm here worried about my life and instead of going out investigating you're sitting safely in your house washing your Fruit of the Loom!"

She heard him give a slight cough. "All right, Angie, what happened today?"

Suddenly, her irritation disappeared, and her voice was tiny, frightened. "Paavo, they're gone! The recipes!"

"What recipes?"

"The last two."

"Last two?"

"I told you about them. George insisted I use them, but Preston didn't think I should. I didn't think so either, because I didn't like him."

"Didn't like who?"

She clutched the receiver more tightly and nearly shouted into it, "Edward Crane—the man with the blue head."

"Blue head?"

"His head was shaved. He's one of the biggest fans of 'Eggs and Egg-onomics.' "

"Ah."

"No, that's not why he's got a blue head. Paavo, I can't find his recipes!"

"Angie, calm down. Start at the beginning."

He listened carefully as she told him about her failed search for the recipes.

"And all that's missing after the burglary are those recipes?" he asked.

"That's what I've been trying to tell you!"

"I'm having a check run on the name Edward G. Crane, but so far we've turned up nothing. Do you know where I can reach this guy?"

"I have no idea."

"This whole thing is nuts."

"No, waffles."

"I think I'd better come right over."

12

Angie wondered what it meant when a man was willing to leave his clothes in the rinse cycle to come to see you. Now that he was on his way, what would she tell him? She felt like a fool. What if Crane's recipes had been thrown away by mistake?

She turned the apartment upside down looking for them, even checking through the trash. Nothing.

A loud knock sounded on the door. Why did cops always knock as if they've come to arrest you on a morals charge? She hovered near the door as Joey opened it.

"Good afternoon," Paavo said as he entered the room. Joey greeted him and then returned to football highlights.

Angie stood with her mouth agape. The inspector was dressed in light-blue jeans, desert boots, and a khaki bush jacket hanging open over a gray wool sweater.

"Your clothes!" She choked out the words.

He looked down. "I'm off duty."

Off duty. Maybe he did have a life beyond policing?

He tossed his jacket over the Hepplewhite. The vertical ribbing on the gray sweater skimmed his chest, outlining his broad, firm muscles.

She led him to the wingback chairs. "Coffee or beer?"

"Since I'm off duty, make it a beer."

She returned from the kitchen and sat across from him, wringing her hands.

He took a swallow. "Tell me what's going on, but slowly."

"Maybe I'm just acting foolishly. This whole thing has me so crazy I'm seeing skeletons in every closet. I'm afraid I disrupted your day off for no good reason." Downcast, she continued quietly. "I really have nothing to add to what I said on the phone. Maybe Edward Crane's recipes got thrown away. No one would steal marshmallow and bean sprout blintzes or peanut butter omelet recipes. Even after a week of Slim-Fast they wouldn't look good."

For a moment he said nothing but simply looked at her. Then he said softly, "Angie, if you ever lost your sense of humor, the world should cry."

The words traveled straight to her heart. She looked at him quizzically, uncertain that he could have meant anything so sweet.

"Let's start with your blue-headed fan. As I understand it, he now brings you some other man's recipes."

"Yes, Sam's—who calls himself Waffles—except Crane claims they were always his recipes."

"So this . . . Crane . . . is saying Waffles is a plagiarist?" His serious voice was belied by the sparkle in his eyes.

She sighed, trying to ignore his skepticism. "I guess so."

"And what does Waffles say about this accusation?"

"I don't know. I was going to meet him, but he didn't show up, and I haven't heard from him since."

"Where'd he go?"

"Crane said Waffles got a job in Carmel."

"As a cook?"

"Who knows? Maybe he ran off to a love nest with Julia Child."

"Take it easy, Angie." He rubbed his temple while she fretted. "Okay, now, Waffles was supposed to meet you but he didn't show, right?"

She nodded.

"But instead he goes off to a ritzy beach resort."

"Correct."

"Do you remember when all this took place?"

"That's easy. It was the day the bomb was delivered. I forgot all about Sam in the aftermath, until Edward Crane showed up and told me what had happened."

Paavo leaned forward in the chair. The look on

his face stopped her from saying more. "Waffles. You said his name was Sam Martin?"

"That's right."

He frowned. "Were you going to meet him here?"

"No. I never invite strangers to my home. I was going to meet him at the park two blocks away."

The only sign that Paavo was stirred was that he began to pace. "Tell me about this Sam Martin." Angie followed his steps back and forth.

"I don't know much. He said he used to be a cook on a freighter. All I know is he's a really sweet man, late sixties or so, very slight, with dyed-black hair."

His step faltered. "You planned to meet him on Sunday. What time?"

"We were supposed to meet at noon. I waited until after one o'clock, then came home. Why? You don't think Sam had anything to do with the bomb, do you? I mean, my God, no. He couldn't. I'd never believe that." She stared at him, waiting.

He ran his hand through his hair, and his piercing blue eyes captured her gaze. She was accustomed to brown eyes. Her whole family had brown eyes. Being studied so intently by such large, pale, blue ones was disconcerting, as if he could see more deeply, learn more about her than she might want to reveal.

He shook his head. "It's too improbable."

He had all her attention now.

"That Sunday, as you waited, did you pass anyone or see anyone in the park or near it?"

"I didn't pay any attention."

He sat and reached across the small space that separated them to take her hands in his.

"Think, Angie. Shut your eyes. Really shut them. That's good. Now picture what I say. . . .

"Go back to that morning. It was a sunny morning. Indian summer. Think of what you were wearing. Your dress. Did you wear a coat? Which shoes? You were doing a lot of walking. You had to walk up to the top of Vallejo Street, then descend those narrow steps down to the park. They're steep. Very steep. You wouldn't want to have to get off the stairs if someone were going up or down them, now would you? No. If you passed someone, you or he would have to move over. You'd probably look down, at your shoes, to be sure you didn't trip. Can you see it? Can you see yourself stepping aside, waiting for someone to pass you? A man, perhaps, approaching you, and you wondering which of you would yield. Maybe he interrupted your thoughts. Maybe you were thinking about your food column, or the view . . . the blue sky, Coit Tower—"

"No!" She opened her eyes and looked at him, blinking. "No. You've got it backwards. I remember now. That day, I got ready early. I'm usually never early for anything, but it was such a warm morning I decided to go down to North Beach for some espresso and croissants for breakfast. I walked back to the park from the opposite direction. Well, the opposite way from where I usually come.

"And I was nearly trampled by a man running

down the steps, away from the park. He seemed startled and looked at me as if he'd seen a ghost. His whole reaction amused me. He didn't stop, and I continued on."

Paavo rubbed his chin. "I wonder if that's it? It must be." He snapped his fingers. "It's got to be."

"What?"

"Describe the man to me."

"Describe him?" She tried to remember. "Dark hair? I'm pretty sure. But the style? I don't know. I didn't pay any attention. He seemed kind of average. Not too tall. I guess he wasn't good-looking or I'd remember." She tried to smile but didn't succeed.

"Come on." He pulled her to her feet. "Grab a jacket."

She jerked her hand free. "Why? Where are we going?" An icy chill came over her.

"The station. Homicide. I want you to look at some pictures."

"Homicide?" Her voice was a whisper. She felt as if all the blood had drained from her face.

"That's where I work, remember? I told you I was investigating a case when I got a call—twice, in fact—to come over here. Last Sunday afternoon, around the time the bomb went off, a man's body was found in that park."

"The man I saw?"

"No. It might . . ." He met her gaze. "The description matches that of your friend Waffles."

His words made no sense to her. "No, Paavo," she said firmly. "Waffles is a nice gentleman. He doesn't even have much money. I used to give him twenty dollars for his recipes. No one would murder him."

"Maybe that's the missing ingredient."

"The what?"

"Let's go."

"No!" She shook her head, backing away from him. "I'm not leaving this apartment."

"Listen to me." Paavo stepped toward her, taking her arms. "You can't hide here the rest of your life. Come with me and we'll try to get this solved and over with."

Her fingers tightened on the sleeves of his sweater. "Paavo, you're saying there's a murderer after me, that's what you're saying! Someone who killed a sweet little man, and now—"

"Yes." His eyes held her rigid.

"The champagne, the sample you took, you haven't told me if it had been . . ."

He nodded.

"No!"

His grip tightened. "That's why we've got to act to stop this as soon as we can."

She pulled back from him. "I can't!"

He moved closer to her and slid his hands up to her shoulders. She bowed her head, feeling her body sway toward him, wanting to lean on him, wanting him to make her feel safe the way he did yesterday. But instead, he dropped his hands and stood very straight. "Miss Amalfi, I'll be with you. The police will be watching you. Believe me, it's safer to cooperate."

The sudden coldness in his voice, this business of being a detective, was more than she could bear. "Cooperate! What do you think I've been doing? You think I like this? Living this way? Being afraid, alone? You might want to live this way, but I don't!"

She saw color darken his cheeks. His jaw stiffened. "Miss Amalfi, to cooperate—"

"My friend Sam was killed and someone's after me, and all you can talk about is for me to cooperate? Who do you think you are, Eliot Ness?"

He paused for a moment. "I'm a police inspector, Miss Amalfi."

"Angie! My name is Angie!" Tears stung her eyes.

"Angie," he whispered.

He said her name softly, almost like a caress. Her heart lurched. She studied his thin face, the lines of world-weariness at the corners of his eyes, the firm, determined set of his jaw. If she were to see this thing out to its end, whatever that might be, she would have to trust this man with her life. She knew she wasn't brave, but maybe she could try to be.

She nodded and turned to get her coat.

13

"*Back again, Paav?* I thought this was your day off."

Paavo glanced at Benson, a first-year inspector who sat on the top of a desk, one foot on the ground, the other dangling in midair. Although he spoke to Paavo, his eyes lingered on Angie's petite body, nicely wrapped in a blousy, cream-colored jacket and matching slacks. Paavo realized he never much liked Benson.

Chief Hollins spared Paavo the trouble of answering. "Smith never takes days off. Didn't you learn that yet, meatball?" The chief was bent double over some reports spread out on a table. The top of his head, his wide nose, and a cigar that rolled from one side of his mouth to the other were all that was visible.

"We may have a break in the Sammy Blade murder," Paavo said as he situated himself between Angie and Benson's line of ogling. "Where's Matt?"

"Dunno. It's his day off, too, remember? I thought you was going to watch his kid?"

"It's next weekend that he and Katie are going away."

The gruff-voiced police chief looked up and, spotting Angie, stood upright, still gnawing his cigar as he studied her through squinty eyes. "Kid's got bad taste, wanting to stay with you, Smith, 'stead of going to Vegas. Anyway, what you got?"

Paavo introduced Angie, and Hollins led them into his office. He quickly told Hollins about Waffles, Crane, and the recipes. Hollins's already pained expression grew worse as the story continued. He removed his cigar and looked slowly from one to the other before speaking. "Could be what you say, Smith. Maybe not. Don't make much sense. But remember, looks like you got guns involved. Plenty of money there. Makes men real mean."

Angie flinched. Paavo shot her a quick glance. "I know. That's why we've got to find Blade's killer."

Hollins continued, "No reason to expect whoever's behind this to give up, you know."

Angie looked even paler, and Paavo felt ready to strangle the man, if that's what it would take to shut him up.

Hollins inhaled his cigar again and let the smoke out slowly, forming big O's in the air. "Better cooperate, little lady. Only way to save your neck."

"So I've heard."

Paavo stood and helped her to her feet, cupping her elbow. "Excuse us, Chief. I'm going to have Miss Amalfi look at some mug shots."

"Fine. Matt said he might stop by later. He's got a lead on the gun angle. I told him don't do nothing until tomorrow, with you. I don't want you guys going off alone on this thing."

Paavo stopped in the doorway. "A lead? Did he say what it was?"

"Not a word."

"Interesting. Would you ask him to call me if he shows up?"

"What am I? A goddamned girl Friday or something?"

"I'll leave him a note."

Paavo brought Angie to a dingy interview room with a wooden table and two chairs. A minute later, Officer Rebecca Mayfield appeared in the doorway, a stack of albums in her arms. She didn't take her eyes off Angie.

"Let me help you." Paavo reached for the albums.

"No need." Her tone was icy as she walked to the table and plopped the albums on top of it. Continuing around the table so that she stood behind Angie's back, she gave Paavo a look that could kill. When he narrowed his eyes, she lifted her chin, marched out the door, and slammed it shut behind her.

Angie looked from the door to Paavo and back

again but refrained from making a comment. He didn't look like he'd have much of a sense of humor at the moment.

Paavo placed his palm on top of the albums. "Look at the pictures here carefully, one at a time. Really study them, because I want you to look for two people: Edward Crane and the man that was on the steps. If you see either man, or anyone with a close resemblance, let me know."

"Crane's no problem, but the other man, I told you, I can't remember."

"You might. Look at the pictures. Want coffee?"

She shook her head and turned to the mug shots, but Paavo put his hand on them. She looked up at him.

"One more thing." He sat on the edge of the table and handed her the picture he had kept separate from the rest.

It was a morgue shot of Sammy Blade.

"Oh, my God!" She threw the photo down on the table and jumped back, wiping her hand frantically against her slacks. "That's Sam," she whispered, every hint of color drained from her face.

"It's Sammy Blade, Angie, a two-bit crook way over his head with some guys who deal in guns. Matt and I were trying to find out about Blade and stumbled right into a federal investigation of a lot of automatic weapons that have been illegally hitting these shores. We're not positive Blade was involved, but it's as good an explanation as any for his sudden unpopularity. Men involved in these things never do last long."

"I can't believe it."

"By the way, when he was in prison, he usually asked for kitchen duty."

She sat down stiffly in the chair, her hands shaking. "May I look at these mug shots now?"

Two hours later she had gone through not only all the albums in the first pile brought to her but another half dozen as well.

"How are you doing?" Paavo stuck his head in the doorway.

"I don't think I could recognize my own mother."

"We'll try another time."

"I didn't see Crane, but the other man I don't remember. I wish I did, but I don't." She stood and rubbed the back of her neck.

"But you do remember that he looked startled. That means the memory of his face is in that head of yours. We just have to find a way to trigger it."

"I don't know."

"I'll take you home now." He led her through the outer office and past the good-byes and raised eyebrows of his fellow officers.

They emerged in the late afternoon sunshine. San Francisco was putting on its usual October display of sunny, warm weather. Winter was rainy, summer was foggy, and spring was windy. Fall was perfect.

Angie stood at the top of the gray granite steps

of the Hall of Justice and looked at the sky. Paavo proceeded two steps ahead of her and then turned and waited.

"What is it?" he asked.

"It's so beautiful out. I hate the idea of going back to the waiting, for I don't even know what. Back to being scared and bored at the same time, I guess." She tilted her head toward the brilliant blue sky. "I wish I could just fade into the day, to go where I want, when I want, do all the things I'd always taken for granted."

"You will again."

She looked into his eyes. "I heard what Chief Hollins said."

Something about the way she looked at him at that moment made him want to wrestle away the ugliness that had entered her world. Strangely, she made him feel as if he could do it. She made him feel as if he could do anything he set his mind to. He could almost hear Rebecca laughing cynically at his weakness.

But at this moment, he didn't care about Rebecca's warning, or even that of his own conscience, reminding him not to become involved with a woman so completely out of his league. He wanted to be with her a little while longer, to bask in the sunshine with her. Tomorrow, he'd be practical again.

He held out his hand. "Let's go for a ride. We'll look at the city. Forget about all this, for a while, at least." For a second she didn't move, and then in a move of utter trust, she placed her hand in his. They continued down the steps toward his car. It was an old sports car, an Austin Healey. In deference to the good weather and Angie's low spirits, he took a minute to wrestle down the canvas top.

"That's heavenly." She shut her eyes and leaned her head against the head rest, feeling the sun on her face.

His chest constricted as he looked at how vulnerable she was, how readily she had placed herself in his power. "Yes," he whispered, wanting to warn her not to trust so easily—not to trust anyone, not even him.

She opened one eye to see him watching her rather than the sky. "Yes, Miss Amalfi," she corrected him pertly.

He grinned as he pulled out of the parking space into the stream of traffic.

"Any place in particular you'd like to go?"

"There is, in fact. You said you grew up in the Mission district. I'm not very familiar with it. What if we went there? You could show me Mission Street, Mission Dolores, Mission High. Even the Paavo Smith ancestral home. How's that?"

"That's easy enough to arrange." He took a left turn. A shadow fluttered across his sharply delineated features. "Except for the latter. There is no Paavo Smith family. Just me."

"Oh? And you sprang full-blown from the air? A regular miracle?"

"Maybe so, Miss Amalfi."

They rode down Mission Street, once the heart of the finest neighborhood in San Francisco. Over the years, though, as the houses grew older, the area had deteriorated into inner city shabbiness. Now, it was a mostly Latin American neighborhood. Mexican groceries, restaurants, and people filled the street.

"*Se habla español*, Paavo?"

"*Si*. I had to survive."

"What else did you have to do to survive?"

A slow grin formed on his mouth. "Plenty."

He stopped the car. "Have you been inside Mission Dolores?"

"Never. Of course, the nuns at school told us how Father Junipero Serra built his missions all along Highway 1 in California. I thought that was awfully considerate. It made it easy for tourists to visit."

He wrinkled his mouth. "Funny. Want to go in?"

She pulled a scarf out of her jacket pocket. Living in San Francisco, she was always ready for a change for the worse in the weather. She saw his surprise as she put the scarf on her head.

"My mother taught me the old way of being a Roman Catholic. I even say my prayers in Latin: *Pater noster qui es in caelis, Sanctificetur nomen tuum. . . .*"

"You'll like the mission. You can almost hear the first padres still at work."

They entered the nave. Angie placed two fingers in the holy water and made the sign of the cross. Paavo hung back, but she felt him watching her as she walked along the far side of the pews to a small alcove with a statue of Mary and a rack of candles in front of it. She put a dollar in the box

and lit two candles, then knelt before the statue
and bowed her head in prayer. A short while
later, she walked toward the altar, genuflected
while making the sign of the cross again, and sat
in a pew.

She took a deep breath, inhaling the scent of
the church and letting its tranquility settle over
her. All old Catholic churches had a similar smell,
a combination of the wax used to keep the pews
and floors glistening, incense, flowers, and burning candles. The familiarity of the scent reminded
her of when she was a little girl. She looked at the
statues, the peaceful expressions on their faces,
and tried to absorb the hope they offered.

She glanced surreptitiously behind her. Paavo
leaned against a wall watching her, one foot
crossed over the other. Policemen must have
enormous patience.

He was an intriguing man. She'd seen flashes
of warmth and wondered if there wasn't much
more carefully hidden behind that cold, reserved
veneer. She had seen a hint of his life today, but
his parents and background remained mysteries.

Maybe all she felt toward him was curiosity.
But even as she considered this, she knew it
wasn't true. She knew that deep within her she
felt a strange affinity with Paavo Smith which
disturbed her as much as it intrigued her. She
glanced up at the statue of the Virgin Mary.
There were times when she could swear she
could read his mind, even though they barely
seemed to speak the same language. Still, whenever she seemed to get at all close to the man,

Inspector Smith appeared, putting a quick stop to it.

She shook her head in disgust for thinking about some man while sitting in church. Sister Mary Ignatius would turn in her grave.

Angie stood and walked to the aisle. Before turning to leave, she gazed once more at the statue of Mary. Her candles burned brightly. "Someday, I'll return, Holy Mother," she whispered. "I promise."

"Where to now?" she asked as they climbed back into Paavo's battered sports car.

He looked thoughtful. "I don't have a family home, as I said. But there's someone you might enjoy meeting. And I'm overdue for a visit. It's been a few weeks."

He was soon driving on Mission Street, heading south.

"Who is he?" Angie asked.

"His name is Aulis Kokkonen. He's Finnish— the one responsible for the name Paavo. He raised me and my sister."

"You have a sister?"

"Had. She's dead."

He said the words so quietly Angie hardly heard him. It took a moment for their meaning to hit her. "I'm so sorry," she said as she thought of how cavalierly she had paraded her own sisters before him.

"It was a long time ago, Angie. She was feisty,

little, kind of like you. In temperament. Not in looks."

She waited and then broke the silence. "What happened to her?"

He shrugged. "An accident." His tone didn't invite further questioning.

He turned off Mission, and two blocks later the car stopped in front of a white building, large enough to house three or four apartments. Paavo didn't go up the stairs to the front entry. Instead, he walked along the side, between the garage and the neighboring house. Just past the garage was a door. He knocked.

After a short while the door opened. A frail-looking old man with snowy white hair, a beard, and eyes the color of Indian turquoise peered cautiously from the doorway. When he saw his visitors, his face broke into a huge smile. "Paavo, my boy, good to see you. Come in, come in."

He reached out and grasped Paavo's arm with a firm grip, despite the pale thinness of his hand. Then he looked in Angie's direction and squinted. "A young lady, too. Good." He shuffled back into the room after Paavo made the introductions.

Paavo had to lower his head to get past the doorway. The room was small, with a bed in the corner, a wooden table and four chairs around it, a T.V., and a dresser. A small kitchen and bathroom completed the living quarters.

Angie sat at the table while Aulis Kokkonen produced a bottle of wine and Paavo set out three glasses.

"Me and my friends made this," the old man said to Angie, pointing at the bottle. "Bet you never had homemade wine before."

"I wouldn't make that bet if I were you. My grandfather made great wine. The only trouble was, he'd be so impatient to 'test' it, it was never quite ready when he poured it. Great three-week-old stuff." Angie smiled and relaxed in the warm presence of this frail old man.

Aulis chuckled. "I know the fault. Yes, I know it well."

He turned to Paavo. "You work too much, boy. I'm glad to see you taking a day off."

Angie spoke up. "I'm afraid not, Mr. Kokkonen. I'm just another case."

Aulis looked surprised. "Is that so?" His eyes danced. "Is that a fact, now? Well, I should be glad Paavo turned out so dedicated to the law. There was a time I'd never take up *that* bet either, believe me."

"Hey, Papa, we don't have to go into that," Paavo said.

"Of course, we do!" Angie's curiosity bubbled over.

The old man seemed amused at her reaction. Glancing quickly at Paavo, he leaned forward in his chair. "Let me tell you, the main reason Paavo is such a good cop is because he learned all their faults as a teenager. Oh, did he give them a merry chase around this neighborhood, him and his buddies. What a group!" He chuckled. "One wilder than the other. They never did anything seriously wrong, they had better sense than that, but they surely thought they were big shots. Paavo got escorted home by the police more times than I can count."

"You're kidding." Angie looked at Paavo. Well, if the mighty Inspector Smith didn't look uncomfortable, even sheepish!

"How's your rheumatism doing?" Paavo asked, obviously trying to change the subject.

The old man winked at Angie. Soon, the three had settled into warm companionship, Aulis pulling Angie into the conversation with a wealth of anecdotes about old times and old friends. As she sat at the table, she witnessed, in Paavo's every gesture, the gentle love and respect he had for the man he called "Papa." For the first time, she saw Paavo relaxed, allowing his own dry humor and wit to appear. The change fascinated and charmed her.

Finally, Paavo stood. "I think it's time we get going. I want to get Miss Amalfi home before it's late—and before you tell her so many stories she demands a new detective on the case."

Angie quickly finished her wine. It did taste a lot like her grandfather's, and it brought back memories of the wonderful times she had had with him as a child. She was sorry to leave the warmth she had found in this tiny apartment.

"Bring her around again, Paavo. This one I like," the old man said as Paavo gave him a quick hug. "Be careful, son," Angie heard him add in a whisper as she and Paavo walked towards the street.

"Thank you, Paavo," she said softly once they

were seated in his car again. "For letting me meet him." And for letting me know another part of you, she thought but didn't dare say to him.

He smiled. "Where to, m'lady? Home?"

Home. The word weighed heavily. Night was falling, and the lights of the city shone with a promise of excitement that only big cities could offer. "I guess so."

She looked up and saw that the yearning in his gaze echoed her own.

"Tell you what," he said. "Let's go to my place so I can change into something better than blue jeans, and I'll take you out to dinner."

Slowly, she smiled. "Just don't order any champagne . . . or squab!"

14

Inspector Paavo Smith's home was in the northwest corner of the city, facing the Pacific Ocean, bordering the lush greenery of the Presidio. He turned up the driveway of a brown-shingled cottage.

"There's no garage," he said. "This place was built before cars were even a twinkle in Henry Ford's eyes."

Angie looked at the trim house lit by the tall streetlamps and the warm, shaded lighting of other homes on the block. "This is quite a change from the hectic pace of the Mission or downtown."

He unlocked the front door, switched on the lights, and stepped aside for her to enter.

The door opened directly into a tiny living room. The sofa and chairs were mismatched, overstuffed, and inviting. Multicolored patchwork cushions were scattered over them, an autumn-toned afghan was draped over the back of a chair, and a red and blue hooked rug lay in front of the fireplace. Books and magazines sat stacked beside an easy chair and on top of the coffee table; cassette tapes and compact disks filled the shelves around a stereo system. One wall had a fireplace with overflowing bookshelves on each side of it, while on other walls hung Impressionist and early Modern prints. It was a comfortable, practical room, Angie thought, except for the surprising touch offered by the prints.

A loud *meow* greeted them. An enormous yellow tabby was curled on a chair. A scar ran from the end of his nose up to his forehead, and he had the most pugnacious face Angie ever saw on a cat.

"That's Hercules." Paavo grinned at the big tom. "Terror of all dogs in the neighborhood. His morning sport is beating up the German Shepherd down the block."

Hercules jumped off the chair, stretched, and rubbed his body against Paavo's leg. Paavo bent and scratched the cat behind the ears before heading toward the kitchen. Hercules ran between his feet, mewling loudly.

Angie followed them to the doorway of the kitchen. The aging appliances were all white, and the five-foot-high refrigerator had only one door. She hadn't seen a kitchen like this since her early childhood, when her father's shoe business had needed every cent of profit plowed right back into it.

Paavo opened a can of 9 Lives. "I leave him dry

food all the time. I'm never sure of my hours, but when I'm home, he knows he gets a special treat. Okay, Herk, chow time."

He put the bowl of cat food on the floor.

"Would you like something to drink?" he asked Angie as he opened the refrigerator and peered inside. "I've got . . . beer." He held it up. "One can."

She smiled. "We'll split it. I'm not very thirsty anyway."

He reached for two glasses from the cupboard and carried them to the living room, placing them side by side on the coffee table.

She sat on the sofa. Hercules leaped onto her lap, and then flopped down. She laughed and stroked his head. Purring loudly, he wriggled onto his back to get his tummy scratched. He was big and tough-looking but also as gentle and affectionate as a kitten. Her gaze lifted to Paavo, who put the one can of beer and a package of Oreo cookies on the coffee table. A warmth tugged at her.

"There." Paavo popped open the can, half filled their glasses, and tore open the cookie wrapper. He faced Angie, and the easy smile he wore vanished. In its place was an odd expression.

"What?" she asked.

"I . . . sorry." He took a sip of his beer.

"It's okay."

"I'd better change so we can get out of here."

"But it's really very nice right here," she said. "I don't mind staying."

"I promised you dinner."

"I'll cook. I love to cook."

"No—"

"My cooking's that bad, huh?" She tried to smile but couldn't help feeling hurt. She dropped her gaze from his and stared instead at the bubbles in her beer glass, absentmindedly petting Hercules. He purred in appreciation, and she glanced down at him. "Well, at least somebody likes my company."

"Angelina." Paavo sighed as he settled his long body back against the sofa, his head cocked as he regarded her. "What to do with you?"

Her gaze went first to his eyes, then to his prominent cheekbones, his straight, winged brows, his mouth, which she had come to find so expressive and sensuous, the funny little bend to his nose, and then his lithe, powerful body.

His question was far too tempting. It made her think of things she'd like him to do with her, and she with him. His nearness made her breath quicken and her pulse throb. There was no way she could answer his question.

"You're sorry I came?" she finally asked in a hushed voice.

He dropped a hand to grip his knee. "The problem's the opposite."

For a moment she couldn't believe what she'd heard. She placed her hand in his and twined their fingers together. Neither spoke. She studied her small, fair hand with long, currently lilac nails, against his large, rough one. She liked the feel of him. She liked everything she had learned about him that day.

"What's wrong, Paavo?"

He rubbed his free hand over his eyes and nose, and held it against his mouth for a moment. "This is crazy."

"What is?"

"This. You. I enjoyed today and yesterday far too much."

"Is that a crime, Inspector?"

He glanced at her, then looked away. "One of the first things you learn as a rookie is to watch out for damsels in distress."

"Oh?"

"They cloud your judgment, making it more dangerous for both of you." His eyes met hers. "For both, do you understand?"

She nodded, knowing, but hating, the truth of what he was saying. She pulled her hand away. "I'm sorry," she whispered.

He cupped her chin. She didn't breathe as he lightly ran his thumb over her lips, a poor substitute for the kiss she wanted. But he held back. The look he gave her deepened and softened, as if he were memorizing her features. Then he dropped his hand and stood up with a shake of his head. "Let's get out of here before my good intentions go by the wayside."

At that, he stood quickly and left the room.

It was moments before her breathing returned to normal. Never before had she known a man whose mere touch had such an effect on her.

She tried to distract herself by looking through his magazines and books. She was surprised at his taste in literature—Mann, Proust, Conrad, as well as murder mysteries and science fiction. The most surprising thing was that the former looked every bit as well worn as the latter.

She heard the shower running as she looked at the books. His words, though, kept sounding in her ears. It was the nicest rejection she had ever received.

A short while later, he came back into the room wearing a black turtleneck sweater and light gray linen slacks, and carrying a darker gray sports jacket. His hair was shining and soft looking.

"Ready," he announced.

"Very nice," she said with frankness.

His eyebrows rose a moment. "Thank you." He stepped toward her. "Ready?"

"Yes."

As he reached for the knob to the front door, the phone rang. Paavo opened the door.

"Shouldn't you answer?" Angie asked.

"The answering machine will click on soon. Maybe we ought to just get out of here. If it's the force, they can use my beeper, anyway."

"Well, whatever." She hated the insistent ringing.

He hesitated, looking at the phone, and then hooked his jacket onto the back of a chair and moved toward the phone.

Suddenly she wanted to tell him to stop, to forget the call, to let them have their evening together. But it was too late. The answering machine had turned on.

"Paavo," the gruff voice of Hollins boomed

over the recorder, "call the station. Ask for me or
Calderon."

Paavo grabbed the receiver. "Wait, I'm here.
What's up?"

Angie felt her stomach knot. Maybe everything
would be all right, maybe she just had a twinge of
nerves, not anything like a premonition at all.

Her heart pounded as she watched him listening to his boss. Something was wrong, she realized almost immediately. He held the phone, first
with one hand, then he lifted the other to grasp
the mouthpiece. There was an imperceptible
stiffening to his stance, and though she was only
twenty feet away from him, he suddenly seemed
an ocean away as the coldness surged across the
room.

"Yes . . . yes, I'm still here. . . ." His voice was
harsh, strained, filled with a bitter anger that
made her cringe inside. "Did you tell Katie?
. . . God. . . ." His gaze lifted to Angie, but
although he was staring directly at her, he didn't
seem to see her. Then the veil dropped from his
eyes, and as his gaze focused on hers, she was
shaken by the pain and sorrow she saw. Her
throat tightened. She stood, wanting to go to him,
to do whatever she could to help, but hesitated,
still feeling the force of the wall he'd built around
himself. He turned his back to her. His voice was
devoid of emotion.

"Where was he? . . . I see. . . . Okay, I'm
coming down. . . . No, I'll be there anyway.
. . . I don't care. . . . All right, all right." He quietly
set the receiver back down.

She waited.

Slowly, he walked to the chair and picked up his jacket. "A change in plans. I've got to go to the station." His voice was flat. He looked at the far wall and stopped speaking.

"Paavo?" she said gently, walking to his side and lightly touching his back.

He grunted and walked into his bedroom. She waited a while, and then, when he didn't return, followed him to the doorway. Her stomach knotted. He stood on the far side of the room with his back to her, wearing his shoulder holster, his shoulders slumped, his arms at his sides. He seemed to be looking at a wall covered with pictures and scrolls, commendations from the force and the city.

She walked across a bedroom that was as warm and cozy as the rest of the house, with Colonial pine furniture and a Paavo-sized bed covered with an old quilted comforter. Tenderly, she placed a hand on his arm. "What is it?"

"There." He pointed at a photo of a boyish-looking, blond-haired policeman with his arm around Paavo's shoulders. They each were wearing blue patrolman's uniforms with brass buttons and shiny badges. Both looked very young, very happy, and very innocent.

"That's my partner, Matt. Eleven years ago we were both rookies. Hired about a month apart. Him first, then me. He liked to say I was the 'junior' partner." He stopped. The room vibrated with the pounding of his heartbeat, the shallow, ragged breathing in his chest. He turned toward her, his eyes now gray, the color of a rainstorm. He searched her face, as if wishing she could tell him it wasn't true, but she couldn't help him, she couldn't stop his pain. "Matt was killed today."

Her grip tightened on his arm. One part of her expected to hear something like this, ever since she had seen his reaction to the telephone call, but another part refused to believe it. Refused to believe in this kind of violence, in this kind of death. Despite all the movies and T.V. shows about the police, despite what Crossen had told her yesterday about shoot-outs, she could not accept that such things really happened.

Her heart ached for Paavo, for the agony she had seen in his eyes, the pain in his voice, and the emptiness he was withdrawing into now. She looked again at the photograph on the wall of the young man with his arm around Paavo, the man so happy and so full of life.

Her eyes locked with his. "I'm sorry," was all she could say, and she knew it wasn't nearly enough.

"Well." He wrapped the keys in his fist and turned away from the picture, breaking her hold on him. "That's the chance we take. We know it can happen any time. We live with it. Every day. Part of the job."

He was shutting himself off, repressing the devastation the news had caused within him. It made his words cut through her all the more. Tears stung her eyes. He was trying so hard to not feel, to lock in his grief, but she had learned enough about him this day—his veneer had cracked just enough—that she knew he was bleeding inside.

"If he was your friend," she said, her throat tight, "I know he was a good cop."

Paavo walked to the door of the bedroom and placed one hand on the jamb. He leaned into his arm, as if barely able to support himself, then looked back at Matt's photo. "He was one of the best, Angie."

He shut the bedroom light and walked into the living room. Angie followed him, feeling helpless and inadequate, wanting to do something but not knowing what.

"I'll take you home," he said, putting on his jacket. "Sorry about dinner."

"No." She stepped toward him, wanting to wrap her arms around him and hold him, but because of his reserve, she didn't dare. Instead she said only, "Take me with you."

His eyes flickered, and then he shook his head. "I've got to go to the hospital, see what I can learn there and at the station. I'll find who did this, whatever it takes. I'll find who . . ." His breath came short and fast. "Sometime I'll have to stop at the house. See Katie. That'll be the hardest."

"Don't go alone, Paavo. Let me go with you. Let me just . . . just be there." Her eyes caught his and she felt as if she were sinking, helplessly, into their blue depths.

He pulled his gaze away. "No," he said brusquely, sounding colder and harder than she had ever heard him sound before.

He drove her home in silence, walked her to

her apartment, made sure Joey was there, and left.

Angie stood in the doorway and watched him until the elevator doors had shut between them. He was stubborn, trying so hard to hide the tremendous capacity for love and pain she had witnessed behind a cold exterior. She didn't ask him to call later, but she had held her door open as a way to convey to him that if he needed her, she'd be there. She only hoped he had understood. Mister Inspector.

She touched her face and felt her cheeks wet with tears.

Before long, she retired for the night, but sleep wouldn't come. As she tossed about for what seemed like hours, all she could think about was Paavo—not Crane or Waffles or bombs or anything else, just Paavo and his friend, Matt, until at last, she fell into a restless slumber.

Hours later, she awoke to the sound of hushed voices in the living room. The bedroom door opened. In the silhouette defined by the light cast by the T.V., she recognized her detective in the doorway.

He shut the door and crossed the darkened room to her dressing table, stopped a moment, then turned to leave.

"Paavo." She sat up, barely able to make out his figure in the moonlit room.

"Angie, I . . ." His voice was hoarse and exhausted. "I didn't mean to wake you." He took a half step toward her, then stopped and withdrew his foot as if he were about to trespass. "I saw so much ugliness tonight." His voice dropped to almost a whisper. "Then I saw something that reminded me of you. I wanted to bring it to you . . . to apologize for involving you. . . ."

He stopped and rubbed his face wearily. "Now I feel like a first-class fool."

"Come here," she said, reaching out her arms toward him. He crossed the room and she clasped his hands, pulling him down to sit on the edge of her bed. "You're anything but a fool, Inspector."

He sat stiffly, unwilling to respond to her or even to acknowledge her touch. Then he turned his face away and drew back. "Go to sleep now."

"Paavo, wait." She grasped his arm, and he looked at her again. As he did, her arms circled his shoulders. "Don't go."

She pressed her cheek to his, holding him, knowing instinctively that despite his abrupt manner, his coming here meant that he realized, on some level, that he needed her.

He put his hands on her waist as if to push her away, but then they stilled, almost caressingly, against her cool, satiny nightgown. Then his hands clenched, crushing the material within his strong fists.

"I'm sorry. I shouldn't be here. I shouldn't have come. I don't even know why I did." He pulled back. Even in the darkness, she could see the agony etched in his face, the torment in his eyes. "Your world is so different from mine," he said. "Here there's light, there's still hope . . ."

"You're in my world now. Try not to think about the other."

"If you saw the other . . ." He shook his head, his eyes shut, as if trying to forget, but the more he tried, the more he seemed to remember.

"I went there." His jaw was clenched, as if the words were being dragged from him. "To the street where it happened. I had to see." He stopped, and the pounding of his heart reverberated through her own body.

She lightly stroked his brow, his cheeks, then lay her hands against his ears as she spoke. "It's all right, Paavo. It's all right to hurt."

He shook his head. "God, Angie!" It was a cry for her from deep within his soul. Wordlessly, she wrapped him in her arms. She held him tightly, fiercely, achingly, as if through sheer physical closeness she could absorb some of the pain and loss he felt.

His arms tightened like a vice, crushing her against him until it almost hurt. "Christ, Angie, I'm a cop. I'm supposed to be used to these things."

She squeezed her eyes shut and twined her fingers in his hair, trying to gather him even closer. "You're a man, too. A very caring man, I think."

He buried his face against her neck, and when he spoke his voice was choked. "Matt was shot in the back, Angie. He was my friend, my best friend, and he died alone on the streets."

She felt the hot tears fall against her shoulder

before she felt him shake with silent sobs, before his whole body wrenched with grief.

His pain seared through her. Her heart ached for him, for Matt, and tears rolled from her eyes too. She lay back on the bed, pulling him down with her, then wrapped her arms firmly around him, her grip strong as he wept for his partner, his friend. Eventually, his agony seemed to ease, and as the first glimmer of dawn lit the sky, exhaustion overcame him, and he slept.

She didn't remember falling asleep. She didn't remember hearing him leave. All she knew was that when she opened her eyes, the room was bright with sunlight, and she was alone.

For a moment, she wondered if she had dreamed the whole thing. Then her gaze caught the dresser, and Paavo's words came back to her, overwhelming her. What an extraordinary man, she thought, as tears filled her eyes, that in the midst of his own grief, he would think of such a thing.

There, lying on the dresser, was a single red rose.

15

"*Miss Angelina,*" *Rico* said, stepping into the den. "You have a telephone call from a Mr. Crane."

"Crane!" Angie hurried to the phone.

"Brussels sprouts and chocolate sauce? Miss Amalfi, where are my recipes?" It sounded like the man was on the verge of tears.

"I'm sorry, I—"

"You're sorry! You don't know what this means!" he whined.

"Let me explain."

"Please. You're so good to me. I just—sardines over eggs, oh, Miss Amalfi!"

"I'm sorry! Listen, someone stole your recipes."

"What?" His high-pitched voice nearly broke her eardrums.

"My apartment was burglarized, and someone took them."

"Took them. I see. Well, thank you."

"Wait!" She had to talk to him, to figure out a way for Paavo to meet him and question him about Sam. "You can give me more recipes."

"No. I really don't think I should come by—"

"I'll come to your place."

"Here?"

"I need those recipes. My readers love them, you know. They're important for my job."

"Well, I do have copies of what was stolen . . ."

"That's great. I'll meet you in a couple of hours. Where are you?"

"Just you?"

"Of course."

"I'm at 501 Third Street, Room eight. Come now. I'll be waiting."

The phone went dead.

"Oh my God!" Angie rubbed her forehead.

"You all right, Miss?" Rico asked.

She looked up at him. "Yes." She reached for the phone to call Paavo, and then hesitated and drew back her hand.

All morning she had hoped he would contact her, but he hadn't. Had she been too pushy last night? Did he regret letting her get so close, letting her see his grief? These questions palgued her. She didn't know where he was and she certainly didn't know if he'd want to speak to her.

Now, though, she had no choice but to contact him.

She telephoned the station. As usual, he wasn't there, but he was working, and the police sergeant said he'd reach him right away.

She waited anxiously, wondering if she had done the right thing. It was almost a half hour later when the phone rang.

"It's me," he said, his voice heavy with weariness.

"Hi. How are you today?" She tried to sound cheerful.

"I'm . . . fine. Yourself?" His manner was stilted, almost irritated.

"I'm fine. But I wanted to know about you. I care about you, you know."

She heard his sudden intake of breath, then a pause as he slowly exhaled. "Look, Angie," he said, his voice flat and expressionless. "That's real nice, but I'm busy."

"I got a call from Edward Crane."

"The recipe writer." He sounded uninterested.

"I'm going to meet him right away in his apartment."

That got a bigger response. "You're going to what?"

"The address is 501 Third Street."

"That neighborhood's too dangerous. You're not going down there."

"Yes, I am."

"I can't get away. I'm working on . . . on Matt's case."

"I see. I just thought you could question Crane about Sam."

"Well, I guess Matt was checking out a lead on Sammy Blade's murder when he was killed. . . . Listen, I'll be right there." He hung up.

Thirty minutes later she heard his loud knock at the door.

She ran to answer it, nearly knocking Rico over in her haste. She pulled open the door and stood, her heart pounding, face to face with him. She needed to see that he was all right and to tell herself that what had happened to Matt couldn't happen to him.

She stepped back to let him enter the room. He looked exhausted. His white shirt was unbuttoned at the neck and his tie loosened, his gray sports jacket was open and hung limply off his shoulders. The skin under his eyes was almost blue with fatigue, and his face had a pale, pinched look to it.

"Are you ready?" he asked.

She wanted to call off the meeting with Crane. All she wanted to do was to have him take off his jacket and lie down so she could rub his neck and shoulders, and let him relax, let him know he didn't have to be Mr. Inspector around her. Just himself, just a man. She ached for him, but she knew better than to even suggest he rest. She nodded and went to get her coat.

Paavo was silent as they rode in his Austin to the address on Third Street, an area full of rundown hotels and homeless winos. He didn't want to think about the woman beside him, or the partner he had lost. Yet he couldn't think of anything else.

They found Crane's room on the first floor.

Paavo lifted his knuckles to the door, but Angie caught his arm just in time. "He'll know you're a cop, Inspector, believe me."

Paavo was surprised, but let Angie knock instead.

"Who is it?" a voice called.

"It's me. Angelina Amalfi."

Crane opened the door a crack and then slammed it just as Paavo's arm shot out to push it open. The door locked. Angie backed out of the way as Paavo gave it a powerful kick.

He rushed into the empty room. The window stood open.

"Wait here," Paavo said to Angie as he climbed out the window.

Crane ran down the alley behind the hotel. Paavo was catching up to him when he heard footsteps behind him, stopped, and spun around, his hand on the butt of his Smith and Wesson.

Angie froze in mid-step. Paavo stared at her in disbelief for a moment and then bolted after Crane again. Crane was far ahead of him now, and, like many small men, he had speed. He turned down an outside stairwell into a basement, and pulled the door shut behind him.

Paavo slammed into it just as he heard the deadbolt click into place. He kicked the door, but it wouldn't budge. He tried his shoulder and winced with pain.

Angie, gasping for breath, caught up to him. He warned her to stay back as he pulled out his gun.

She held her fingers to her ears, her eyes shut tight as he pointed at the lock and fired.

With his gun pointing upward, he carefully pushed the door open and entered the building. "Wait here," he ordered her.

He hurried through the basement, then climbed a staircase to the main floor. It was a warehouse, full of unopened crates stacked high. This time, he recognized the footsteps behind him as Angie's. Didn't that woman ever listen?

A door on the main floor was open, leading to the street. Paavo caught Angie's eye, pointed at it, and slowly they walked toward the door.

He lowered his gun, then slid it back in his holster as they stepped outside. The street was empty.

"He's gone. Damn!"

They crossed to the other side of the street, unsure as to which direction they should go. There was no sign of movement or anything else to give them a hint.

"I'll take you home," he said. "Then I'll go down to the station and do a little investigating on my own about Mr. Edward G. Crane. He looks familiar. I'm surprised he didn't turn up in the mug shots, though the shaved head may have thrown you off."

"I'm very good at faces, Inspector Smith," she said. "I'll come along and look again."

He saw the alert, hopeful expression in her eyes and remembered the innocent trust with which she had followed him during the chase.

But if Crane, who surely carried a gun, had turned and fired. . . .

"I'm taking you home. I can't waste any more time. I've got other cases to investigate."

"What do you mean, waste time?"

He strode quickly toward his car, and Angie hurried along beside him, taking two steps to his one. "I've got work to do. Some of us have to, you know. It's the way we bring in money to live on."

"Why are you saying this to me?"

He steeled himself before he stopped walking, and then he faced her. Her hurt, baffled look was more than he could bear. He turned, scanning the buildings, the pedestrians, the passing cars, anything but her as he spoke. "I want you to understand. I'm a detective. Your case is my work, and so's Sammy Blade's murder, and most of all, so is finding Matt's killer."

She said nothing until, unable to bear the silence, he looked at her again. Only then did she speak. "This is about more than that."

"Oh?"

"It's about last night—"

"Stop." His face flushed in anger.

"It's about letting yourself feel and cry—"

"Angie!" He grabbed her arms, furious, unwilling to listen to one more word from her. "That's far enough."

She flung her head back to look at him. "No, it's not. There's nothing wrong with how you felt. I liked you—"

"You were convenient." His voice was low and deadly, and it stopped her cold.

"What?"

He let go of her arms. "You were there, easy to use. A soft shoulder when I needed one. Got it?"

He watched her proud jaw jut out. "You don't fight fair, Inspector. That one was below the belt."

"Look, I'm not some hotshot lawyer or doctor like you're used to. I grew up on the streets. Don't try to fight me, or even understand me, because you wouldn't know where to begin."

Her cheeks flamed as his words struck. "I don't believe you, Paavo. I understand much more than you may think."

"The world isn't rosy or nice. It's brutal. And so are the people in it. Keep away from me, and if you're lucky, you'll never find out just how savage things really are."

She folded her arms. "All right, Inspector. I've got the message. I think you're wrong, but heaven forbid I waste your time or get too close to you." She spun on her heel. "Don't bother to take me home!"

She marched off. He watched until she got into a taxi, and then he called Rico and told him to get out on the sidewalk, watch for Angie, and get her into her apartment, fast.

16

Angie looked at the clock: it was four-thirty. Paavo had called at ten that morning and spoken only to Rico, telling him to be especially on guard—not even to open the door. The fact that Paavo hadn't asked to speak to her and hadn't called back suited her fine. She didn't want to talk to him anyway. Not ever seeing him again wouldn't have bothered her in the least.

She spent the morning on the telephone to Bodega Bay searching for a house to rent. Then she packed her suitcases. Bodega Bay, a small fishing village on the Sonoma coast, was isolated and quiet, although only about two hours north of San Francisco.

It was the ideal place to hide, to run away from the whirlpool her life and her emotions had fallen into. She couldn't possibly continue, the way things were.

Convenient! Her face burned with pain, rage, and embarrassment all over again whenever she remembered Paavo's hateful word. How could she have been so mistaken about the man?

The decision to leave San Francisco gave her a feeling of release. Even a little giddiness. She'd be free of this anxiety, this constant tension of worrying about herself—and Paavo. Worrying about some man just didn't fit into her lifestyle.

She kicked the sofa and threw herself onto it, her face in her hands. A scared, sick feeling churned in her stomach. Paavo's world of violence, criminals, and ugly, senseless death was still too near to dismiss easily. But she would. And very soon.

At six o'clock, she heard a knock at the door. Rico ordered her back into the bedroom and stood beside the front door, gun poised. "Who is it?" he called.

There was a moment of silence. "It's . . ." a meek voice started, and then there was the sound of a throat being cleared. "It's Stan Bonnette. Is Angie home?"

Angie started out of the bedroom. Rico waved her to stop. He unlocked the bolt, held his gun in front of him, and opened the door a crack.

"Don't shoot!" Stan yelled. "I'll go!"

"Come in. It's okay," Rico opened the door to let Stan enter.

"Stan!" Angie said, as a rush of relief filled her. He was a figure from the past, when her life had been simple and carefree. She had always wanted to find a man like Stan to marry one day. Not Stan

himself—she had never cared for him that way—
but like him. Wealthy, suave, with a business free
of murders, guns, and crooks. A nice, staid business that wouldn't interfere with her idea of a
good time. She gave her perfect hostess smile.
"How nice of you to drop by."

Stan's face was ashen. "Hello, there! Well, I
don't want to intrude, so I think I'd better be on
my way."

Rico was already back at the T.V.

"No intrusion." Angie took his arm and yanked
him into the apartment, kicking the door shut as
she led him to the chairs by the bay window.
"Rico's my bodyguard."

"You still need a bodyguard? What's wrong
with the police? Why can't they do something?
Bunch of incompetents!"

Angie's smile froze as she looked at Stan without saying a word. Not long ago she probably
would have joined him, railing against the vagar-
ies of law and order. Now all she could think of
was Paavo—and Matt.

Instead of replying, she asked, "Can I get you
a drink?"

"Scotch."

She had just poured a Diet Coke for herself
and set the drinks on the table when the brusque
rap she'd waited for all day sounded against the
front door. No, she corrected herself, she had *not*
waited for him all day. She stared at the door. A
wild, silly hope surged in her that, just perhaps,
he was here to apologize for his horrible words.
Just perhaps he was going to charge in, sweep her

into his arms, and whisper words of regret, of remorse, of passion. . . .

"Rico, Smith here. Open up." The cold, perfunctory voice shattered her fantasy.

Stan groaned as Rico crossed the living room to the door.

A moment later, Paavo strode into the room, taking in the cozy scene with Stan in one sweep before his eyes met hers. The look in them was cold, and maybe something more. Disappointed? Or was he merely resigned?

He appeared even more tired than he had been yesterday. She wanted to greet him casually, to show how little he mattered to her, but the words stuck in her throat. She lowered her gaze to her drink and let silence hang in the air.

"I see Bonnet's back again," Paavo said.

Stan stood. Angie looked up as he puffed out his chest. "Listen, Smith, you've no right to keep sending me out of here! I think I better stick around and listen to just what you're planning to do about this situation. It's intolerable, do you hear, intolerable that Miss Amalfi is still being threatened. I demand you get busy!"

She saw the anger growing in Paavo's eyes. After his past two days and his exhaustion, he would have no tolerance for Stan's sudden heroics.

"Stan!" she cried, jumping up.

But Stan was on a roll. "When are you police going to get off your duffs, stop visiting this attractive woman, and find whoever's after her?"

"Bonnet." Paavo's voice was a low rumble. "Time for you to say bye-bye."

Stan's face reddened with fury. "I said I will not be ordered—"

"Thanks for stopping by." Angie grabbed his arm and pushed him toward the door. "Go home now, Stanfield. Please."

The anger on his face turned into astonishment as he gaped at her. With an indignant sniff, he squared his shoulders and marched solemnly from the room, slamming the door behind him.

Paavo's cold glare now fixed on Angie.

Fury and pain converged as she looked at him. "You'll have to ignore Stan. He was just being chivalrous."

"So I saw." His mouth curved into a sneer.

"At least he knows how!"

"Fine, now that we've established what an ace among men he is, I can get on with business."

"That suits me just fine." She plopped down on the yellow Hepplewhite.

He remained standing. "I wanted to give you the latest breakthrough. The man's name isn't Edward G. Crane. It's Edmund Banner. He's been here about a year, from the East Coast, where he's been in and out of jail more times than you can count. Small-time stuff. Have you ever heard the name Edmund Banner before, Miss Amalfi?"

Her heart flinched at the formal address. So we're back to "Miss Amalfi" now, she thought. Why not, now that she was no longer convenient? Anger licked at the edges of her control. "No, I've never heard of Edmund Banner, or Edward Banner, or any other Banner, *Inspector Smith.*" Two could play at this game.

He raised one eyebrow. "I'd like a copy of every recipe Sammy Blade gave you."

Without a word, she went into the den, where she pulled copies of Sam's recipes from her files. There were only fourteen items. She made two sets, using her personal-sized copier: one set to bring to Bodega Bay—if Paavo wanted to study them, she would, too—and the other set to give him.

She returned to the living room and gave him his set. He shuffled through the papers. "I've had this place patroled all day, in case you were worried," he said.

"My worries are almost over."

"Oh?" His attention was on her now.

"I've decided I can't stay here."

His black brows locked, and he scowled at her. "What do you mean?"

"Just that." She lifted her chin. "Think of me as a coward all you want, but I'm scared. I don't mind admitting it." She took a deep breath before continuing. "I've rented a house at Bodega Bay. I'm already packed and I'm going there."

"You're what?" He slowly circled closer, reminding her of a panther carefully, menacingly, stalking its prey.

She refused to react to him or back down. "I'm going away until things blow over."

He stared at her without word or expression,

his eyes penetrating and his lips drawn in a tight, thin line. "If someone is determined to kill you, they'll try to find you wherever you go."

"Once I'm away, I'm sure they'll leave me alone. I know nothing."

The ceiling lights outlined his long, lanky figure. He seemed to loom over her. "But you do know something," he said. "That's the problem. You've been in the middle of this from the time you printed Sammy Blade's first recipe. You saw his murderer. Crane contacted you. And not only that, the ballistics suggest that Blade and Matt were killed by the same gun."

Angie hated this Sherlock Holmes act. "Rather 'elementary,' is it?"

He shrugged, as if the answer was too obvious to bother with words.

"I don't care!" She spit her words out through gritted teeth. "I'm leaving."

His face darkened as he leaned over her. "Right now, Miss Amalfi, you're my only lead."

Her eyes widened a moment, then narrowed. "So I'm just bait for your trap!"

"That's not the way it is."

"Like hell!" She stood, brushed him aside, and then spun around to face him, carefully enunciating each word. "A lead, you said! Your best lead. Well you, *and* your leads, *and* your police business, and all the rest of it can be damned! I'm through with all of you." She marched to the door and placed her hand on the knob, ready to open it and throw him out.

Instead, she watched him walk to the window

and look out, his back an unrelenting, rigid outline against the darkening sky. He turned toward her again. "I wouldn't do anything that might harm you."

He was so infuriatingly controlled that she wanted to scream. "Of course not. Lose me and the department might look bad. To think that I trusted you, that I cared. My God, I've been a fool!"

His eyes dulled and a look—could it possibly have been longing?—flickered briefly in them before they became shuttered and emotionless again. "We need you here," he said.

She could feel the blood throbbing in her ears, her breathing fast and heavy. He's a cop just doing his job, she told herself for the umpteenth time.

"I'm driving to Bodega Bay. No one will know where I am. I'll be able to breathe again."

"Will you for once just *listen* to me?"

"No!" She stabbed the air in front of his chest with her finger. "You listen. You're the one who said we were from different worlds. So you can jolly well think of my going as a victory. Angie's going to cut and run, just as you always predicted. I won't be here to be used, to be convenient, for *anything,* any longer!"

"Enough!" He gripped her hand, her accusing finger crushed in his barely contained fury. But the moment their hands touched, she felt a jolt arc between them like an electric current. An angry, smoldering gaze raked her from head to toe as his hand drew her toward him. But she held herself back, stiff and unbending. Time seemed to stop as he weighed his response. Then his shoulders eased, and he let her go. "All right," he whispered.

She seethed, breathing hard, unsure she'd heard him. "What?"

"I said, *all right.*"

"You can't mean that."

"You told me you're packed. When did you plan to leave?"

"You agree?"

"You might be safer if you're away, out of sight. It might have been shortsighted of me to insist that you stay here."

"Because I might be safer somewhere else?"

His blue eyes pierced her. She'd almost forgotten, arguing with him so much, the effect a simple glance from him had on her. "Of course," he said. "Why else would I want you away from here?"

The emotion in his voice rocked her, weakening her defenses. She fought any softening of her feelings, though, and gave him a steely stare. "I'm leaving tonight."

"Tonight! No way."

"Shall we bet on it?"

He folded his arms, suddenly every bit as stubborn as she. "I won't let you go to Bodega unless I go up there and talk to the local police. But I can't leave tonight."

She folded hers in return. "Then you'd better come up with another solution real fast, Inspector, because I'm not staying in this apartment any longer."

17

Angie couldn't believe she was doing this—skulking around some dingy back alley. One moment, she had been anticipating a cozy little retreat at Bodega Bay, peaceful and safe. The next, she'd been persuaded to hide out in the city for a couple more days. Why had she turned into such a marshmallow when he turned those baby blues on her and suggested she stay at his home? Even his obvious reluctance to have her there hadn't defused her ready agreement. Damn! She didn't know what angered her more: him or her reaction to him.

Did she honestly think she'd have a second chance at melting his cold heart? Whom was she kidding? But, on the other hand, as her niggling inner voice pointed out, he must care at least a little bit, or he would have simply sent her packing. It couldn't *all* be out of duty.

So here she was, standing among bulging Hefty garbage bags and trash cans, in a dark alley, imagining assailants lurking behind every dark corner and waiting for Prince Charming to find them a taxi cab.

She'd handed Rico her car keys and her suitcases. Rico would take Angie's car, drive around for about a half hour, and, when he was sure he wasn't being followed, meet them at a parking lot across town. She and Paavo had taken the stairs from her apartment to the basement, and then run to a side door exit.

She'd held her breath as Paavo raised his gun, opened the door, and bobbed his head outside. When no one tried to remove it, she had followed him into the darkness.

They had scrambled over three backyard fences before they reached the street on the opposite side of the block from Angie's apartment. Every muscle in her body ached. Going over the fences wasn't so bad—Paavo had given her a boost up and steadied her as she got both legs on the other side of the fence—but landing on that other side had caused her teeth to rattle. She was amazed she hadn't broken a leg, if not her neck, doing it.

Now they huddled in an alley off of a busy street until a taxi drove by. Paavo ran into the street and hailed it. It stopped.

Sore and exhausted, she flopped back against the cab's seat, wondering what she was doing. Was she the crazy one, or was it the cop beside

her? The cop who made her so angry she scarcely
knew her own mind. . . .

He'd promised to drive her, using her car, to
Bodega as soon as he was free to go. As they
neared the rendezvous point with Rico, she realized he hadn't ever actually seen her car. "My
car's pretty small," she said. "It's Italian, and a
couple of years old already. Anyway, since the trip
to Bodega is fairly long, if you prefer, I could rent
something bigger to drive up there."

The cab pulled into the lot. Rico was leaning
against Angie's white Ferrari.

"No," Paavo said with a little catch in his voice,
"your car will do just fine."

Thanking Rico for all his help, Angie gave him
her father's card, in case she wasn't able to send
the payment due him and Joey.

His eyes took on a sad cast as he nodded, then
left.

She turned to hand her car keys to Paavo, but
he was already halfway in the car, checking out its
dials and running his hands lingeringly over the
soft leather interior. She'd never dreamed she'd
be envious of a car.

"I can't wait to get away," Angie said shortly
after they arrived at Paavo's cottage. "Can't you
do something, pull a few strings, so we can leave
tomorrow?"

Paavo sat on the sofa, his hands clasped. A
sudden shadow came over his face. "Tomorrow
morning is Matt's funeral."

"I hadn't realized," she whispered. "Would you like me to go with you?"

"No."

She nodded. Why had she expected any other answer? Again, she wrapped herself in her rancor at him, making it a shield against the compassion she also felt, but in this proximity, her anger was difficult to hold. Holding a grudge didn't come naturally to her. She preferred to have a simple, cleansing tantrum, and then get over it and go back to being friendly once more. But Paavo wouldn't allow her to get close enough even for that.

Hercules was kicking up a ruckus. The cat's hunger made Angie remember that she hadn't eaten all day either, and probably, neither had Paavo.

Within minutes, Hercules was devouring his canned food as she scrambled eggs, made toast, and heated a can of chili. Paavo's pitiful pantry offered little choice.

She set the kitchen table, dished out the food, and returned to the living room to call Paavo.

He was curled up on the sofa, sound asleep, his brow unlined, the sadness and worry momentarily gone. She stood over him a moment, realizing that he needed sleep far more than dinner. She suspected he hadn't slept well last night, and she knew he had spent the night before that at the hospital, at the station, and with her. She stood there a long time, just watching him. He could be brusque, cold, and bossy, but underneath, his heart was warm—with others, at least. Matt must have known that, and Matt's wife. She remembered Chief Hollins saying Matt's son liked visiting Paavo. It seemed Paavo wasn't doing nearly as good a job as he imagined at hiding his true nature. Poor man.

She found the linen closet and an extra blanket. Perhaps her being there relaxed him in some way he didn't even realize. She hoped it was so, because that was how she felt. In fact, she had to admit she liked being there more than the thought of being alone in Bodega. She covered him, smoothing the blanket over his long, powerful frame. Maybe he'd ask . . . no, *demand* . . . that she stay right there until her own place was safe again. Of course, she'd say "no" for a little while. . . .

She ate dinner alone. After cleaning up the kitchen, she moved her suitcase into the bedroom. It was a comfortable room. The whole house was comfortable, as Paavo was under that steely surface.

She read the plaques and certificates on his wall, all of which had to do with the police force. Aulis Kokkonen must have been a good influence, but what makes a kid go from the streets to the force? Whatever it was, being a cop meant a lot to him. He clearly was proud of his work and his accomplishments, and he believed in them. Looking at his mementos, she felt a stirring of affinity. She couldn't have explained it, but it was there.

After changing into a long, heavy, flannel nightgown—brought along especially for cold

Bodega nights—she switched on the lamp by the nightstand, propped up pillows, and took Sam's recipes from her handbag. She had decided to read through them to see if she could spot some code or clue, as Paavo had suggested. There had to be some hint, some ingredient. . . .

The next morning, the smell of freshly brewed coffee gently nudged her awake. Across the room, Paavo stood at his dresser, his back to her, putting on cufflinks. That done, he looked in the mirror, adjusted his tie, and picked up his hairbrush.

Angling her head just a bit, she could see his reflection in the mirror. She stared, struck by how handsome he looked in his charcoal suit, dark tie, and white shirt. She hadn't spent much time simply observing the man before. Usually she had been too busy being irritated by him to pay much attention. But as always, he had a magnetism that she couldn't deny.

Deep in thought, he held a faraway look that softened his features and erased the wariness that too often defined his expression.

She noticed the gentle waves appearing in his hair now that it was a bit longer than when she had first met him. The skin at the inner corners of his eyes and below was a shade darker than the surrounding area, making his eyes look especially deep set and intense. She loved his eyes.

Her gaze caught his in the mirror. He had been watching her through the glass with an odd expression on his face. She smiled and tried to appear nonchalant, as if she hadn't been staring at him so openly, so admiringly.

"Good morning," she said.

He put down the hairbrush and faced her. His gaze traveled the length of her there, in his bed, wrapped in his blankets. When he raised his eyes to hers again, they were like blue flames. Their heat traveled straight to her heart.

He turned abruptly to the dresser and began to rummage through the things on top of it. "Where are the keys? . . . Ah!"

"Did you eat, Inspector?" she asked, wrapping her pink quilted robe over her gown as she got out of bed.

"I'm not hungry." He left the bedroom and walked toward the front door. "I won't be gone long. I'll use your car, if you don't mind. Mine is still at your place."

"Fine." She followed right behind him.

"Don't go out. A patrolman will be driving by at least every half hour. He'll keep an eye on things."

"Thank you," she said. He reached for the doorknob, looking so alone that her heart ached for him and she moved closer to him. All of yesterday's resolutions had vanished, and she couldn't let him go without saying something. "Paavo." Her voice was a choked whisper.

He turned, and she wrapped her arms around his neck and pressed her lips to his, tightly, not even quite sure how she had gotten there. The clean, spicy scent of his aftershave, and the warm, firm feel of his lips made her knees weak. Almost as quickly, she let go of him. She was embarrassed but nonetheless glad she had kissed him. "Take very, very good care of yourself," she murmured.

He nodded, his blue eyes capturing hers a moment, and then he hurried from the house.

18

Angie cleaned out the refrigerator while waiting for Paavo to come home. She had never seen so much mold outside of a botany laboratory. Later, she thumbed through some magazines and looked over his books, but all she could think of was Paavo. Where was he?

At about three in the afternoon, the phone rang. Angie ran to it and picked it up on the second ring.

"Hello?" She was breathless.

"Who's this?" a woman's voice asked.

Angie frowned. "Who are you?"

"I'm trying to reach Paavo Smith. Perhaps I dialed wrong?" The voice was low with a Swedish accent.

"This is his number."

"Oh." The woman hesitated. "Are you the cleaning woman?"

"I beg your pardon."

"Is Paavo there? I'd like to speak to him."

Angie's stomach knotted at the imperious, yet seductive-sounding voice. Her imagination assigned a face and figure to the speaker. Seven feet tall, beautiful, with long, silky white-blond hair, and a voluptuous body, the woman probably pumped iron while skiing on one foot down the Matterhorn. Just Paavo's type.

"He's not home. Can I give him a message?"

"So, who are you, then?"

The woman was impossible. "I'm his ex-wife. His *third* ex-wife. Me and the kids are here to get all the back child-support payments he owes us."

"Oh!"

"May I tell him who called?"

"No. No, that's all right." The woman hung up.

Angie slammed down the phone. Her guilt was fleeting.

Another two hours passed before she heard her car pull onto the driveway. She wanted to run to the door, but considering the way she had seen him off, she decided a little discretion was called for. She waited, none too patiently, on the sofa.

Paavo opened the front door and walked in. "Hi."

"You were gone longer than I expected." God, I sound like a wife, she thought.

His blue eyes glinted, but he said only, "I guess so. I checked in a few times with the patrol."

"Where did you go?" Again? Her voice clearly

had become possessed, and these questions popped out, uninvited.

"To the zoo."

"What?" Was the man mad? While she had sat there worried half to death, he had decided to go look at wild animals?

He took off his jacket as he spoke, turning his back to her. "Actually, things were kind of . . . rough . . . at Matt's house, and he has, had, a four-year-old, a great kid, named Micky. I took him. It was good to get him away for a while."

She looked at him with astonishment at first, but then her eyes became misty, and her heart went out to him.

She rushed away to get him a cup of coffee while he changed into a blue heavy-knit sweater and light gray slacks. He'd eaten little that day, and she convinced him to take her out to the dinner he had promised days ago. They went to a small neighborhood cafe where he was known and the food was good and plentiful. She kept reminding herself that she was still angry at him, but the reasons why were growing dimmer.

It was dark when they arrived back at his house. He lit a fire and fed Hercules while Angie poured them each a brandy.

"What's this?" he asked, picking up the dollar bills by the phone.

"I called my mother today. I had to tell her about my going to Bodega Bay. It was a long conversation."

"I'm not a pauper, Miss Amalfi." He slammed the money onto the table.

"I know! But I sleep here. I eat your food. I couldn't use your phone like that, too."

"I wouldn't have cared."

"I know, but . . . have you done this kind of thing much?"

He looked at her with eyes narrowed and dangerous. "What do you mean?"

"This. Bringing someone like me here to your house."

He braced his hands against his hips, a towering figure in the small room. "Oh, sure. It's a regular bed and breakfast. Can't you tell? It's how I make my pin money." His voice was too quiet. Angie knew that inside he was seething at her.

She shrank back into the sofa cushions. "I didn't mean there was anything wrong with it. I was serious."

"Never."

"Never what?"

His eyes caught hers and slowly his cold anger seemed to vanish. "You are never serious, Miss Amalfi."

Would she ever get past this aloofness of his? She knew others did—Aulis, Matt's child, and even Angie's own mother, but he'd built a wall between them Joshua's horn couldn't bring down. Why? Was it simply because deep down he just didn't care for her, or was there some other reason? She couldn't face the fact that she was no more than a case to him—the case of the woman who was rapidly making a first-class fool of herself over him!

Men had always thrown themselves at her,

pursued her until she grew tired of running. This one treated her as if she had all the feminine appeal of a mushroom.

"By the way," she said, "you got a call today. A woman with a heavy Swedish-sounding accent. Tell her your cousin was here and she was just joking on the phone."

"My cousin?"

"She'll understand."

He gave her a quizzical look. "I see."

"It sounded like she really wanted to talk to you," Angie said with forced casualness. "You should call her."

"Angie, I—"

"Call her. Really. Go see her tonight if you want. I don't mind."

"Angie—"

"I realize you have a life. I never thought you lived like a monk, you know. Just because you are around me—"

"Miss Amalfi!" He crossed the room to stand in front of her, glaring down at her as she sank further back on the sofa.

"Yes, Inspector Smith?"

He stood for a moment longer and then sat by her side. Slowly, wonder filled his eyes, and all the cold aloofness vanished.

"Miss Amalfi," he said with a grin that on anyone else would have been labeled goofy, "I do believe you're jealous."

Hot rage filled her. "Of all the arrogant—!"

He placed a finger against her lips and suddenly the memory of her simple kiss that morning leaped between them. She stopped talking, her anger fizzling as quickly as it had erupted, and she stayed absolutely still as his head bent toward her. He lifted his finger and in its spot placed his lips. He didn't put his arms around her, didn't hold her. Only their lips met.

Her breath caught in her throat, and her body leaned toward his as her eyes shut. His kiss was gentle, soft, right. Yes, she thought, as her hands lifted to his head and her fingers spread to touch his high, proud cheekbones, then his ears, his hair. She liked the feel of the soft, springy waves of his hair and ran her fingers along the sides of his head, to the back, and then circled her arms around his neck.

He lifted his head, his eyes dark and burning as they traveled over her face. "Damn," he whispered.

"Paavo . . ." Her arms tightened.

He slipped his arms around her back and pulled her against him as his mouth descended with crushing force on hers, unleashing the tension that had pulsated between them for so long. Her fingers twisted in his hair as her lips parted and his tongue plunged to meet hers, hot and urgent. There was no gentleness here, no softness. She felt as if she held a caldron in her arms. Just as her heart had opened to his gentleness earlier, she responded to his passion and returned his kisses with equal reckless fury. His mouth traveled over her cheeks, her eyes, then back again to her lips, sending shooting sparks of desire throughout her body that left her gasping for breath.

He shifted his weight, turning to tuck her body against his, her back pressing the back of the sofa. His hand descended to her breasts, her waist, her hips, and her body burned wherever he touched her. His devouring kisses, and the long, lean, hard feel of his body, his soapy, spicy scent were intoxicating. She slid down on the sofa, so that he covered her. She wanted to feel his weight, his strength protecting her, surrounding her . . . within her. She arched toward him, aching for his nearness, needing more.

He stopped suddenly and lifted himself from her, his breathing ragged and his eyes clouded with desire—a desire, she knew, that mirrored her own. She could see the struggle raging within him.

"I must be crazy," he said finally, sitting up, turning away from her as his fingers raked his hair.

"Yes." The word rolled off her tongue, and her eyes met his as she leaned toward him, her hand pressed lightly against his back.

"I didn't bring you to my house for this."

"I know."

"I can't take advantage of this situation."

"This isn't taking advantage, Paavo."

She sat up beside him and reached out to touch his hair, but he grabbed her hand in midair. His tone was hard. "Stop. Sometimes you are so naive, for all your outward sophistication."

She felt as if she'd been slapped. She blinked,

straightened, and pulled her hand away. "Naive?" What was he trying to tell her? Convenient? Naive? Every time she opened herself to him, tried to show warmth, responsiveness, he cut her off at the knees. Well, no more. Her cheeks burned from his rejection. "You don't have to make excuses to me, you know! A warm fire, good brandy, and a presumably functioning male. It meant no more than a way to pass some time. Convenient, in fact. You needn't take it personally, Inspector."

"I didn't mean—"

She crossed the room, her back to him. "Forget it. It doesn't matter. Not anymore."

He stood as well, his lips tight as the full impact of her words struck him. "We should get some sleep. We've got a lot of traveling to do tomorrow."

"Yes." The word was choked. So he was sending her away, as she had requested, after all. "We have much to do." She didn't want to leave, but she had no choice. The obstacles were insurmountable. Throughout all this, he'd thrown nothing but accusations at her, though she'd done nothing to deserve them. Childish and naive, he'd said, even pampered. She surreptitiously eyed him standing there looking so angry. And now he meant to shunt her and all her faults far away from him. She shut her eyes a moment, her fingernails digging into her palms. Maybe once she was gone he'd appreciate the real Angie, the Angie his stubbornness had lost him forever.

Nose in the air, eyebrows arched, she said, "Good night," then sashayed into the bedroom with all the regalness of a queen dismissing a lowly servant.

19

The ocean fog had burned off by eight o'clock the next morning, and by nine, the sun was shining.

Angie smiled continuously, saying nothing as she cooked breakfast. Paavo kept a wary eye on her, his expression filled with awkwardness and perhaps even a little guilt over all that had passed between them the night before, as well as a degree of uncertainty over her changed demeanor. As she cleaned up the kitchen she sang, in her off-key voice, one Barry Manilow hit after the other. Paavo's wince told her he wasn't one of Barry's biggest fans. When she got to the song about Lola the showgirl, he looked ready to writhe in agony.

"Are you ready to go?" he asked as she hung the dishcloth on the rod.

"It's so early." Her voice was sweet as sugar-water.

"It's nine-fifteen. It'll take a couple of hours to get there, and I need to get back to the department some time today."

"Oh, you need to work? I should have realized. Silly me!" Without giving him a chance to reply, she went into his bedroom and shut the door.

She let an additional fifteen minutes pass before she opened the door and came out. Inspector Smith had paced a groove into his carpet.

"All right." She nearly sang the words.

"Finally."

She gave him an innocent smile. "I'm so sorry. I'd hate for you to waste time on my case."

"Angie—"

"Miss Amalfi, if you don't mind. I've decided you're quite correct. We don't know each other in the slightest, and keeping a strictly professional relationship is important. After all, once this case is over with, our paths certainly won't cross again." She had the keys to her Ferrari in her hand, and now held them in the air, between her thumb and forefinger. "You'll drive, Inspector?"

"Sure . . . Miss Amalfi." He took the keys. "Look, I know you're upset about last night—"

"Upset? You flatter yourself, Inspector." She breezed out his front door, then glanced over her shoulder at him and batted her eyelashes. "My bags are in the bedroom."

She sauntered to her car and then leaned against the passenger door and waited. Convenient, was she? Naive? Upset? We'll see, Inspector, she thought.

He came out of his house carrying her bags,

four small pieces of fitted Ferrari luggage. He put them down, locked the deadbolt on the front door of his house, carried the bags to the Ferrari, and put them down again as he unlocked the trunk in the front of her car. She pointed to where the pieces were designed to fit—two in the trunk and two behind the seats. He then opened her car door and swept his arm toward the car seat in a way that would have done Serefina's chauffeur proud. Angie ignored his sarcasm.

His expression was immobile as he got into the driver's seat beside her. The interior of the car felt tiny.

Paavo drove in silence. As they crossed the Golden Gate Bridge, leaving the city, Angie suddenly felt sentimental.

"I've always loved the view from this bridge," she said. "The city looks so white, like a dove. St. Francis would approve of his namesake, I think."

"Soon you'll be able to enjoy the city again, just like you used to do."

"Right." She sank back against the plush leather seat. Why didn't the thought of the way she used to live please her?

She stole a glance at Paavo, his gaze fixed upon the roadway. He looked foreboding, brooding, even sexy. She sighed and turned her attention to the rolling hills and bay inlets that were Marin County. She didn't want to notice him any longer. Why was it that the more she pushed him away, the more she wanted him to wrap his arms around her and make her fears vanish? Why did she continue to throw herself against a brick wall—hell, a *steel* wall—with this man?

She tightened her jaw. He'd been a challenge, and nothing more. Other men threw themselves at her, but he didn't, *ergo* she wanted him. He was a sort of sexual Rubik's cube to her, and now playtime was over. No big deal.

She looked at his strong hands gripping the steering wheel and folded her own hands on her lap. He glanced at her, his gaze drifting upward, leaving a trail of heat in its wake until his eyes met hers. He quickly turned away.

Her throat tightened. She kept her eyes forward, not daring to look at him again as the Ferrari carried them over the coastal mountains and through groves of California redwoods to the twisting, narrow cliffside highway that edged the Pacific Ocean.

In the heart of Bodega Bay, a once-flourishing fishing village turned artists' colony, they found the realtor from whom Angie had rented a house. The realtor turned over the key and instructions, and Angie turned over a healthy deposit.

Paavo swung the Ferrari into the driveway of a modern, ranch-style house on a beautiful setting overlooking the ocean. The house, the town, the hills, and the ocean carried the serenity and peacefulness Angie longed for. But they also held loneliness.

Paavo got out of the car and looked at the

house, then at Angie. "It's rather nice," he said wryly.

Whatever was the man thinking of now? The place wasn't particularly large. The realtor had told her it had only two bedrooms, a living/dining room combination, kitchen, and small den. There was a laundry room, two and a half baths, and a hot tub. The garage fit only two cars.

She shrugged and got out of the car. "It's only a modest place. But if I'm not going to live in an apartment, I need some amenities."

"Without a doubt."

Paavo picked up two of her suitcases and followed her into the living room. A wall of windows and glass doors leading to a rear patio framed a majestic view of the ocean. The room was richly furnished in rustic modern style, with leather and heavy hand-rubbed woods that looked both comfortable and functional.

Paavo said nothing, but she'd come to know him well enough to see the subtle softening of his eyes as he looked over the room, and the hint of a smile as he absorbed the view. She knew he liked what lay before him.

If only he'd stay, she thought, her heart wrenching as she watched him quickly check out the house. She had to admit that the more she learned about him, the more she cared, and the more she wanted to find a way to bring him some happiness. His will was strong and his heart, she had learned, was as big as he was. Even when she had been annoying him that morning, she wanted him with her. She felt lost when he wasn't near.

She remembered his kisses, the feel of his arms and hands holding her, caressing her, just last night. Yes, she wanted him—for more than companionship.

Flustered by her thoughts, she carried a suitcase into the master bedroom. She heard Paavo go out to the car to pick up the rest of her things. In a moment he was behind her, putting down her other suitcases.

"If you'll drop me off at the police station," he said, "I'll talk to the police, then get a rental car back to the city."

She took a deep breath. He really was leaving her. "Of course, I'll drive you," she whispered.

She suddenly felt like a traitor, hiding in safety while Paavo went out there, looking for the one who had killed Matt and Sam, and for whoever it was who wanted to kill her. "I don't suppose you'd like some lunch before you go?"

He stepped toward her as if drawn without volition, and then his shoulders stiffened and he turned away. "I'd better not. It's a long drive back, and I've got a lot of work to do."

"I see." She grabbed her car keys and hurried from the house. Paavo followed.

A few minutes later, she pulled up in front of the police station. "Do you want me to wait?" she asked.

"No. They'll help me get a car back."

"I see. Well, I guess that's it then."

He nodded.

"You'll let me know when it's safe to go home, right?"

"Someone will contact you."

Someone. She nodded.

He put his hand on the car door-handle. "Good-bye, Miss Amalfi."

"Take care of yourself, Inspector."

He got out of the car and walked toward the police station. Angie drove off before he reached it. Some things were too hard to watch.

20

Angie slammed her pen down on the desk and leaned back in her chair, folding her arms in exasperation. She had tried to work on her San Francisco history, but this archaic means of writing was hopeless. Before she could get an idea on paper she would lose her train of thought.

Some things couldn't wait, however. She picked up her pen and a fresh sheet of paper and carefully wrote across the top " 'EGGS AND EGG-ONOMICS' by Angelina Amalfi." An essay on consciousness-raising with kiwis followed. To this, she added a recipe for Snicker Doodles from a Mrs. Barra in El Cerrito and Baba Rum Balls from a Cloris Barnes in Hayward.

Pleased with her effort, she slipped the papers in an envelope and put it aside to mail the next day. It was already six in the evening, too late for that day's mail pickup. She had decided that even though she was forced to hide out in Bodega Bay, she wouldn't disappoint either her boss or her readers. In fact, she had mailed in a column on the very day she had arrived. This would be her second from the seaside.

She went into the living room and stood by the glass wall facing the ocean to watch the sun set over the Pacific. The waves crashed against the rocks far below the cliff that edged her property.

In the three days that she had been in Bodega Bay, she had come to find the sound comforting. No matter what happened to her, the waves would slap against those rocks for eternity. In the end, she was no more than a speck of sand on a beach.

Three days and two nights in Bodega Bay. It sounded like an ad for a lost weekend. She had never been alone like this before; there had always been friends or relatives close at hand. She talked to her family by telephone, telling them she had gone on a writer's vacation so that she could work in peace on her history book. Their only reaction was astonishment at her dedication to her work. Their clumsy attempts at trying to find out if Paavo was with her were dismissed with an emphatic, Garbo-esque, "I vant to be alone."

She had quite a shock the first time she attempted to use the television set. There was no cable in the area, so her choice was limited to three stations: snow, snowier, or snowiest, and even the voices were full of static and garbled.

She found herself reading more than she had in years.

Soon, she'd learn to forget Paavo Smith. Their good-bye had been final, and she accepted it. She was out of his jurisdiction now, and since she no longer provided human bait for Matt's killer, he no longer needed to contact her. She could see that she'd deluded herself into thinking he'd ever done anything for her personally. Oh, sure, he didn't want her killed, but that was his job. The extra part, the motivation from the heart, was because of Matt. It hurt, more than she wanted to admit.

The feelings Inspector Paavo Smith aroused in her were impossible to understand. Oh, he was nice looking—but she knew plenty of good-looking men, some so handsome she felt plain when she was with them. No, it wasn't his appearance that caused this strange, confusing reaction.

He was obviously intelligent, although he had no college training. Ph.D.'s in all kinds of specialties had waltzed into, and then out of, her life. In fact, she had always been rather attracted to the ascetic, intellectual type—at least she thought so. No, it wasn't his intellect.

Most of the men she knew had great elegance in their manner, and always treated her like a delicate lady of leisure. Paavo glared at her, criticized her, laughed at her, and threw her over fences in the dead of night. No, it certainly wasn't his manner.

She knew it wasn't his money. And it definitely wasn't his profession.

Yet somehow, she had been able to laugh around him and feel safe when she was in the most frightening predicament of her life. She was able to care about him and his friends rather than just herself. When she was scared, he made her feel brave, even if it was because he made her so darn angry that her anger was all she could think of.

How did he manage that?

He did have charm. Yes, he did. And maybe he wasn't another Clark Gable, but she found his looks exceptionally appealing. And, frankly, she found his conversation more interesting than that of a whole roomful of Ph.D.'s.

In many ways he was a lot like her father. Her father had far less education than Paavo, but he knew more about life and more about people than anyone she had ever met. He was a self-made man and had spent a lifetime working hard for everything he had. It was only in the last two years, since his bypass surgery, that he had allowed himself to slow down at all. And he was tough. No one could push around Sal Amalfi; no one dared.

She thought Sal Amalfi would like Paavo Smith.

She tried to keep her mind off Paavo as she set out dinner: lettuce leaves, one hard-boiled egg (no salt), and brown rice. She was already so depressed she figured dieting, a food columnist's perennial curse, couldn't lower her spirits any further.

After dinner she worked again on trying to find

a clue in Sam's recipes. She was getting nowhere. All of his recipes were for breakfast foods: pancakes, waffles, omelets, or blintzes. But beyond that, she saw nothing. Frustrated, she curled up on the sofa and read a mystery until ten o'clock. She finished the book in bed around midnight. Nero Wolfe stories were difficult to put down. Maybe she should write a mystery someday, starring a strong, wonderful hero. She could call him something truly heroic, like Rex Truheart. She smiled. He would be tall and broad-shouldered, with wavy brown hair and big, blue eyes. . . .

She turned off the lamp beside her bed and shut her eyes. She turned onto her left side, then onto her right, then to her stomach, her back, left, right, front, back, until she sat up, exhausted.

This hiding out was so leisurely, she wasn't tired enough to sleep!

She took a few deep breaths and then lay down again, but the racing of her mind would not stop.

Unbidden, her thoughts turned to Paavo, and the emptiness that had become so familiar to her descended again. How she missed—

Her thoughts were interrupted by a faint sound.

No, it couldn't have been anything. She listened carefully. The dull roar of the waves lapping against the rocks lent their rhythmic hum to the night.

She relaxed a little.

Paavo. . . . She shut her eyes and began to doze off as she remembered his every feature, every nuance of his expression. She never needed to be afraid when he was near, no matter what was happening—

Again, a light scratching sound cut through the air.

She sat up, her heart pounding, every nerve in her body alert, straining to hear. Maybe it's the police checking on her, as Paavo said he'd ask them to do. The fluorescent numbers on her clock showed two A.M. It's just an animal of some kind, she told herself. A very small animal.

A sharp squeal, like a fingernail against a blackboard, pierced the silence. A silent sob caught in her throat as she listened. Someone was trying to break in.

The bedroom could trap her. She had to get out of there and hide.

She slid out of bed and put on her slippers. Should she risk using the phone? Even a whisper, in this silence, could be heard if anyone was nearby, and the noise of the old-fashioned rotary dial itself might be enough to alert the intruder. A sixth sense told her to keep quiet. The intruder might be willing to do his work fast and noisily if he thought she'd called for help.

Slowly, she inched across the darkened bedroom to the wall, then used it to guide her toward the doorway. Her pulse raced, making her head light.

Why hadn't she listened to Paavo? Why wasn't she back home, with Joey and Rico to guard the apartment and Paavo nearby?

The hallway was windowless. She hurried down it to the living room. There, through the sheer drapery covering the sliding glass doors, silhouetted by moonlight, she saw the shape of a man.

She froze and then pressed her hands to her mouth, stifling a scream as she stumbled backward into the hall. She could run out the front door, but from where he stood, he could see the door open and might be able to run around the house and catch her. No, it was safer inside. He might not be able to enter. He might give up and leave.

But if he didn't . . . if he entered. . . . She had to protect herself, find something to use as a weapon. Knives were in the kitchen, on the opposite side of the living room. She dropped to her hands and knees and began to crawl, hardly breathing, praying he wouldn't see her.

As she reached the kitchen, the lock on the glass door clicked open. She had put the wooden pole in its place between the sliding door and the doorframe, hadn't she? Hadn't she? She'd meant to. . . .

The glass door slid open. She pressed her knuckles against her teeth. A slight thud sounded as the pole was pushed into the window frame. She had remembered it! She heard the door slide shut, then open again. Once more, the thud—a little louder this time.

Cold perspiration broke out over her body.

The noises from the glass door stopped.

She had a terrible urge to shriek, to laugh or cry, to do anything to end this cat-and-mouse game.

She ran across the kitchen. Her hands shook. First, second, third drawer over, to where the knives were kept. Her fingers were stiff, scarcely able to grip the drawer handle. She yanked the drawer open.

Too loud! The contents of the drawer clanged against one another. She gasped. Had he heard it?

She reached into the drawer, touching the knives with quivering fingertips until she found what she wanted—the meat cleaver.

She clutched the handle with both hands as her eyes fixed on the back door. She crept toward it.

All was quiet outside. Perhaps he hadn't heard her, and she was safe. Please, God, she prayed, make him go away!

The back door was right in front of her. If he was still at the sliding glass door, or even the front door, she could sneak out this one. Her car was parked just beyond the door, a spare key under the floor mat. The back door became her safety valve, her escape, and she inched toward it, scarcely breathing, the meat cleaver held upright in front of her.

Her fingers touched the door handle just as a heavy weight crashed against it from the outside. She screamed. She clutched the meat cleaver tighter, staring, unable to move as he hit the door again.

The sound of splintering wood jarred her.

She ran from the kitchen as the door gave way. The sofa stood in the middle of the living room, facing the fireplace. She dropped behind it. Pressed hard against it, she could only hope he wouldn't be able to find her in the darkness.

Heavy footsteps sounded in the kitchen, the floorboards creaking beneath his weight as he searched.

Footsteps tapped on the hardwood floors as he walked into the living room, then when the sound grew muffled, she knew he had reached the carpeted area nearby. Her eyes wanted to squeeze shut, but she forced them open, unwilling to give up without a fight. She waited.

His breathing was low and raspy as he stalked her.

When she saw the toe of his shoe, she jumped up and threw the meat cleaver at him. He cried out. She tried to run, but her feet got tangled up in her nightgown, tripping her. The blast from his gun was the last thing she heard.

21

Paavo hadn't gotten home that evening until after eleven o'clock. He'd stayed at police headquarters, going over leads, shuffling through reports, trying to do anything to make himself feel useful. It didn't work. Nothing did anymore. He felt a weary emptiness as he dragged through each day.

He couldn't believe how many times a day he'd see something, or get an idea, and think, "I've got to tell Matt," or "I wonder what Matt'd say about that," and then it would hit him all over again that Matt was dead. The pain, ever present, would grow sharp once more. Christ, but he missed him.

At least when Angie had still been in the city, she distracted him. Not that she interested him, he told himself, but he could work on her case and, doing so, enter a world he had only read about up until then. It wasn't often, in Homicide, that he got to hobnob with the upper crust of the city. Angie had provided him with a diversion, that was all. But she, too, was gone now.

He called the Bodega police every day for a report, and they put an extra patrol on her place. If anyone had followed her, Paavo would know about it by now. She was safe in Bodega.

It was probably best that she was gone. He was growing far too . . . attached to her. God knows he hadn't expected anything like that to happen, and he certainly hadn't wanted it. But, damn, he missed her. Even her bad jokes. And her smiles, her tears, the way her eyes had filled with compassion over Matt, whom she hadn't even met. Somehow, she'd managed to help him through one of blackest periods he'd ever known. But with her gone, and Matt dead, the blackness was total now.

He had his job, but what else? It used to be enough. It would have to be again.

In Bodega, she was out of his jurisdiction, no longer his concern. That's how he'd wanted it. He'd arranged it so that they'd never have to see each other again.

Finito, as her mother would say.

Hell.

A copy of the *Bay Area Shopper* had been left on his doorstep that day, free to him as it was to every household in the city, filled with advertisements and coupons. He always used to throw it away, unread. Since he'd met Angie, Jon Preston,

Meyers, and the others, he'd flip through it for a minute or two, *then* throw it away.

He opened a can of 9 Lives for Hercules, made himself a cup of instant coffee, and then sat down to look over the day's mail. After that, he picked up the *Shopper* and thumbed through the pages. When he reached an inside page, he stopped and stared, his coffee cup poised against his lips. There, in front of him, was "Eggs and Egg-onomics" by Angelina Amalfi.

He jumped to his feet. "What the hell does she think she's doing?" he exclaimed aloud.

Hercules, who had polished off his canned food and curled into a sleeping ball on a kitchen chair, suddenly jumped to the floor, crouched, ears back. With his stomach nearly touching the ground, he scuttled out of the room.

Paavo paced a moment, telling himself he was overreacting, that there was no danger. She couldn't have been foolish enough to let people at her paper know where she was staying.

But he wasn't sure. He should phone her . . . and say what? Are you still alive? Be careful? Get the hell out of that house. And if he did say that, where could he tell her to go?

He didn't know what such a phone call would accomplish, except to scare her and maybe make things worse. She was only two hours away. He could look over the situation in person, talk to her, find out exactly how many people she had told where she was hiding. He called the Bodega police and asked them to check on her. He said he'd get there as soon as he could.

He pushed the old Austin as fast as he dared along the precarious coastal highway. Why hadn't he warned her against doing anything that could give her pursuer a way to trace her? He'd been more concerned about leaving her before he made a fool out of himself than he'd been about her safety. Never before had he been so negligent. Why now? Why with Angie?

He arrived at the police station at 1:50 A.M.

"Anything?" he asked the night lieutenant.

"Been quiet as a mouse out there, Inspector. Nothing's gonna happen tonight." The lanky, sandy-haired officer tilted his swivel rocker back and lifted his feet onto his desk. "Coffee?"

Paavo ran his fingers through his hair. "She's probably sleeping like a baby. I don't know if I should wake her up or just go to a motel and see her first thing in the morning."

The lieutenant's face spread wide in a grin. "I don't know, but seems to me a fellow rides up here in the dead of night, hell bent for leather, to see a pretty woman, he ought to see her."

Paavo gave him one of his steely stares. "It's not that way!"

"Oh, no, Inspector. I wasn't implying anything. The coffee's fresh made. I figured you'd need some. Want me to call the motel for you?"

Paavo walked over to the coffee maker and poured himself a cup. It was strong and black, just what he needed. "Yeah. I'll need a place to sleep tonight whether I see Miss Amalfi or not."

The lieutenant smirked as he picked up the phone. Paavo chose to ignore him.

It was nearly two o'clock before the lieutenant finished talking to the motel desk clerk. "They got plenty of rooms available. I didn't bother with a reservation—in case you get hung up with the investigation," he added with mock innocence.

Paavo grimaced. "When's your patrol due to report in?"

"Any minute. He's been calling in every half hour since you phoned."

"Your man's on it alone?"

"This is just a small town, Inspector. There's only two men on night duty besides me, so I split them up. We often have to work alone."

It was 2:01. "Shouldn't he have called by now?" Paavo asked.

"We'll give him a minute or two."

"Try to reach him."

"Bill's hardly late," the lieutenant muttered as he made a call over his radio. No answer.

Paavo paced.

"Hell, Inspector, the man's probably taking a leak!"

"Try again."

No answer.

At 2:05 Paavo and the lieutenant jumped into their cars to ride to Angie's place. Paavo never pushed his Austin so hard. If anything happened to her, he thought, how could he forgive himself? How could he live with himself? He had never even told her how much he enjoyed being with her.

He was the professional, the one who knew the dangers. She was just . . . just Angie. Smiling, laughing, enjoying life even through this madness. It had been bad enough going to bed alone on their last night together, after he'd kissed her and felt her wriggle beneath him, knowing she wanted him as much as he did her. Then to see her looking so appealing and sexy the next day, even as she rebuffed him. . . . He couldn't remember the last time he had felt so desperate about a woman. Maybe never.

Why had he left her alone in this wilderness? He should have known better. He *did* know better. And he had never even told her. . . .

He pressed the accelerator harder. She was beautiful, she was sexy, but much more. There was an emptiness in his life that she alone seemed to have the ability to fill. Somehow, sometime, somewhere she had taken hold of his heart. . . .

No! The thought shook him to the core. He'd never given his heart before. It hurt too much to love . . . and then lose. But Angie was a woman who deserved to be loved, a woman to grow old with. She was a woman who could make life seem worth all the ugliness that went along with the good.

She was a woman *he* could love.

In less than five minutes, he stood beside the patrolman's car. The officer was slumped over in the seat, dead. He'd been shot through the temple.

A horrible emptiness drained Paavo as he stared at Angie's dark, silent house. As the lieutenant called for assistance, Paavo quietly crept closer.

He wanted to burst in there, yelling for Angie, but too many years of training kicked in, and he was automatically cautious, though raw with fear.

As he approached the side of the house, he heard a loud crash. A scream, then the sound of splintering wood . . .

The front door was solid, with a dead bolt, he remembered, but the back door was flimsier. He ran toward the back. The splintered door hung open ominously.

A man cried out. Paavo hurled himself through the kitchen to the living room just in time to see a small blur of white and a dark, hulking figure raise his gun and shoot. Paavo heard the distinctive *ping* of the silencer.

"No!" His cry shattered the air. "Drop the gun."

The man spun and aimed his gun at Paavo.

Desperate to stop him, Paavo fired, and the intruder fell. But the small, white figure remained absolutely still where it had fallen. Paavo lowered his arm.

The lieutenant stepped to Paavo's side, his gun drawn, then switched on a lamp.

Paavo stood motionless, his chest constricted and aching as he looked at Angie lying face down on the floor. All the life went out of him in that moment, and with it, all hope.

He stepped toward her on leaden legs. His fault . . . this was all his fault. . . .

He saw no blood, though, and his heart began

to beat again. He dropped to her side, down on one knee, touching her shoulder, her back. She was alive. Gently, he turned her over. She's alive, his heart shouted as his breathing came hard and fast.

"Angie," he said, his voice choked as his hands carefully moved over her, checking for injuries. No blood, no bullet wound. How could the gunman have missed at that range? "Angie, wake up. Angie, please."

Her eyelids fluttered, and her head rolled slowly from side to side. She lifted her hand to her forehead and winced.

"What's wrong, Angel? Tell me. Where are you hurt?"

She opened her eyes. "Paavo."

Relief washed over him. He realized his hands were shaking as he clutched hers tighter. "Do you hurt anywhere?"

She tried to sit up. He put his arm around her for support. She blinked hard, looking dizzy, and then gave up and slumped against him. "My head. I was trying to run, but I tripped . . ."

"You tripped?" He chuckled. "Tripped? That's wonderful!"

She looked at him strangely.

He ran his fingertips over her forehead and lightly probed her scalp. "I don't feel any lump."

She touched his wrist, stopping him. "I didn't knock myself out! I think I may have . . . fainted."

Their eyes met, and he smiled.

"It was so scary!"

"I know." His voice had a peculiar catch to it. "It's all right now."

"She okay?" The lieutenant asked. Paavo looked at the officer, and then over at the man he had shot. Only then did he realize the man who had broken into the house was dead. Paavo's eyes turned to the lieutenant's with the question all cops understood. The lieutenant answered. "I was right behind you, Inspector. If you hadn't gotten him, I would have. In fact, I wish I had. How's she doing?"

"She's just scared," Paavo said. "She's tough. She'll be all right." He looked back at Angie. "You ready to get off this cold floor yet?"

"Okay." She tried to get up on her own, but Paavo didn't let her. He lifted her in his arms and carried her to the sofa. He was struck again by how slight she was. He was reminded once more of the small, battered bird she had been sent, and of the aching despair he felt when he thought she had been killed. Gently, he put her down, then hovered over her, brushing her hair back from her brow.

"Sheriff should be here any minute, Inspector. I told him about Bill—"

Paavo jumped to his feet and motioned him to the farthest corner of the living room.

"I don't want her to know about the policeman who was killed." Paavo's voice was hushed.

"Why not?"

"She'd feel responsible. It'd . . . I think it'd tear her apart. I don't want that to happen to her."

"It'll be in the papers," the lieutenant said.

"Bill and I worked together a lot of years. He was a good friend. Do you know what it's like to lose a man like that?"

Paavo's heart twisted. "I know," he whispered.

The lieutenant eyed him a moment. "I'll do what I can."

"Thanks."

Paavo went back to Angie. She lay with her arm across her eyes. "Angie," he said, "Angie, listen to me." She lowered her arm and looked at him.

He spoke slowly. "I know it's not easy, but I want you to look at the man who's lying on the floor. Tell me if you recognize him. Okay?"

She nodded, raised herself up on her elbow, and glanced where he pointed. The man lying on the carpet was skinny and had black hair, and his chest was saturated with deep red blood. She quickly shut her eyes.

"Do you know him?" Paavo asked again.

She shook her head.

"Have you ever seen him before?"

She forced herself to look at the man again, to look carefully, this time, at his face. He had bushy black eyebrows, his nose was long, and his mouth, even in death, was mocking and twisted. She raised her eyes to his open, vacant ones, and a shock of recognition surged through her.

"It's him," she whispered, shutting her eyes, trying to block out the sight before her as she lay back on the sofa. "On the Vallejo steps, the day Sam was killed. It's him. Oh, God," she cried, her face turning deathly white and clammy, and her hands going to her mouth. Paavo knew what was happening; he'd seen it often when people came face to face with this kind of death. He grabbed the handiest thing, a huge candy-dish, dumped out the mints, put the dish on the floor beside her, then rolled her onto her stomach, her head hanging over the edge of the sofa. He patted her shoulder as her stomach turned over and over. When she was through, he took away the dish, got a damp washcloth and passed it over her face. "I'm sorry," she whispered. Her eyes were bewildered and wet with tears.

"It's okay. Rest now." He took off his overcoat and covered her with it. The sound of cars pulling into her driveway caught his attention, and he went to the door to meet the sheriff.

22

There he was again, the thin man with black hair, his gun silhouetted against the misty, yellow lights of the long tunnel. She ran. His footsteps echoed against the walls, coming ever closer, but she pushed on, feeling her heart would burst. *Paavo, where are you?*

"Angie!"

A gunshot filled the night. It hit her. No, she screamed. *No!*

"Wake up, Angie."

Stop! Let go of me. Paavo!

"It's me. It's Paavo. Stop struggling. It's just a dream, Angie. A dream."

Slowly, the words began to make sense. She opened her eyes and saw Paavo sitting on the sofa beside her.

"Angie, it's okay now."

She sat up, her arms wrapping around him. "It felt so real," she whispered.

"I know," he murmured, stroking her back, his voice warm and comforting, "I know."

She tried to relax, but the dream lingered. The sun was already filling the room. She was safe. Paavo was here. She let go of him and leaned back against the cushions, trying to make sense of what had happened. In a way, her dream seemed more real than what had really happened here last night.

She knew Paavo had tried to hurry things along, but it had seemed to take forever before the noise stopped, the lights dimmed, and the last men from the sheriff's department and county coroner's office walked out the door. Then she had only dozed, emotionally and physically exhausted.

She remembered how Paavo had somehow managed to fit his big frame beside her on the sofa. He had held her close, ignoring his own discomfort, until her trembling ceased. She had leaned her head against his chest, listening to his strong heartbeat and realizing that, once again, he had been there when she needed him. In his arms, she had finally slept.

This morning, his hair was more tousled than usual and his five o'clock shadow had gone into overtime, but other than that he looked wide awake and energetic—quite the opposite of how she felt.

"I can't believe you're here," she said, reaching for his hands. "I thought you weren't coming back."

"Last night, when I saw your column in the

Shopper, I called the police and told them to be on the alert, and I drove up."

"Thank goodness," she exclaimed. She thought about his explanation. It was very odd. "I don't understand," she began. "Why you were concerned just because you saw my column?"

"I don't understand why you submitted it."

"It's my job!"

"And your safety is mine!"

"But—" she stopped, uncertain of what he meant.

"Who did you give this address to?"

"No one." What kind of a dummy did he think she was?

"Your boss?"

"No!"

"Did you put a return address when you sent out your column?"

"Of course not! I mailed it at the post office."

"The postmark—then a few phone calls to local realtors. . . ."

She shut her eyes in disgust. How could she have been so stupid!

"We have to go to the station," he said. "You need to make a statement."

She rubbed her forehead. The whole thing revolved around the *Shopper.* She'd sent her column to George Meyers, but there was no way he could be involved in anything criminal.

"It won't take long," he said.

She sighed and looked away. She didn't want to hear it. She wanted to blot everything out, but he wouldn't let her.

"I don't have to go back to the city until tomorrow," he added. "I think you should return with me."

She sighed. "You're probably right. Tomorrow, then."

"We have today," he said quietly.

She glanced at him. It sounded as if, *almost* as if, he wanted to be with her. She stood up and went into the bedroom, shutting the door behind her.

"Yes," she whispered. "We have today."

The afternoon air was cold and heavy with the fog that seemed to constantly hover over the village. She was dressed in jeans, a heavy fisherman's knit sweater, and boots.

That morning at the police station, Paavo had guided her through the red tape with a minimum of time and frustration. She couldn't have helped but notice the deference many officers gave him. Afterward, she had sat in an empty office, alone, for over a half hour while he concluded "police business." She had thought it strange, but he had said she wouldn't want to hear some of the gorier details. He was right.

He had taken her to a diner for a good-sized brunch, and then they had driven to the beach. Although the sun peeked now and again through the fog, the air was cool and brisk, the wind sharp. Except for a couple of fishermen and the ever-present gulls, they had the beach entirely to themselves.

He held her hand as they walked along the shore now, the silence comfortable between them. Angie needed the silence. She needed to be there, her hand in his, away from the world which seemed so threatening.

"I guess it's no good to hide, is it Paavo?" she said finally.

He glanced at her and then turned his gaze to the waves breaking far from shore. "The man who broke into your place last night has a long record of arrests for everything from muggings to armed robberies. He also has a reputation as a hit man, a gun for hire. We were never able to pin anything on him, though."

"A hired killer?" She stared at him. "What does that mean? Was he after me because I saw him at the scene when Sam was killed, or because someone else wants me dead?"

"We don't know."

She stopped walking and faced the water. "My God!"

"I wish I didn't have to tell you that," he said. "But you needed to know it."

The breezes lashed at her face, turning her cheeks red, whipping her hair about as she pondered his words. She looked back at him. "If only I wasn't so afraid," she said quietly.

"Anyone would be. There's nothing wrong with the way you feel."

"I don't know what to do."

"You have faith, Angie. It makes all the difference."

They walked again, and she watched her shoes

sink into the sand with each step. "Do you, Paavo?"

He was thoughtful. "Most of the time, I guess not. But other times, like when Matt was killed, I want life to be more than just a fluke."

"Policemen need God," she said. "Maybe more than most people."

He glanced at her with a sad, haunted smile on his face. "That sounds like something Aulis would say." His words were little more than a whisper.

They found a boulder with a flat top and sat side by side on it, facing the ocean. "I'm not clear about Aulis's relationship to you," Angie said. "Is he an uncle or something?"

"No, nothing. In fact, I'm probably not even Finnish."

"But you said he raised you. A person just doesn't raise someone else's kid."

Paavo shrugged. "Aulis did. Maybe because he was a foreigner and didn't know any better. Or maybe he kept us because he understood a lot more than anyone thought."

"You mean, you and your sister?"

Paavo gazed at the sea as he spoke. "Jessica was five years older than me. I was about four when we went to Aulis."

"What happened to your parents?"

A long time passed before he said, "I didn't know my father, and I doubt his name was Smith. The only things I remember about my mother were her drinking, and crying, and the way she liked to get all dressed up and go out. One day she took me and Jessica to Aulis, who lived in the next apartment. She left, and I never saw her again."

Angie drew in her breath. "But why? What happened to her?"

"Those are the questions I grew up with, Angie."

She didn't know what to say. She couldn't imagine a mother doing that, she simply couldn't imagine it.

"Jessica was older. Didn't she remember your father?"

"We didn't have the same father. Jessie's father was black. She had only the vaguest memory of him. Then lots of different men started coming around, and before long, there I was."

"I . . . I see."

Paavo's gaze flickered over her face. "No, Angelina, I don't think you do. I don't think you could ever begin to."

She wasn't sure what he meant. "I'm sorry."

"Don't be. I like the way you are—to me, you're like a ray of sunshine. God! What a thing to say!" He grinned and shook his head.

She studied his profile. The smile had vanished, and in its place there was a wistfulness, as arresting as it was heartbreaking.

"Were you very young when your sister died?" she asked softly.

He didn't respond for a long time, and then, when he did, he didn't look at her. But slowly, in his clipped, direct way of speaking, as the waves rolled onto the shore at their feet, he told her about his past. Every word he spoke, and especially the many he left unsaid, she caught and held and studied, until, in her heart, she understood.

Paavo sounded like the kind of little boy perhaps every classroom has. He was the boy who was always getting into trouble, the skinny kid whose shirts were usually two sizes too big or too small, whose jeans were torn, and whose socks didn't always quite match. The other kids, the ones who lived in nice houses and had parents who cared about them, didn't exactly snub him; they simply didn't see him. Angie remembered a boy in her school like that. She felt her throat tighten as she wondered how many times her own thoughtless remarks and disdainful looks hurt the child in her class.

For hurt it did. That came through very clearly in Paavo's tale, even though he spoke not a single word of self-pity or unhappiness. But there was no talk of joy either, or of fun.

His world, he explained, had revolved around two people, Aulis, and his sister, whom he adored. He told her how, as he had grown older, he'd met other boys like himself, outcasts, and they'd associated only with each other. But he knew the life those boys were growing into wasn't what he wanted.

When he spoke of his sister Jessica, his voice held a tone close to anger. And frustration, and helplessness—almost more than Angie could bear to hear.

Paavo saw what his sister was doing. She liked to go to parties and to what she called "good" times, much as their mother used to do. He saw the kind of people she was running around with and tried to stop her. They were bad people, he would warn her, but she would laugh him off. "Don't worry, Paavo. I know what I'm doing," she would say.

There was nothing he could do, for he was only fourteen, and she was his very beautiful, very grown-up, nineteen-year-old sister. And he believed her.

Then, one night, she didn't come home. She'd stayed out all night before, lots of times, and Paavo knew why. But this time he had seen the man she had gone with and felt uneasy, so uneasy that he went looking for her.

By the time he found her, it was too late. The man had passed out, and Jessie was dead. There wasn't even a phone in the cheap apartment for him to call for help. He shook her, again and again, desperately trying to awaken her, but he knew he could not. Finally, he held his sister in his arms and cried. When his tears stopped, he felt old.

The coroner said it was a heroin overdose.

Paavo's story stopped there. He didn't say anything more—not how he'd felt, or how he'd told Aulis, or even how he'd continued his life without the person who meant the world to him.

Angie's eyes filled with tears. She gazed out to sea, forcing herself not to cry. She couldn't let him see her emotion.

Finally, she took a deep breath and turned again toward him, taking in his soft wavy hair, his strong jaw, the fine contours of his face. "You've come a long way, Inspector Smith."

He scooped up a handful of sand and watched it slide through his fingers until just a little was left on his palm, then he tossed it away. His voice held a forced merriment. "Maybe it's just two sides of the same coin. What do you think, Angel?" He glanced at her quickly, but not quick enough to hide the need showing on his face.

"I think . . . I think you shouldn't sell yourself short, Inspector. You can be proud."

He bowed his head in silent thought. She watched, unable to take her eyes from his face, once again finding her admiration and her heart going out to this solitary man.

He reached over and took her hand from her lap. Raising it to his lips, he softly placed a kiss on the back of it, then lowered it again.

Her throat tightened.

He stood and held out his hand to help her up. "Shall we go?"

As they walked, he draped an arm over her shoulder. She put her arm around his waist. Their steps slowed as they walked back to the car.

Paavo opened up the Ferrari and roared along the highway. Angie had asked him to drive, knowing how much he'd enjoy it. She found a lot to laugh about, maybe as an antidote for yesterday, she thought, or to wipe away the pain of the past he had revealed to her, or simply because he was with her once more. They went to some antique shops and art galleries in the town of Bodega, holding hands and playing tourist. Angie smiled almost continuously, and her mind raced as if she was trying to fit a lifetime into one, all too short afternoon. She even got Paavo to concede that a couple of her jokes were funny. At a deli, they selected a mix of prosciutto, galantina, and gorgonzola cheese, plus freshly baked sourdough bread. Finally, they returned to the house.

While Paavo built a roaring fire, she spread the food on the coffee table and added a bottle of chilled white wine.

They sank down on the thick, flokati rug, and sat cross-legged, facing each other, in front of the fireplace. The light from the fire played against Paavo's features, surrounding him with a warm glow. Her eyes drank him in, the sight more heady than any wine. The gentleness of the man, his caring and thoughtfulness, filled her senses.

She cared too much, she knew that, and she knew he cared not nearly enough. She was a tool for him, a pawn. He had given her no reason to think otherwise. But now, just for this day, this night, he'd opened himself to her and let himself feel. Tomorrow he would be Mister Inspector again, but today, none of that mattered. "We have today," he'd said earlier. Today.

She reached for the wine, carefully filling their glasses. They picked them up and leaned toward each other, clinking the glasses in a toast. As they raised the wine to their lips, they looked up, their eyes locking. A quickening began in her stomach and she lowered her glass, her hand suddenly unsteady.

Paavo watched her every movement. She knew

everything was written in her eyes, and knew there was no way she could hide the desire she felt. Nor did she want to.

He reached over and took the wine from her, setting the glass on the hearth beside his own. Neither of them breathed. He got to his knees and took her arms, pulling her toward him as his lips met hers with a fire and urgency far beyond her expectations. It left her shaken and breathless and in need of more.

He tasted like fine wine and smelled of the sun and the sea. She held his shoulders as his hands circled her waist, his kiss deepening as she softened in his arms. Her fingertips traced the strength of his back and wrapped themselves in his hair as she returned his kisses twofold.

His eyes captured hers as his hands ran along the length of her body, to her hips and lower. He molded her to him, letting her feel the rapid pounding of his heartbeat, his hard need pressing against her body.

"Are you sure?" he asked.

"Sometimes, Inspector, you ask too many questions." She replied with a kiss that left him no doubt.

He lifted off her bulky sweater and eased her onto the soft rug as gently as if she were fine crystal. Stretching out beside her, he lightly ran his hand over her silky camisole, along her stomach, her midriff, her breasts. His eyes grew dark and languorous, and she raised her hands to his neck, pulling him down to kiss her again.

His kisses seared with intensity. As his hand

slid under her top, she lifted it away, needing to feel the coolness of the evening air against her skin, and needing to feel his touch.

She twisted her fingers into his hair as his mouth lowered to her neck, her shoulders, her breasts.

He unzipped her jeans and removed them, then slid his hand over the soft skin of her belly to her hips.

"You're a beautiful woman, Angel. Your body is every bit as beautiful as your soul. That's rare. It's something a man can treasure."

She lifted his sweater over his head and began to unbutton his shirt. He relaxed, seeming to enjoy watching her undress him. She outlined his shoulders, then ran her hands over his broad, hard chest and flat stomach, watching his muscles ripple as she touched him. "What do you treasure, Paavo?" she asked.

He removed the rest of his clothes and stretched out beside her. He was a handsome man, lean and strong. Her pulse throbbed in anticipation.

His kisses ranged over her as did his hands, slipping between her legs and inside her. Her desire for him was as strong and immediate as his was for her. "You," he answered finally. "I treasure you."

Her lips trembled as she kissed the mouth that so often spoke words that went straight to her heart. Her fingers ran over his stomach, then lower. She felt a tremor rush through him at her touch, felt his kiss deepen until he broke it off to slowly trail kisses down her body, from her breasts to her waist to the spot where his fingers worked their magic.

Her body arched and tightened, both to pull away and to press closer, in agony and pleasure, not daring to allow him to continue, yet unable to bear to have him stop until, finally, her world wound tighter and tighter then snapped and shattered into glorious relief.

She couldn't move, could scarcely even breathe for a long while. "Paavo," she whispered, and wrapped her arms around him. She ached to taste him, keep him, hold him, protect him, feel him deep inside her.

He lowered himself into her slowly, cautiously, as if, even then, he remembered that he was a big man, and she was just a little woman.

"It's all right," she whispered, her arms tightening. He lifted his head, and the look in his eyes sent her soul soaring.

She was lost in him—a vortex of the man, the fire beside them, and the loud crashing of the waves onto the beach nearby. He made love intimately, expertly, with every bit of the seriousness and intensity he brought to everything else, and she found herself consumed by him, physically, mentally—spiritually, if such a thing were possible. Until, finally, in each other's arms, their worlds spun wildly out of control, the sea and the fire blending with them, the sound and the heat swirling about until the chaos ended, and the world became still once more.

He was everything to her that night. Only in

his arms did she feel complete. Away from him, not touching him, she felt bereft.

After a while they rekindled the fire, and eventually they crawled under the warm quilts on the bed when the night air became too damp. She didn't want to sleep that night, but she lay in his arms, unwilling to move, listening to the strong, steady rhythm of his heartbeat.

He rolled her onto her back. "Hungry?" he asked.

She ran her fingers over his shoulders. "Only for you."

His look was open and warm. "Angel," he whispered as he kissed her, pulling her close to him again.

She mouthed his name silently, squeezing her eyes shut, holding him to her. The way she felt about him scared her. It was too strong. Not this man, she prayed. If she had to fall in love, she couldn't let it be with this man, whose life was so different from hers, and far too frightening.

But she knew her prayer was already too late.

23

The rain beating against the windows awakened Paavo. The bed was empty, but the smell of coffee was in the air, and he could hear a radio in another part of the house. Easing himself off the bed, he crossed the room to the window and watched the rivulets of rainwater form and run down the pane. They seemed appropriate for his mood.

You're supposed to feel good now, dummy, he told himself, like the conquering hero. After all, Angie wasn't the first woman to fall for her blue knight and act on those feelings. Hell, for a lot of cops it was an occupational hazard, and a lot of them enjoyed the hazardous-duty payoff. He'd always been more careful. He knew that in the long run, what had happened last night wouldn't mean a damn thing to her beyond the danger and excitement of the moment.

Last night, he'd let his emotions take over. He was supposed to know better. He had made a mistake, but he would rectify it soon.

He took a shower and walked into the kitchen. He found her in front of the stove, concentrating hard on turning over an enormous ham and cheese omelet.

"Good morning," he said.

She turned from the stove to greet him with a hug and a light kiss. "You smell good," she said as she nuzzled his ear.

All his good intentions about her evaporated at the feel of her body against his. The dampness of her hair from her earlier shower and the soapy cleanliness of her skin, soft and fresh without makeup, were like aphrodisiacs.

His hands trembled as he set her from him and stepped back.

She glanced at him quickly.

"I've got to leave right away," he said.

"Paavo?" The look of bewilderment on her face tore at him. "What's wrong?"

"I think you should come back to the city with me. We need to wrap this up. Having you there will be useful."

"Useful?" Her face paled and she turned away to nudge at the edges of the omelet with her spatula. "I don't understand."

"It's time to go back to work, back to the way things are supposed to be."

She shut her eyes for a moment, and then nodded silently. She divided the omelet in two, giving him the larger portion.

"Angie?"

She sighed, her hands over her eyes a moment. "I'm just . . . I'll go back to San Francisco with you, okay?"

Her face no longer held the warmth of the morning. He lowered his head and looked away, knowing he was the reason the cold, damp air of the ocean seemed to have seeped into the room.

They ate breakfast in silence. She didn't look at him.

"I'll clean up the kitchen, then pack," she said, picking up the dishes. "We should leave soon."

"I'll do these." He took the dishes from her hands.

She hurried away from him to her bedroom and shut the door.

A half hour later, he'd finished in the kitchen and was standing by the picture window looking at the gray ocean, the waves white and choppy from the storm, when she walked into the living room with one of her bags. "I'm ready," she said softly.

"Even in a storm it's beautiful," he murmured as he turned to face her.

The emotion in her eyes reached across the room in that unguarded moment. The last thing he wanted to do was hurt her—or himself—more than he had already. He went to her and cupped her face with his hands.

"Angie," he whispered, touching her gently, "yesterday was perfect."

She nodded, her eyes swimming.

"The weather."

"Yes."

"The scenery."

"Yes."

"The company."

She lowered her gaze.

He continued. "At times like that, it's easy to do things . . . out of character."

She searched his eyes, as if to seek some feeling toward her, but his training had been too good for that.

She stepped back. "I have no regrets, Paavo."

"Good." The word was a whisper.

He took her hand and held it gently in both of his. "Hey, look at this," he said, running his fingers over hers. She looked down. "Your nails. They're short and not purple anymore. I'd better get you back to the city fast. This will never do."

She gave him a small, sad smile, then reached for her bag. He went into her bedroom to pick up the others.

He had Angie go ahead in her Ferrari, and he followed in his Austin, keeping a close eye on her and on any driver who ventured too near.

Angie had called the bodyguard service from Bodega. Joey was already waiting for them, leaning against a blue Thunderbird in the basement garage, as Paavo pulled into an open parking space near Angie's.

The two men greeted each other warmly, but Angie had nothing to say as they rode up the elevator to her apartment. Once inside, she

checked her belongings, which appeared undis-
turbed since her hurried departure. Paavo and
Joey looked over the entire apartment, while
Angie paced, holding her elbows, in front of the
bay windows.

"Everything's fine, Angie."

Her eyes jerked to Paavo at the sound of his
voice. He held his jacket loosely over his left
shoulder, trying to look casual. He turned to Joey,
his right hand outstretched.

"Take good care of her, my man," he said as
they shook hands.

"Sure thing, Inspector."

Paavo glanced at Angie for just a moment and
then walked out the door without a word, shutting it quietly after him.

Angie stood, motionless, in the center of the
room.

"You all right, Miss Angelina?" Joey asked.

"Sure, Joey. . . . Say, why don't we watch some
T.V.?" He gave her a funny look. The T.V. was
already on.

The man who had been after her had been
caught. It was all over, she decided. The "hit
man" theory was nonsense. She didn't really need
Joey, but it was probably best to be cautious for
a while. Soon, it would be time to get back into
the swing of things. Dates! Action! Good times!

Her eyes filled with tears. She spent the afternoon with Joey watching reruns of 1950s T.V.
shows on Nickelodeon. It was true misery.

Around dinnertime, she went into the kitchen,
smeared peanut butter on saltine crackers, and

stuck some chocolate chips on top. She was battling despair and losing—badly.

To hell with everything, she decided, and grabbed the whole bag of semi-sweet chocolate chips. In the living room, "Gomer Pyle, USMC" was just starting.

Halfway through the bag, the sound of the telephone jarred her out of her chocolate-and-TV-induced stupor. She spun toward the phone, hesitated a moment, and then picked up the receiver. "Hello?"

Nothing.

She swallowed hard, then repeated, "Hello?" in a more tentative voice this time.

"Ang——" Then nothing.

"Who is this? Paavo, Paavo is that you? Are you hurt?"

"George . . . it's George." The words were slurred, coming out like "zzgiorr," but she recognized her editor's voice.

"George! What happened? Where are you?"

"Be careful, be—"

Her whole body jerked with the sound of the receiver banging, as if dropped on the floor. "George!" She screamed into the phone. "George! Answer me!"

Silence.

She looked at Joey. "What should we do?"

"Do?" He was standing now. "Who's it? What happened?"

She clutched the receiver tighter, giving it a hard shake. "George? George, please answer me! Where are you? Oh, God!"

She waited, listening, not wanting to break off the connection, but realizing that precious minutes were being wasted. She decided what she had to do and prayed she was right as she hung up the phone.

Immediately, she dialed George's office. The line was busy. That meant he may well have been calling her from his office when—what? A heart attack? He was in the high-risk years, and was certainly tense enough. But why call her, and why tell her to be careful?

She dialed 9-1-1, alerting the police to the call she'd received and telling them where George's office was located. Next, she called Paavo's home, but got the answering machine and hung up in frustration. Finally, she called Homicide and spoke to an Inspector Calderon, who seemed to know all about her and the case. That done, she and Joey rushed to the *Bay Area Shopper* building.

When she got there, the street was already filled with police cars and an ambulance. She left Joey with the car. After explaining that she was the person who had made the call to the police, she was admitted. Everyone, it seemed, wanted to speak with her.

A policeman led her up the stairs to the second floor, toward George's office. She was about to enter it when she saw Paavo hurrying toward her. She stopped and stared at him. He caught her arm and led her away.

"You don't want to go in there," he said.

"What do you mean? Where's George? How is he?" She tried to free her arm.

He put both hands on her shoulders. "George is dead, Angie. He was shot."

A roaring began in her ears. "No, Paavo. It's not true. You want to scare me, but it's not going to work. I want to see George."

"Angie," he said softly, and she knew he was being truthful with her. At the moment she saw the number of police cars at the *Shopper,* she began to suspect something like this had happened.

Another policeman wheeled over a desk chair and placed it directly behind her. Paavo helped her sit.

"Angie, you called in the report on George. How did you know about it? Angie?" He crouched down so that he was level with her eyes and took her hand. "Listen to me. Tell me what happened."

She placed her other hand on his but sat staring at the carpet. He had said George was dead, but who would shoot George? He was a good man—not a great editor, even he knew that—but why would anyone kill him?

She knew Paavo had been speaking to her, but it wasn't making much sense. Nothing had made much sense for a long time now. She gazed in his direction. He had such a look of compassion, it made her heart ache. Not for me, Paavo, she wanted to say, for George. She felt her lower lip begin to tremble, and Paavo's hand lightly stroked her cheek.

Another man pulled up a chair and sat in front of her. He had black eyes and heavy brows, and hair the color of charcoal, pomaded in an unsuccessful attempt to control it. "Miss Amalfi," he began, "I'm Inspector Calderon. Do you hear me?"

She nodded.

"I spoke to you on the phone, remember?" Again, the nod. "I want you to tell me what happened tonight."

She couldn't think, her mind was blank, and she shook her head.

"Miss Amalfi, a man has been murdered. He's lying in there in his own blood with bullet holes in the chest and stomach. You were the last one he talked to. I want to know why."

Purple and black spots appeared before her eyes and next thing she knew, Paavo was patting her face and another officer was handing her a glass of water. As she sipped the water, her head cleared enough to hear Paavo yelling at Calderon for being too rough with her and Calderon shouting back at him.

Chief Hollins stormed toward them. If an expression could look like a growl, his did then. "Isn't it bad enough a newspaper editor gets shot in his own office in the middle of this city without two of my own men squabbling like a couple of wet hens!"

Angie looked from Paavo to Calderon, both men now silent.

"I'm sorry," she said to them.

Paavo knelt beside her, and she placed a hand

on his shoulder as she began to tell him about George's call—what little there was to tell. Calderon and Hollins sat across from her, listening.

The detectives looked at each other when she had finished. "He had to warn her," Calderon said, "but of what?"

"Back to square one," Paavo said.

"Square two, man. Like two dead bodies now."

"Body!" Angie glared at Calderon. "What's just another body to you is a man who was very good to me. He had a wife and a couple of grown sons. Now he's dead. He's not a body! He's George. Paavo," she whispered, gripping the lapels of his jacket as tears rolled down her cheeks. "He's George!"

Paavo's arms went around her, holding her close. She buried her head against his neck as her hands formed into fists, her anguish coming out in great, shaking sobs.

Hollins addressed Paavo. "You're too close to this case, Smith. I think I better pull you off."

"I know what I'm doing." Paavo's voice smoldered, but his hands remained gentle as he patted her back and stroked her hair.

"So far, but it's too dangerous. Situations like this—with her—and you make mistakes. One cop's already dead."

"Forget it!"

Angie lifted her head to look at Paavo. Something in Hollins's words reminded her of something she had heard before. What was it?

Hollins removed the wrapping from a cigar, put it in his mouth to wet the tip, and then took it out and looked at Paavo. "She knows two guys and now they're dead." He struck a match and lit the cigar, puffed on it a few times, then took it out of his mouth and stared at the glowing embers. "Maybe Meyers didn't call her to warn her. Maybe she shot him and called us to throw us off the track."

"That won't wash, Hollins!"

His eyes narrowed as he looked at Paavo. "You wouldn't know if it did! You're too involved, both with her and with wanting to find out who killed Matt. I know you'll do anything to find his killer. And that don't make for a smart cop. You could end up dead!"

"Damn it, I can handle it!"

"You're off the case, Smith." Hollins put the cigar back in his mouth.

"No! I won't—"

"One more word," Hollins said through clenched teeth, "and you're suspended. Right now, you're on vacation. Two weeks, Smith. Now get the hell out of here."

Paavo seethed. He didn't say a word. He didn't have to; his eyes spoke volumes. He stood and pulled Angie to her feet, took her arm, and hurried her to the stairs and out of the building.

As they walked toward her car, she remembered where she had heard Hollins's words before—Paavo had said them. He had told her he couldn't get involved with her because even a rookie knew it would be too dangerous—too dangerous for them both.

24

A *few hours* later, Angie lay alone in Paavo's big bed.

He had insisted she return home with him. George's murder might mean that whoever was after her would be even more desperate, and Paavo didn't want to take any chances. Angie sent Joey back to her apartment to lock it up for a few days and inform Rico about all that had occurred. She tried to convince Paavo she'd be safe in her own apartment, but he was so furious over what Hollins had said and done, he wasn't amenable to either conversation or reason. He sent her to his bedroom while he spread out a blanket for himself on the sofa.

Over an hour passed. She lay still, her mind racing when the door to the bedroom opened slightly, casting a ray of light into the room from the hallway. "Angie?" he whispered.

"Yes, I'm still awake."

He opened the door a little wider. "I want to apologize. Here I've been, acting like a jerk, and you just lost a friend. I hope you can forgive me—about everything tonight."

He sounded so dejected that she got out of bed and approached him. The pajamas he had lent her, rolled up at the wrists and ankles, billowed around her as she crossed the room. Halfway there, she stopped.

"You have no need to apologize. You were wonderful. I'm sorry about Hollins, Paavo. I know how you must feel, and I realize, too, that everything you did and said was for me." She stepped closer. "Do you think I'm so blind I couldn't see that?"

He stared at her in the darkness. "Thank you. You'd better go back to bed now, Angel. Good night."

Before he could leave, she reached his side and took his hand. She hadn't hesitated a moment. It was that simple; she couldn't let him walk away from her again. Leading him to the bed, she placed her hands against his shoulders and eased him onto the mattress, and then stretched her body on top of his. "Just because I accepted your apology so quickly doesn't mean you're getting off scot-free, you know." She tried to say it jokingly, to hide the tremor that shook her body as she touched him, but her voice was husky.

As she kissed him, his arms slowly went around her, their pressure increasing with the intensity of her kiss, until he crushed her against him and

rolled her body under his. The bed creaked with
the weight of the two of them, and Hercules
protested loudly from the foot of the bed at the
disturbance to his peaceful slumber.

The next morning she got out of bed and put
on Paavo's pajamas again, having shed them during the night. She liked them, even though she
herself favored Christian Dior nightwear. She
padded out to the kitchen.

"Good morning," she said. Paavo was dressed
and hunched over a cup of coffee.

"We've got to find Crane," he said, his chin
resting on his hand as he gazed out the kitchen
window at the jungle that used to be his garden.

"You know," she said, pouring herself some
black coffee and sitting across from him at the
table, "I really ought to bring a bunch of clothes
over here. I feel like I spend more time at your
place than my own."

Paavo rubbed his eyes wearily. "It's madden-
ing the way Crane disappeared. But he's got to be
around here somewhere. I feel it! There's no
other reason for George Meyers to have been
killed. The two must have been partners." He
took another sip of coffee.

"I like your house very much." Angie yawned.
"Maybe we can forget all this detective stuff. You
know, we wouldn't have to worry about anyone
trying to kill me if I just moved in here with you."

"On the one hand, we have the illegal guns
connected to Sammy Blade and Sammy Blade

connected to Crane. And we know that the bullet that killed Matt was from the same gun as the bullet that killed Blade. On the other hand, we have George Meyers, the *Shopper,* and the fact that the man who killed Sammy Blade was also able to track you down in Bodega because your address went to the *Shopper.* That means he had to be connected somehow to the *Shopper,* or to George Meyers. . . ."

"It goes round and round and makes no sense, Paavo." Angie got up and walked to the window.

"The link between the two of them has to be you, the *Shopper,* and Crane's recipes."

"The recipes, yes. . . . You know, I could easily write my food column from this house. That's the nice thing about being a writer. I can live anywhere. I think I'd like it here, in fact."

He stroked his chin. "Maybe we should be trying to find out more about Blade. He knew Crane. Something in his past might just lead us to Crane. If only we knew where he was from, where he lived, anything."

She sat across from him at the kitchen table. Their eyes met. "What did you say?" she asked.

"No . . . you," he looked at her quizzically. "I don't think I heard you right."

"I said . . . I said . . . ," No, she couldn't repeat what she had said. "I said they might know something at the Ben Lomond Inn near Carmel, since Sam was once a chef there. Did you ask them?"

"I thought you said you wanted to live . . . I mean . . . he was?" He jumped up. "How long have you known this?"

"How long? He told me when we first met. Why?"

"Why? Why didn't you tell me!?"

"Why didn't you ask? How was I supposed to know you didn't know something so simple!"

"Simple!" He sank back in his chair. "I give up. Are you sure?"

"Well, I have no proof. But then, if he were going to lie, wouldn't he come up with something really fancy? I mean, why lie about a bed-and-breakfast inn for eight guests?"

"Have some breakfast, Angie. It's a long ride to Carmel."

Her mouth turned downward. "It's not your problem anymore. You're off the case and it's too dangerous—"

He placed his finger against her lips and she stopped speaking. "I'm not abandoning you in this, Angie. I couldn't do it to you—or to Matt."

By afternoon, they were on their way to Carmel, after a quick stop at Neiman-Marcus. She swore she wasn't going to Carmel without a suitable wardrobe, and Paavo wouldn't let her go back to her apartment to get anything.

As Paavo drove the Ferrari toward Carmel, he told her that he was convinced Crane had to be the link in all this, and that Sammy Blade was their link to Crane. He also believed that whoever was behind Blade's death was behind George Meyers's, maybe for the same reason—whatever it was. The man who had tried to kill Angie had to have been no more than a hired gun who made the mistake of allowing her to see him. Paavo doubted he was the brain behind whatever was going on.

Perhaps the man behind it all was Crane. But, if so, why kill Sammy Blade? Blade and Crane were friends, cohorts, or so everyone thought.

Paavo explained that he couldn't go barging in to the Ben Lomond Inn, asking questions about Sammy Blade. If anyone knew, they might keep quiet in order to stay uninvolved. No, what he and Angie had to do was check in as guests. Angie would be a part of his cover, and this way he could keep an eye on her.

"Don't worry about me. I know all about investigative reporting," she said.

"You're not Lois Lane, Angie."

"What I'm referring to is that I took a journalism class that had three or four sessions on how to be subtle when investigating."

"Miss Amalfi, I hate to disillusion you, but you're about as subtle as Henny Youngman."

"Inspector Smith, I intend to be a real asset in this investigation."

"Seriously, Angie, you just stay out of the way, enjoy the sea and sunshine and leave the police business to me."

She raised an eyebrow and pursed her lips. "Sure, Inspector. Anything you say."

"Why do I *know* you're lying?"

◆　　◆　　◆

They got off the highway about a mile past town and turned toward the ocean. Near the edge of a cliff overlooking the water stood a large gray and white house, its New England colonial architecture strangely out of place against the soft, California seascape. A blue and red sign in the shape of a coat of arms pronounced it to be the Ben Lomond Inn.

As they walked up the front steps, Paavo asked Angie to wait outside while he spoke to the innkeeper. "You're kidding!" she said.

Paavo entered with Angie behind him, but not too closely, only because he turned and glared at her.

A large woman with a cherubic face and gray hair pulled into a topknot emerged from the parlor. She wore a black dress with a crisp, white apron over it.

"I'm Mrs. Ward," she said, marching across the room with long strides, extending her hand to Paavo. The power in the woman's voice astonished Angie. She hadn't heard a pair of lungs like that since Birgit Nilsson had performed at the San Francisco Opera House. "Forgive my appearance," Mrs. Ward bellowed, gesturing toward the apron. Then she smiled prettily at Paavo. The voice and the face were totally incongruous.

Before Paavo could respond, Carmel's Brunhilde continued, "You must be Mr. Smith."

"Yes," Paavo's voice was hushed, as if trying to tone her down by example. "Thank you for providing a room on such short notice, I—"

"Think nothing of it. Newlyweds! It's the least I could do!" Angie knew her mouth hung open, but she was too stunned to shut it. The woman turned to her. "Congratulations, Mrs. Smith. Right this way, please."

As Angie passed Paavo to follow Mrs. Ward up the stairs, she saw that his complexion had turned pale. She sniffed loudly as she walked by him, and he followed like the proverbial lamb to the slaughter.

The room was perfect for honeymooners. It had a four-poster double bed with a white lace coverlet, an antique dresser, and a lowboy with mirror. On the dresser stood an old-fashioned pitcher and water bowl set. A fireplace provided heat, and the gabled windows looked out over the ocean.

Mrs. Ward showed them where everything was, including the communal bathroom down the hall. She explained that the Ben Lomond was more than just a bed-and-breakfast inn; the management also ran a very nice restaurant next door, which was open Thursday through Sunday. Angie and Paavo exchanged glances but said nothing. It was Wednesday—one day until mealtime.

"I hope everything meets with your approval." Mrs. Ward nodded at them as she turned toward the door.

"It's quite lovely," Angie replied.

"Good-day, Mr. Smith, Mrs. Smith," she murmured as she left them alone, shutting the door behind her.

Angie spun around to face Paavo as soon as she

thought Mrs. Ward was out of earshot. "Mrs. Smith!" she cried. "Why did you say we were married? What century are you living in, Inspector?"

"Shush, not so loud."

"Don't you shush me. Answer me!"

"I didn't expect you'd hear about it."

"No kidding!" She folded her arms and sat on the bed.

He paced the room. "Policemen tend to be very conservative about such things."

"Policemen, Inspector?"

"All right, *I* am. *Me.* All right? Are you happy now?"

She looked up at him, and slowly a smile crept across her face. "Yes. I'm happy."

He seemed completely puzzled by her reaction. They unpacked in silence.

It was dusk when they made the short trip to Carmel to find a restaurant for dinner. They picked an unimposing place in the middle of town, with a few tables and a good-sized bar filled with locals. Paavo told her he knew the owner, an actor who sometimes played a San Francisco homicide inspector, but the man wasn't there that night.

After dinner they returned to the inn. Everything was quiet. Angie and Paavo hurried to their room and lit a fire, leaving the lamps off.

They sat before the firelight and let the charm of the old house work its magic, giving Angie a feeling of peace and safety in its cozy warmth. Soon it was time to retire.

She had made a purchase at Neiman-Marcus which, at the time, had seemed somewhat foolish, but which she was now glad to have made. It could have been for a trousseau—a lacy, cream-colored negligee. She went to the hall bathroom to change clothes and then returned. As Paavo watched the fire, she removed her robe and stepped closer to him. When he turned his head toward her, the look in his eyes told her everything she wanted to know. He stood up slowly, his gaze fixed upon her, and as she stepped into his arms, she did feel like a bride.

25

Angie awoke in the middle of the night. The sea air was damp and chilly. She got out of bed to stoke the fire and add more wood, then sat in front of the blaze, her long gown tucked under her toes and her arms wrapped around her legs. She rested her head against her knees. In the daylight hours, she could pretend that she was coping wonderfully with the whole terrible mess surrounding her—even with the idea that there was some madman out there trying to kill her, and that someone had killed George. She could put on a brave front then. But in the night, when she slept, the whole ugly business would catch up with her. That was when ghosts tormented her, when her fears rose up and turned into sightless, faceless monsters. She tried to run from them, but they could run faster. She tried to hide, but they always found her. That's when she'd awaken, more exhausted than when she'd gone to sleep.

"Another nightmare, Angie?" Paavo whispered. The flickering light of the fire barely reached the dark shadows where Paavo lay.

"I'm sorry, I didn't mean to wake you up."

"It's okay. Are you all right?"

"Oh, Paavo," she cried, burying her face in her hands. "Let's go away. Far, far away, you and I."

He shrugged on his robe and joined her, settling down cross-legged on the floor. Gently, he stroked her hair.

"You and I," she pleaded. "Let's leave all this craziness. I've got money. We can go wherever we want, do whatever we want—whatever *you* want! What do you say? Let's do it, okay?"

"Angie," he said, placing his finger against her chin, "that's the nicest proposition anyone's ever given me."

She shoved his hand away. "I mean it!"

"I know you do. Now. But believe me, little Angel, when this is over—I mean truly over—you'll walk away from it with a big sigh of relief and never want to see a cop again. I've seen it happen before. You'll just see the color blue and you'll run."

"Never!" Her hands grabbed both of his. "I don't want to leave you."

"I know."

"You don't believe me," she whispered. "For you, this is just a job, isn't it? Nothing more."

"No! No, Angie, never think that. You mean . . . very much to me."

"But . . ." the words caught in her throat. They

were so hard, so very hard, to say . . . to admit.
. . . "You don't love me."

He didn't answer right away, and when he did,
his voice was distant. "What good would it do for
me to speak of loving you? You know we have no
future together. It would only mean more pain."

"But we can have a future, we just need to go
away where you don't have to risk your life!"

"I'm a cop, Angie."

Those few words said it all. She let go of him,
clasping her hands together. "I'm making a fool
of myself again, aren't I?"

"Listen to me," he covered her hands with his,
and as she raised her face, their eyes met. "You're
warm, generous, and witty, and you wear your
emotions on your sleeve. You're strong, yet with
a vulnerability that makes a man want to take care
of you. I can't tell you how good it's been having
you in my life, even though I know it's only for a
few weeks, and that's all it can ever be. You're
easy to love, Angel, but the differences between
us are too great."

"What differences really matter, Paavo?" She
dropped her gaze. It hurt too much to look at
him, but she had to tell him how she felt. "We
enjoy being together . . . or so it's seemed to me.
We enjoy talking. At times, we've even laughed in
the midst of all this madness. I believe there's
something special between us, Paavo, something
I've never felt before with anyone. Serefina saw it
and, I think, so did Aulis. I admire you, who you
are and what you do. There are differences be-

tween us, but they're our strength, not our weakness."

"Ah, Angie," he sighed and then stood and walked around the room, his hand rubbing the back of his neck. "Listen to me. You're living in the middle of a nightmare. You don't know your own mind or heart."

"But you can't be sure of that."

"No." He stopped pacing and put his hands in the pockets of his robe. She could see an aching emptiness in his eyes. "But I can be sure that our worlds, our lives, would clash more horribly than you could bear. Believe me when I say that. And believe how sorry I am that it's true. I don't want to watch what we have now die slowly. When it's over, it's all over. Recognize that, and promise me."

"I can't."

"You can. Promise."

"I promise you I'll try to do as you wish. Is that good enough?"

He sighed, then gave an indulgent, half-smile. "I guess it'll have to do. Can I add stubbornness to the qualities I was praising a little while ago?"

"Of course. It's part of my devastating charm." Her eyes filled with tears, and she shut them and quickly turned toward the fire, away from him, not letting him know the effect of his words.

Angie awoke the next morning feeling drained. Paavo was sitting on the floor with Sam's recipes spread out around him. His chin rested on his hand, and he was lost in deep thought. He looked as if he hadn't slept at all. This crazy situation between the two of them couldn't possibly be affecting him in that way, could it? After all, he was the one who kept pushing her away.

She shrugged off the thought. It was obviously the unsolved murders that bothered him, not her. She rolled to her side and propped herself up on an elbow.

He looked up at the sound of movement. "I saw these lying on top of your luggage," he said, gesturing toward the recipes.

She yawned. "I brought them to work on. Since you're so sure they carry the clue, I plan to crack them and solve the case."

He shuffled the papers around a bit. "You crack codes, not clues, Angie," he replied absently.

The thought seemed to strike both of them at the same time. Angie scrambled from the bed to sit beside Paavo.

"If it *is* a code, it has to say who, what, when, and where," Paavo began.

"Every one of these is one of four foods— waffles, pancakes, omelets, or blintzes." They stacked them accordingly.

"They all are made with eggs—" Paavo added. "Get some paper, Angie, I'll read off how many eggs in each recipe."

Milk, too, was in every recipe. They stared at the sheets before them.

"You know," Angie mused, "there's an awful lot of lemon in these recipes. Over half of them.

That's unusual. And those without have cinnamon or nutmeg."

She ticked off her fingers. "We have four types of recipes. All have one of three spices, one to six eggs, lots of milk—and lots and lots of other ingredients! Maybe we're on the wrong track."

"Is 9T of milk an odd way to write a recipe?"

"Yes . . . but it's just a fluke. Look, almost all of them are in cups: 1, 2, 2½, 2⅞ . . . Hey, that's a weird one."

"You printed it!"

"Well, chefs are so tempermental about revisions."

He stood and paced, every so often stopping to stare at Angie's notes. Then he paced, then stared again. She kept quiet.

"Look at the milk," he said.

"What?"

"The milk! Yes! All the numbers make sense for dates. If you ignore the bottom of the fraction, then there's 1 cup, 2, 2½ might be twenty-one, 2⅞ could be twenty-seven, and 9T for nine. I don't see anything higher than twenty-seven. Dates, Angie! The milk just might represent dates."

"Too weird," she replied.

"It's got to be!"

It was almost noon before they left their room, but Mrs. Ward insisted they have coffee and croissants before leaving the inn, even though they had missed breakfast. They weren't about to argue with her.

"I understand you'll be serving dinner here

tonight," Paavo said as Mrs. Ward placed enormous, warm croissants on the table in the dining room.

"That's right. I hope you give us a try."

Angie decided then and there that she was tired of cat-and-mouse games. She looked directly up at Mrs. Ward. "An old friend of ours used to be a chef here. He recommended we stay here, in fact."

"Really? What was his name?"

"Sam. He was an older man, and was once a sailor."

"Sam Larson! Of course I remember him."

"I'd really like to see him again. He was a sweetheart."

"That's true. He wasn't the most reliable chef, but such a sweet little man." Mrs. Ward beamed as Paavo's head turned from one woman to the next.

"Do you know where I can find him?"

"Oh my, no. It's been months, but I suppose his friend in Monterey would know."

"I didn't know he had one."

"Oh my, yes. Blackie. He's the bartender at the Blue Whale. He'll know where to find Sam, I'm sure." She picked up the tray. "Well, I'll leave you two young folks alone. I'm sure newlyweds don't want some old lady like me standing around gossiping."

As Mrs. Ward walked away, Angie looked smugly at Paavo. "Well, Inspector, how did I do?"

"Impressive. We may make a cop out of you yet, Mrs. Smith."

"Be careful with that name-calling. You may get to like it."

Paavo told Angie they had been incredibly lucky that Mrs. Ward knew Sammy and was willing to talk about him. He didn't expect such helpfulness from Blackie. The only way to handle the case now was straight, he said. No more roleplaying. He would go to the Monterey police, explain who he was and what he was doing there, and then question Blackie, legally, as a police officer. He would, of course, forget to mention that he was on vacation.

Then he gave Angie a quick demotion from her "almost-cop" status of early afternoon back to "civilian," in the hope of keeping her safe. First, he made her sit in the outer office when he went inside to talk with the police chief about the case. Later, she sat in the car as he entered the Blue Whale bar to talk to Blackie. He came out in a couple of minutes. Blackie wasn't to come on duty until eight at night. Angie's next job was to join Paavo for dinner to help pass the time. He decided the only reason she wasn't livid was that she was preoccupied by her hunger.

At about nine o'clock, they returned to the Blue Whale. Paavo didn't think it was safe for Angie to remain alone in the car when it was dark, so he had her sit at a table in a corner. He asked the cocktail waitress if the bartender was Blackie. He was.

Paavo left Angie fuming at being left out while

he took his scotch to the far end of the bar and sat down. He wasn't going to leave until he got all the information he could out of Blackie. He took a sip of his drink. Something told him it was going to be a long evening.

"When Blackie finally got it through his head that I meant business, he remembered the names of a few bars that Blade frequented in San Francisco," Paavo said as he drove along Highway 1 toward Carmel, a few hours later. "Apparently, after going to those bars, Blade would return to Carmel with a lot more money than when he left. The bars are all in the Tenderloin. Chances are, so's Crane."

"The Tenderloin—the red-light district?"

"Where you find prostitutes, you can be sure pimps, drugs, and guns are also nearby. It'd be as good a place for Crane to hide out as anywhere else, I suppose."

"Now what?" Angie asked with trepidation.

"Now? Back to the city. I'll find someplace safe for you, then look for Crane. I can't help but suspect that if I watch him for a few days, he'll do something, make some mistake, that'll link him to the murders or to the smuggled guns. Then I can move in with an arrest."

Paavo made it sound so simple: find Crane, watch Crane, arrest Crane. He ignored the other part, the dangerous part—the part that had left his own partner dead. The Tenderloin was the district where Matt had been killed. The facts were starting to fit together now, she thought, like pieces of a jigsaw puzzle. She saw the grim determination on Paavo's face as he drove, and also saw the slow stirrings of a pain too fresh to be forgotten.

She reached out and patted his shoulder, then brushed her hand over the back of his head, finally twisting a lock of his hair around her finger. She liked the soft, springy way his hair felt—the way all of him felt, the scent of him, the taste of him. Everything about him was a treasure to her, but one she could not keep, despite her wealth. She was finding out what made one feel truly rich in life.

"It'll be late by the time we get back to the inn," she said. "Let's wait until tomorrow to go back to the city and allow ourselves one more night of escaping whatever's waiting for us back there. Would that be all right?"

Their eyes met briefly, and Paavo reached over and squeezed her hand. "One more night."

Early the next morning they checked out of the inn, explaining to Mrs. Ward that some unexpected business had come up. Mrs. Ward said she was sorry it had to interfere with their honeymoon.

Two hours later the world once again consisted of skyscrapers, paved hills, and gridlock. They had entered San Francisco.

"There's got to be a better way to live," Angie said.

"There is, but you'd be bored silly in two weeks if you tried it."

"No I wouldn't. I could live at the Ben Lomond Inn forever."

"Face it, Angie. You have the same goofy love-hate affection for this city that I do."

As they came to the crest of a hill, Angie caught a glimpse of the Bay Bridge and San Francisco Bay. She sighed. He was right.

26

All afternoon, Paavo was strangely quiet, but she felt his gaze on her as she walked around, straightening up his house, taking care of the laundry, and then later putting away the groceries he'd bought. He left the house again for about an hour. When he returned, he was even quieter. He wouldn't say a word to her about what he was planning.

That evening, his face scruffy since he hadn't shaved that day, his hair uncombed, wearing old jeans, a Levi's jacket, and a plaid shirt, Paavo said good-bye.

"I don't know how long I'll be gone," he told her. "Wait here for me. Remember, if you hear nothing, everything's all right. If I were to get hurt or anything happened with Crane, the police would contact you."

"Yes, but—"

"No *buts*. Don't worry. I've got to find Crane, Angie. And when I do I'm going to learn what's going on. Who killed Matt, who killed George Meyers, and why. Meyers—that's the one that really makes no sense. He had to have been working with Crane to get those crazy recipes published on time. So why would Crane kill him? It doesn't add up."

"I guess only Crane can explain it."

"Exactly." His gaze softened. "Good-bye, Angie. You'll be safe here, since no one but Inspector Calderon knows where you're hiding."

"I'll wait for you, Paavo. You should know that by now."

Then he was gone.

She waited for two days, but he didn't return, and he didn't call. It became more than she could bear. She telephoned her mother, her sisters, some friends—one she hadn't talked to since high school. She even became fascinated by a 900 number that told horoscopes. She did a lot of weed pulling in the backyard, despite the constant fog. Without her notes, she couldn't even work on her book, and of course she knew better than to write recipes now.

She was in the garden, wiping the tears that threatened to splash onto the begonias, when she decided she was tired of sitting around, cooped up and waiting to be rescued like some princess in a tower. Paavo was out there in the real world, knowing exactly what was happening, facing adventure, danger, intrigue, and probably enjoying every second of it. She certainly wasn't doing what she enjoyed. She was bored to death, and . . .

She sank back on her heels, her knuckles pressed against her teeth.

And worried sick about him. Where could he be? What was taking him so long?

She returned to the house, but she couldn't sit still. In the bedroom, she looked in the mirror at her red, puffy eyes, shiny nose, and dirt-smudged face. What a mess, and all due to some man! She looked out the window and saw a trickle of sunshine peeking through the fog. That made it harder than ever to sit around and do nothing.

She had never been an idle person; she hated trying to stay put. The need to go out grew in her, along with her fears about Paavo. She had to find him and be sure he was okay.

A plan began to formulate in her mind. She knew it was dangerous—Paavo would rage at her if he found out—and she knew a whole lot better than to do it. . . .

It was taking a chance, a foolish chance maybe. But so was Paavo, and this was her battle, not his. It was hers and George's. But George had lost.

It wasn't as if Angie knew *nothing* about the Tenderloin. She had driven through it many times with her car doors locked, trying to avoid looking at the derelicts and hookers on the streets, the pornographic book shops, and the old hotels. There were a number of legitimate thea-

ters along the edge of it, with a few not-so-legiti
mate ones inside.

Angie knew she had to be careful. She couldn't
simply waltz into the area at night looking for
Paavo. She'd be an easy target and probably
wouldn't make it from one block to the next without losing her purse—not to consider what else
she might lose. The only way to be safe was to fit
in, just as Paavo had done. Or so she hoped.

She planned her wardrobe more carefully than
she'd planned her last outfit for the Black and
White Ball.

She put on slacks, a sweater, a pair of sneakers,
and then covered as much as she could with
Paavo's old army jacket. She stuffed about a hundred dollars in her pockets and hid Paavo's house
key in the garden so she could get back into the
house when she returned. No purse, no credit
cards, no identification. She felt positively naked.

She called a taxi and had the cab drop her off
in front of a tacky-looking discount store on the
edge of the Tenderloin. They had just what she
wanted: a platinum-blond afro wig, shimmering
black tights, a long-sleeved yellow leotard, false
eyelashes, plenty of garish makeup, and a large,
black canvas drawstring bag. From there she
went to a store that seemed to sell only leather,
where she found a red leather miniskirt and a pair
of black sandals with ankle straps and narrow,
four-inch heels.

She ate at a diner and drank several cups of
coffee while waiting for nightfall.

At about nine o'clock, she walked toward the

theater district and found a gas station on the way. She went into the ladies' room, changed into her new clothes, and stuffed everything she'd been wearing into the canvas bag. She globbed on the makeup and even added a couple of beauty marks. She stepped back from the tiny mirror to survey the results. What a looker! Would Sister Mary Ignatius have considered this outfit merely a venial sin or an out-and-out mortal one? She poked her head out of the restroom, wondering if she really had the nerve to appear in public like this.

She had no choice. Paavo was out there alone, and so was Crane. She stepped through the doorway and hesitated. The skies didn't open up, and not a single lightning bolt struck her. She headed across the station to the sidewalk, and then up the street toward the Tenderloin.

Slow down, she told herself. You've got to fit in, to act like one of the regulars and not call attention to yourself.

Coming toward her were two women, arm in arm. When Angie saw them she stopped walking and her mouth dropped open as she stared. One had bright purple hair, the top straight up and spiky, the sides slicked back. She wore white face powder, with black lips and blue circles around her eyes. Her clothes were black—a tee-shirt and leggings, with a low-slung, wide, silver belt—and heavy aluminum rings were around her neck and forearms.

The other woman's hair was turquoise, almost shaved over the left ear and hanging to the earlobe of the right ear. She was also dressed in black—a tank top, the shortest miniskirt Angie had ever seen, and boots with metal studs down the sides. She wore a silver pentagon-shaped medallion and silver earrings that fell to her shoulders. Her eyebrows were shaved off.

Damn! Angie thought. I'm out-of-date, passé. How mortifying!

She tried to ignore the derisive expressions on the faces of the two women as they eyed her outfit. The medallion caught Angie's eye. It looked Satanic. She felt as if a cold hand had touched her. She dropped her gaze and hurried on. This was going to be more difficult than she had expected.

The Tenderloin was small—about six blocks long, all centered around two main streets. In one night she could cover the whole thing. If Crane was there, she'd find him. If he wasn't, she didn't even want to think about it.

She started at one end of the district and methodically went into every bar and dirty bookstore on one side of the street to the end of the district, and then she crossed the street and started down the opposite side. She received many strange looks, some very frightening. It wouldn't do. Although going into the bars and clubs seemed to be the easiest way to find Crane, it was probably the easiest way to get into serious trouble.

When she saw two women vacate a centrally located doorway and get into an enormous white car, she took their place, leaning against a wall. Now she just had to hope she didn't get arrested.

A car pulled up and stopped. A middle-aged man reached over and rolled down the passenger-side window. "Nice night, isn't it?" he called.

"Get lost!" she yelled.

"Say, er, would you—"

"No! Leave me alone, or I'll scream!" She was shaking. Maybe this wasn't such a great idea after all.

The man's eyebrows shot up. He looked confused and flustered as he stepped on the gas and drove off.

"You musta know'd I was comin' baby. I seed you get ridda that john." A black man swaggered up to her, hands on his belt.

"Stuff it!"

"I can take care a you. Your prayers is answered, baby."

She hadn't expected so much attention so soon, and her initial upset was quickly turning to irritation. She scowled. "I don't know you, and Leon don't know you, so you get the hell away from me."

"I don't care 'bout no Leon," he said, smirking.

"You will, sucker." She looked at him and smiled. That must have been what did it—her smile. The man just shook his head and moved on, muttering something about a "bad news broad."

Time passed. A couple of men stopped and looked in her direction, but she averted her eyes, and they left without saying a word.

The street became quiet. The night swallowed up the other "girls," and eventually, only Angie still stood there, unwilling to give up, certain that Crane or Paavo might yet walk by. Her legs, feet, and back all ached from standing for so many hours. No more than three or four johns spoke to her. She was glad she wasn't doing this for a living; she would probably have starved to death.

No Crane, no Paavo. And she thought finding them would be easy. When two-thirty A.M. rolled around, she was chilled to the bone and dejected. An empty taxi rode by. That decided it. She ran out to hail it, but it kept right on going.

"Wait!" she screamed, running down the street after the rapidly departing cab.

"What's wrong, honey?" a low, mellifluous female voice called from the shadows. "Don't you have anyone to give you a ride?"

"I've had more than enough rides for one evening, I guess," Angie said, squinting into the darkness, trying to see whom she was talking to.

A throaty laugh filled the quiet street and then stopped as quickly as it began. "You new here, honey?"

"Yes." Angie hesitated to say more. She wondered if she shouldn't just move on.

"From?"

Good question, she thought. "San Jose."

The woman began to sing an old song about the way to San Jose. Her voice was deep and off-key. Then she stepped forward, in front of the red and yellow neon lights from a shop window. All Angie could see was the fiery silhouette of a very tall, large, and amply endowed woman with hair like a lion's mane and a long, thick boa over her shoulders. Her face was shrouded in darkness. Angie shrank back, saying nothing.

"You can't get a taxi to take you all that way, honey. Come with me. I'll help."

"I can take care of myself, thanks, anyway."

"Not here you can't honey. I'll take care of you. I can introduce you to people. This can turn into a good, profitable relationship."

"You know lots of people around here?"

" 'Course, honey. In fact, I was going to an after-hours place now. Why don't you come along?"

Angie's stomach flip-flopped. Something told her she should just go back to Paavo's house and forget this. She just might be getting in way over her head. On the other hand, what better place to find someone like Crane than inside the world she was only seeing the periphery of?

The woman stepped up to her, dwarfing her. Angie was surprised to see a face heavy with powder, rouge, and mascara—a face that had lost the battle against years of rough living.

27

The woman's name was Rachel. Angie called herself Star, and told Rachel a long story of unhappiness which culminated in the streets of the Tenderloin. Rachel didn't say much but was sympathetic and friendly. She reminded Angie of a crocodile crying before dispatching its victim.

When Rachel turned into a dark alley, Angie hung back. It seemed too dangerous, too forbidding. "Don't worry, honey," Rachel's voice rumbled. "We're here."

She knocked on a door which immediately opened and then beckoned to Angie. Cautiously, Angie followed.

The massive room was hazy with smoke and filled with people. The lighting was dim, consisting only of shaded bulbs casting cold glares. In the shadows, Angie made out a long bar lined with people, a number of tables with card games in progress, a band dressed in black leather, and a dance floor. It reminded her of a movie she had seen years ago that had depicted a modern-day Orpheus going to Hades to find Eurydice. But Hades had nothing on this place; the evil that lurked here was palpable.

Rachel introduced her to a tall, thin man named Fish. He had greasy, slicked-back hair, cirrhotic skin color, and a shiny, gold front tooth. He smiled broadly, the tooth twinkling, and extended a hand toward her. She grasped it and found it as cold and scaly as his name suggested.

"Pleased to meet you," she said.

Surprise flickered in his eyes, then he laughed. "You're new here?"

"That's right."

His eyes raked her body and then met her glance. "Maybe we can talk?"

"Maybe. Later. I'd like to check out the scene, you know?"

"She's from San Jose," Rachel said. Angie assumed this was an explanation of her hopelessly dated patois.

The man nodded. "Okay, Star. Check it out. But anybody asks, you tell them to see Fish."

Angie gulped and forced a smile, and then moved away from the two, blindly heading toward the bar. It suddenly occurred to her that it might be considerably more difficult getting out of this place than it had been getting in. Her heart beat faster.

The bartender handed her a Chivas Regal on the rocks. "It's from Fish," he said.

Angie lifted the glass in the man's direction and nodded her head slightly in thanks. He returned the gesture. She took a large sip of the amber liquid. It was just what she needed to calm her nerves. It went down smoothly, warming her. She moved away from the bar toward the band.

Crane had to be here, he absolutely had to. She slowly wandered through the room, looking at the men, hoping that she'd see him. She didn't.

On the other side of the room, she spotted the rest rooms and went into the one marked Women. It was filthy and windowless—no escape here. She hurried out again and stood beside the door, trying to figure out what to do.

Rachel came up to her and looked at the door next to Angie. "This is always such a hard choice, honey," she said. Then, to Angie's astonishment, Rachel walked into the men's room.

Angie found a chair and sat in it with a thud. She took a long sip of her scotch. What she had just seen explained everything about the strange way Rachel acted and sounded. But it also gave her an idea: with Crane's high voice and small build, what better way to hide?

Angie downed the scotch and then stood, feeling just a little wobbly. Slowly, she made her way across the room, scrutinizing every woman—or possible woman—in the place.

It was the voice that gave him away. Angie knew she would recognize that voice if she ever heard it again, and she did. She turned around, stepping back into the shadows as her gaze fixed on the body with Edward G. Crane's voice. It was him, wearing a short, red-haired wig in a shag cut, a glittery black and silver dress with a turtleneck and long sleeves, nylons, and high heels. Angie felt sick. She stumbled toward the bar and asked for another drink. It was too much, too crazy. She longed to be suddenly whisked away from all this and safe at home again.

"You ready to talk yet, babe?"

Her fingers tightened on the glass as she felt something press against her shoulder and looked down. Fish's long, thin finger rested lightly on it, causing a chill to creep along her back. "Not yet." Her voice was breathless.

"You're wasting time, you know. Fish don't like that." His long razorlike fingernail trailed from her shoulder down her arm.

Her stomach curled, but she smiled, trying to hide the quaking she felt. She had to keep on his good side so she could sneak out of here when the opportunity arose, if ever. "Let me finish my drink, okay? I'll come find you." She took a big sip, feeling the whiskey's fire all the way to the pit of her stomach.

He gave her a long, hard stare and then gestured for the bartender to fill up her glass. He watched as she drank a little more. "Fifteen minutes," he ordered and then walked away.

Her hand trembled as she faced the bar, cold perspiration breaking out on her upper lip. The hard liquor was making her dizzy. She had to get out of this hellhole.

When she turned toward the crowd again, Fish

had disappeared. There must be a back exit, she reasoned, a means of escape.

Squinting to see through the smoke and haze that filled the room, she spotted a door in one corner and prayed it didn't lead to a closet. Now she just had to get to it. An empty table in front of the door gave her an idea.

There were always any number of men looking at any woman standing alone at a bar. She checked over the men and made her choice—a small one, thirtyish, scruffy and dirty, clearly under the influence—a man she thought she could handle.

She let go of the bar, swaying dizzily, and then approached him. She cast him a look guaranteed to rattle his teeth. "Me?" he mouthed.

She nodded.

He moved toward her as she slipped her arm in his. "Why don't we go find a nice table for two?" she murmured.

"Sure," his diction was slurred. As he tried to walk he stumbled a bit, so she gripped his waist, and he slung an arm over her shoulders, pulling her close to him. She had to hold her breath to keep from gagging from the fumes of a long night's bout of drinking.

He threw his other arm across her chest as she tried to maneuver him toward the table and began to nuzzle at her ear. His hand slipped lower. She pushed it away, but he clutched her against him with far more strength than she had expected him to possess. Disgusting suggestions of intimacy were whispered in her ear, his hands moving freely over her body as she struggled to control him. Relentlessly, though, she managed to move him toward the back door.

Suddenly, they were pushed apart. Fish figured out my plan, she thought. Stumbling, she tried to run when she was grabbed again, this time spun around so that she faced her assailant—Paavo. She nearly fell over, out of surprise and from the influence of the whiskey.

Angie's drunken friend, in the meantime, was loudly decrying Paavo's legitimacy.

"The lady made a mistake," Paavo said quietly, palming a crumpled ten-dollar bill into the man's hand. He staggered away without another word.

Paavo then turned to face Angie. He didn't touch her. His stance remained nonchalant for the benefit of the roomful of people watching them, but his eyes blazed. "What the hell do you think you're doing?" His voice was hushed, but tense and furious.

"Nothing! I—"

"Nothing!" In one fluid motion he had all but scooped her up and led her to the empty table.

"Sit down before you fall down. You're drunk," he said, his teeth clenched as his hand clamped tightly on her wrist. "Look at you! These are pimps, junkies. How in the hell did you get in here?"

"I didn't *do* anything, if that's what you're implying!" Her eyes smarted. "I was looking for you. I was worried about you, and scared!"

"Keep your voice down," he warned, his look softening as he listened to her words. He let go of her and then shook his head, angry again. "My God, woman, don't you realize the danger?"

Her head felt clouded and dizzy as she looked at him. She had found Crane—she had done it!—and now here Paavo was to help her get away, but he had turned on her like an adversary.

He watched her wordlessly, his face stony, his eyes emotionless. She couldn't bear it. She reached out to stroke his thin, noble face, but he caught her hand in a crushing grip and flung it back to the table.

"We're being watched," he said, and she felt the glances upon them. "Let's dance."

He grasped her hand, pulling her to the dance floor as the band played a slow, swirling cacophony of sound with a heavy metal beat. He took her roughly into his arms. She wrapped both of hers around his neck, a shudder of relief going through her body as she let herself melt against him. His expression showed irritation, almost pain as he clutched her. She felt the tension in his body as they danced, but also his desire for her.

He pushed her away, keeping inches between them, while continuing the dance. "You know I should wring your neck," he said.

"Yes." She paused. "But before you do, I found Crane."

His step faltered. "You what?"

"He's here. In drag."

"Drag? No wonder I couldn't find him!"

As they turned around the dance floor Angie pointed out which "lady" Crane was.

"You're sure?" Paavo asked, grimacing.

"Yes."

"He's been here each night. If only I'd known. Damn!"

"We need to follow him."

"He—she—stayed till dawn the last couple of nights. I've got time to get you out of here first."

"That might not be so easy. There's this guy called Fish who appointed himself my pimp."

Paavo let out a sardonic snort. Angie was not amused.

"Let's go." Unsmiling, he put his arm around her waist and headed for the door.

Fish met them halfway. "You leaving, Star?"

"Just give me ten minutes," she said.

Paavo looked shocked. Then he nuzzled her neck. "That's all? What do you think I am? I should get at least twenty."

"You don't go nowhere with the lady till I say so." Fish studied Paavo.

"How much for you to say so?" he asked.

Fish pursed his lips. "Fifty."

"For her? Ten."

"Forty."

"Twenty."

Fish looked slowly at Angie, head to toe, then back again. He shrugged. "Deal."

Paavo handed him the money. "Hey, that's mine," Angie reached for it.

"When you come back, babe. When you come back." Fish put the cash in his pocket and walked away.

"Thank God we're out of there!" Angie sighed

with relief as they went through the exit to the alley.

"I'll get you a cab back to my place."

She hurried to keep up with his long strides. The cold, impassive inspector was back, and Paavo, friend and lover, was gone. She hadn't heard from the inspector for a while—not since Bodega Bay, the last time Paavo had been deeply upset by her.

The street glistened with dampness from the night fog and echoed with their footsteps. The brick walls of the alley took on an eerie shine above the layers of old exhaust smoke. The pungent garbage smell around them mixed with the saltiness of the night air.

"Why are you angry?" she cried, running and stumbling, trying to ignore the way the scotch made her feel. She grabbed his sleeve to stop him from going farther.

His look blackened. "I don't like, and I don't need, you putting yourself in danger to help me."

"If you were worried about me," she cried, "then tell me you care! Don't shut me out."

He looked at her and she dropped her hands, but her heart pounded. She didn't understand what was wrong.

"I do care," he said.

He turned away from her and resumed walking. She followed close behind, the echoes of her footsteps matching the hollowness within her body. She pulled off the wig, that stupid blond mess, and toyed with it. Her voice, when she found it, was tiny, childlike. "Really?" she asked.

He spun toward her, gripping her shoulders, his face contorted with inner turmoil. "What are you trying to do?"

"I just want to help you, to be with you."

"I don't need your help. I want you to leave me alone!"

"Paavo!"

"I'll get you a cab."

"I don't want a cab!"

"What do you want then? What do you want from me? I've got nothing to offer you, Angie. Nothing! Not much money, few friends, and little time to find any, either. I can't even remember the last time I went to a party."

She was shocked. "I don't want your money! And I don't even like parties. What are you talking about?"

His voice grew soft and his eyes, intense. "You can have anything you want, do anything you want. I can't. Don't make it harder on me than it is."

She stopped walking, unable to believe she had heard him right. Then she remembered something he had once told her. He had likened her to his sister, who had liked to go off and have good times. One of his few memories of his mother was of her getting dressed up and going away from him. And Angie, too, had talked to him about her dates, the theater, and using her money to run from any danger. But she had never dreamed how he would see it.

She ran to him, grabbed his sleeve, and made him turn and face her. He looked surprised as their eyes met. "I don't want to leave you." Her voice caught. "Nothing else matters."

"Because you've always had everything else." He jerked his arm free and continued down the street.

At the corner, he stopped beside a lamppost and stuffed his hands in his pockets, his shoulders hunched, watching her as she neared him.

She reached his side. The street was absolutely silent. The streetlamp cast its pale glow down on them. He said nothing as she stood breathlessly watching him, waiting, knowing he was carefully weighing her words and praying that he would believe her.

"You won't listen, will you?" he asked.

"No."

He reached his hand toward her, lightly touching her hair, and then rested it against the back of her head, its slight pressure bringing her closer to him. His lips brushed hers, he drew back, and then he kissed her again. His hand moved to her cheek as he lifted her face, holding it mere inches away, gazing into her eyes. His lips parted as if to speak, but he couldn't. When he finally found his voice, it was husky, filled with tenderness. "Angel," he whispered, "the well-named little Angel."

She squeezed her eyes shut, put her arms around his shoulders, and lay her head against his neck. His arms held her close as he kissed her hair and forehead, his fingers running over her body and finally grasping her hair. He gently brought her head back, and his lips found hers in a long kiss, a real kiss.

He broke it off and searched her face. "I've got to send you back to my place."

"There's a couple hours until dawn."

Despite himself, she saw a hint of a smile in his granite expression. "Let's go inside," he said.

"Your room?"

"This way, m'lady, or—" his eyes sparkled mischievously as he draped an arm over her shoulders and tucked her against his side "—should I call you Star?"

"A real comedian, aren't you?" She scowled, snuggling beside him where she knew she belonged.

He chuckled to himself as he led her to a cheap hotel and up the stairs to his room.

"Will you stop laughing!" she said finally. "It wasn't that funny."

"That's not what I'm laughing about."

"No? What then?"

"I don't think I should tell you."

"Why not?"

"You'll be insulted."

"Insulted? That's nonsense. I never get insulted!"

"All right," he said. "Angie, for a hooker, your price is really cheap."

She let out a squawk of outrage, and he collapsed on the bed, laughing so hard he had to hold his stomach. She climbed on top of him. "Laugh at me, will you! You should be taught a lesson."

He laughed harder, rolling to his side. "By you and what army?"

She tugged at him until he rolled onto his back. His laughter stopped, replaced by an all-too-sexy smile as she began to unbutton his shirt. "I should simply take that taxi you threatened to put me in," she said. "But that would punish me, too."

He lifted his shoulders off the bed as she removed his shirt and undershirt, and then he lay down again. Still sitting on his hips, she ran her hands over his chest.

"Leaving me would be a punishment to you, too, would it?" he asked, his fingers inching up her thighs to the hem of her miniskirt. "Hearing an admission like that'll make me swell-headed."

"As I sit here, Inspector Smith, I can tell something's getting swollen—and your head has nothing to do with it."

He laughed. "Ah, Angie love, whatever will I do once you've gone from me?"

Her heart twisted as if it would break in two. She could feel her face crumble. She stood up quickly, needing to separate herself from him, to not look at him, not touch him, in order to regain control. She looked at herself in the mirror that hung over the dresser against the far wall. With the clothes and makeup, she looked like a clown—an ugly, garish clown.

He approached her, and she turned away, lowering her head so he couldn't see her face. He placed his hands on her shoulders and kissed her neck. She felt lost as she allowed her head to loll back against his shoulder. He ran his hands over her cheeks, her throat, her shoulders, and then cupped her breasts as his breath blew hot against her neck.

Her breasts grew taut and hard under his fingers, and she pressed back against him. He slid his hands along her sides, her hips, then under the brief mini she wore. Her body went weak. "I don't want to leave you, Paavo," she whispered. "Not ever." Her eyes shut. She could feel his arousal pressing against her.

"Soon you'll be free of worry and fear, Angie. Free to do as you please."

She turned in his arms, keeping her arms tight against her sides, her voice low. "I know what I please. You. I love you."

"Don't Angie."

"Paavo!" She touched his hair. Her hand went to his face, his bent nose, his lips. But his countenance was hard.

"Don't."

She squared her shoulders and moved away from him. "It's all right," she said. "I'm sorry. I shouldn't have said anything."

He took her hands. "You have a million and one rich men after you. You don't really want one poor cop."

She shut her eyes. "I don't?"

"You'll forget about me in a matter of days—hours, maybe."

That stung. "You really think I'm so shallow, Paavo?"

His eyes were so soft, so caring, her anger at him vanished. "You live in a sunny glow, Angie.

I'd only cast a shadow over everything you know and love." As he lifted the palms of her hands to his lips, tears filled her eyes. This would be good-bye, then. He had made up his mind. This was where it would end. Crane would be caught, and she'd be free to go back to the life she had led before this happened.

She dropped her arms to her sides, and he slowly slid his hands down her arms until they caught her fingers and interlaced.

She raised her face and he lowered his, tipping his head to one side so that their lips met. She closed her eyes, her tears spilling over, her fingers tightening on his until they ached. His kiss was soft, light as he traced her lips with his tongue.

Her mouth opened as she swayed toward him. He pulled her against him as his tongue plunged deep. She could feel the heat rising in her body, building a fire more intense than anything she had ever experienced. Where her covered breasts met his bare chest, she felt seared.

Still holding her wrists, he rained kisses from her throat, to her shoulders, to her breasts. Then he unfastened her skirt and let it drop. He placed his hands under the neckline of her leotard and slid it off her shoulders.

His eyes met hers, and his look softened. Ever so slowly, he undressed her completely, as if every movement was precious to him. He traced his fingers over her back and her stomach, as if trying to memorize them with his fingertips. He lifted her arms to his shoulders as he caressed her, his hands increasingly probing, increasingly intimate.

"Wait," she whispered. She undressed him, then, much as he had done, she traced her fingers over his body and followed her fingers with her tongue. She heard his low moan of pleasure as she reached the center of his desire.

She felt him throb as he suddenly pulled her up, lifted her into his arms, and then carried her to the bed and gently placed her on it. She tried to etch his face forever in her heart.

He kissed her eyelids, forcing her eyes shut, and then returned hungrily to her mouth.

She opened herself to him, and he thrust deeply as if he couldn't get enough of her, as if he needed enough to last a lifetime. She gave herself to him completely, with no holding back. The wonder was, as much as she gave, he returned in kind.

28

Paavo held open the door to the taxi cab. Angie was dressed in her slacks and Paavo's army jacket once again, her "hooker clothes" left behind in the waste basket in his room. She was ready to leave, but not yet willing.

She fought the sudden tightness in her throat and the pressure against her eyes as she approached the cab.

"Wait." He reached toward her and his fingertips lightly brushed against her cheek. "You be careful."

"Sure, I have nothing to worry about, right?" She couldn't stop the bitter tone in her words. "George is dead, so the newspaper office is safe. You'll soon arrest Crane, so when I do go back to my apartment, I won't need Rico or Joey anymore. Everything's coming up roses. . . ."

"Just stay at my place until it's all over and we're sure we've got the right man."

She looked into his eyes, her heart filled with regret that they had come to this. "Of course," she whispered.

He coiled his fingers into the back of her hair, his arm resting on her shoulder. The blueness of his eyes was clouded, and his voice deep and soft as he spoke. "I'm not arresting Crane yet. We've got nothing to hold him on. But I'll watch him and see who he leads us to. As soon as we have him and I'm sure your apartment is safe, I'll send a squad car by to take you home."

She lowered her eyes a moment and then raised them again to his. "I understand," she said. She wanted to say more, anything that would convince him he was wrong about the two of them. But she knew no words could penetrate his belief that her feelings for him were ephemeral, simply a result of the current situation. And his feelings for her? He had never spoken words of love; perhaps there were none to be spoken.

She climbed into the cab. She turned to close the door, but Paavo held it ajar, as he stood watching her.

"Good-bye, Paavo," she said, her voice hushed. She waited, the silence hanging between them, and then he shut the door and backed away.

Later that morning, Angie made the usual calls to her mother and sisters. She didn't have much to say. Serefina was back in Palm Springs with Salvatore and, as usual, asked about Paavo. Angie said he was fine, working hard. Then she hung up, feeling worse than ever.

She was restless. Something about Paavo's plan was wrong, very wrong. Whatever it was had bothered her for days, but it was always just beyond her comprehension.

She checked her watch. It was early afternoon. Paavo was probably asleep again, knowing he'd have a long night of Crane-watching. Angie, though, was keyed up. She paced around the house, but it didn't help.

Finally, she decided to go down to the *Bay Area Shopper* to find out what was happening there. Paavo had told her to stay in his house, but she hadn't listened to him before. Why start now? Besides, she hadn't turned in a column since the one from Bodega Bay and, in fact, didn't even know if she still had a job.

As she pushed open the revolving doors at the entrance to the building that housed the *Shopper*, she realized what it was that had bothered her for so long about the police department's explanation of what was going on. George was innocent.

Paavo and all the others were so sure that because George had requested Crane's recipes from her, and then George was killed, he must have been involved. But they hadn't known George.

The police had wrapped up a neat little package and she had gone along with it. After all,

George was dead, he couldn't be hurt by it. But the premise was wrong, and she—and others—could be very hurt by such a mistake. Here, in this building, George's murderer had lurked that terrible night, and perhaps he—or she—was still here. Angie agreed with the police that the case involved the *Shopper* and her recipes, so the key had to be in these offices. She would have to find it on her own.

She rode the elevator to the second floor. A shudder rippled through her as she realized how empty George's desk would seem, but she straightened her shoulders and held her head high.

Every eye in the room seemed to be on her as she walked through the double doors to the main office. That was good, she wanted lots of attention. The police were off the track, and the killer felt safe. Maybe if Angie made enough noise, whoever the contact at the *Shopper* was would get nervous and give Crane a signal. Then Paavo would at least be able to catch Crane in the act of doing something other than parading around the Tenderloin as a transvestite.

If her plan worked, then whoever was behind this was going to think Angie was on her way to meet her loyal fan Edward G. Crane. George's killer had to know about Crane and might be nervous at the idea of her meeting him. Paavo would probably notice if someone among the *Shopper* personnel contacted Crane.

She plunged into her act, not allowing herself to debate what she was doing. If she did, she'd

surely see the flaws in her argument and the
danger she could be subjecting herself to. But
then, wasn't she in danger, anyway, if the guilty
person wasn't apprehended?

"Hello there, Bill," she said to the startled copy
boy, who stood surrounded by a group of coworkers. Her gaze swept over them quickly, and Bill's
ears turned bright red as he croaked out a short
hello.

The group around him included another boy as
youthful as Bill, a stooped, white-haired man who
stared at her with a vacant expression, and several
others. "I'm so excited, Bill," Angie continued.

This made Bill stand a little straighter and his
friends huddle closer. "Really?" he said.

"Yes. I'm going to meet my biggest fan, the
number one contributor to my column."

"That's really neat."

"Isn't it? His name is Edward Crane."

"Oh."

"See you later, love," she said as she breezed
off. That would give his friends plenty to talk
about.

There, that wasn't so hard, she decided, quite
sure what had passed was just an exercise. No one
in that group could possibly have anything to do
with murder, could they?

"Mrs. Cruz!" she cried, walking up to Jon Preston's secretary.

"What a surprise, Angie," the older woman
said. "We've missed you."

"I've got such exciting news!" she practically
shouted, catching the attention of the women in

the typing pool. She then launched into her plans to meet Crane and was given a thorough dressing down by Mrs. Cruz for being so foolish as to even think about meeting a strange man—especially since George had been murdered by an unknown assailant. The secretary told Angie she should call the police immediately. Edward G. Crane's recipes were clearly those of a perverted mind.

"What is going on?" Jon Preston peered out his office door. He sounded irritated at the noise level in the outer office. When he saw Angie, his eyes widened and he ran his palm over the blond hair above his ear, as if to assure himself it was still perfectly in place.

Mrs. Cruz repeated Angie's story to him, saving Angie from having to go through it again.

"—and I told her it was sheer madness to go through with this," she concluded.

"You should listen to good advice, Miss Amalfi," Mr. Preston said, fingering his tie. "There are strange goings-on here." He went back into his office and shut the door.

One last stop. She went down to the pressmen's area. Everyone was busy at work since the paper was due out the next day.

She found Mr. O'Malley, the foreman of the group, a beer-bellied, balding man who was sweating profusely. "Hello, there," she said loudly, interrupting everyone. The typesetters looked up, then down again, and continued to work. It wasn't often one of the writers came down there, but they didn't appear impressed.

"Yes, ma'am," O'Malley said, acknowledging

her presence as he dabbed his brow with a once-white handkerchief.

"I just wanted you to know my column will be starting up again."

He scowled. "It's up to the people upstairs to get things down to me on time. I'm not holding up my paper."

"I know, I just—"

"Good, then. They do their job, I do mine." He turned around.

"But—" Angie had to shout to make herself heard over the machinery. "But I'm going to meet my best fan."

O'Malley turned toward her again, looking at her as if she were crazy. He said nothing.

"Edward Crane, my biggest fan," she repeated. "He's going to give me more recipes."

O'Malley remained silent. Then he took a step toward her, his barrel chest puffing as his face tightened. "Lady, I don't care if you're going to meet the Pope."

She turned and hurried out of there, her face burning. At least I tried, she thought, as she rode the elevator up to the main offices.

She sat down at a desk with a heavy sigh. They all looked innocent, every one of them, but she knew George was innocent! Nothing made sense. Why would someone kill George and want her dead, too? Sam gave her recipes, but Crane wrote them. Crane must have known about George's murder and then gone into hiding. Was he the murderer, or another potential victim?

Her head hurt. Maybe what she needed to do

was simply go back to writing her columns and let
the detectives do the detecting. But at the same
time, her plan hadn't been a bad one. Someone
was behind this mess, and she needed to find out
who that was. If she gave it more time, that someone might crack.

She rolled a sheet of paper into the type-
writer—such a quaint machine!—and began to
compose what she hoped would be a humorous
column about the effect of saffron on sex appeal
and red dye number three as an acne deterrent.
Words glided from her fingertips, and she felt
pleased that all the recent trouble hadn't
squelched her creativity.

"Oh, you're still here, Miss Amalfi." Jon Preston stood just outside the door of his office.

She looked up. The room was empty; she
hadn't realized how engrossed she had become,
nor how late the hour was. Her night in the Tenderloin had her internal clock out of kilter.

"I'm sorry, I didn't realize it was past quitting
time."

He walked toward her carefully, as if sidestep-
ping specks of dirt on the carpet. The man was
meticulous, with never a thread out of place. "It's
quite all right. I'm surprised to see a young, attractive woman take such an interest in her job
these days."

Angie leaned back in her chair. "Really? These
days I would have thought quite the opposite."

He laughed, revealing a perfect set of teeth.
"Forgive me, Miss Amalfi, I seem to have struck
an antifeminist chord. Purely unintentional, be-

lieve me." He sighed, patting his sideburns before continuing. "George—poor George—told me many times that you were quite exceptional at your work."

Now he had Angie's attention. "How kind!"

"Oh, yes, he was all heart. Unfortunately, now that he's gone, there's no one to do his job."

"You haven't filled it temporarily?"

"I'm doing both jobs, Miss Amalfi. May I call you Angie?"

"Oh, yes, sir." She was taken aback; Mr. Preston was never familiar with his employees.

"I'd like to ask a favor of you, Angie, if I might?"

"Why, of course, Mr. Preston."

"Would you be my feature editor? Temporarily, of course. You do have a good eye for the offbeat and humorous, even though you're not a real newspaper type. Actually, you might work out at it quite well. Then the job would be yours permanently, if you were interested."

Her jaw fell. "Me?"

"I would appreciate it greatly. Got to keep things shipshape, you know, and that requires a top-notch first mate. I'm not one to run the day-to-day operation. Not my style. I prefer publishing to editing. What do you say, Angie? For George's sake?"

"For George?" Her head was spinning. Feature editor of the *Bay Area Shopper*. Could she handle it? Damn right she could! She was thrilled.

"I think your offer is overwhelming, Mr. Preston. Since, as you say, it is just temporary, I would be willing to do the job, just to help you out until you find a permanent replacement for George."

"Wonderful! Now, let me take you to dinner to celebrate!" He extended his hand to help her out of her chair.

She should go to Paavo's house in case he called. She took Preston's proffered hand and stood. "I'm sorry, but I—"

"Really, we must. I have lots of information and materials to give you. The sooner, the better and, frankly, I'm hungry." He lifted her jacket off the back of her chair and held it for her to slip on. She did so and then glanced at her watch.

"Won't it be a little late? I mean, won't your wife mind your talking business in the evening?"

"I was divorced last year." He smoothed the jacket over her shoulders, placed his hand against the small of her back, and guided her out the door. Her uneasiness grew.

The man was cloyingly well mannered, hovering over her as if ready to fulfill her smallest wish, while producing a constant stream of chatter as they rode down the elevator to the employee parking lot where his oversized Mercedes waited.

They went to an intimate and understated haute cuisine restaurant, where her casual Oscar de la Renta dress didn't appear out of place. He ordered dinner after carefully quizzing her about her feelings on each dish. When she looked at him with some exasperation, he said, "Some meals must be memorable, Angie," which struck her as rather odd.

The food was probably quite good, but she had no appetite and picked at it with her fork. As excited as she was about her new position, she couldn't keep her mind off Paavo. She wondered what he was doing, where he was—if he was safe. Had he arrested Crane yet? Was he home? What would he say when she told him she would be an editor?

Finally, she put down her fork. "I'm very tired, Mr. Preston. I must be terrible company. I really think I should go home. Perhaps we can continue our discussion tomorrow?"

"Of course I understand. I'm really quite grateful, Angie. The last thing in the world I want is that editor's job hanging over my head one more day! Believe me, I'll make it up to you."

He called for the check and then whisked her out of the restaurant.

The night was quite dark. The fog had rolled in early from the ocean, masking the stars and moonlight and blanketing the streets with a fine mist.

Preston put an arm around her shoulders. Angie found this offensive and stepped away from him. He flashed her a look—no, it couldn't have been as hostile as it had appeared. The fog surrounding the street lights must have created shadows on his face that made it look menacing. She shook away the start he had given her.

The man reeked with charm, money, and good looks. There was no reason she should feel uneasy around him. She gave him a bright smile as she climbed into his car.

29

"*Why are we* stopping here?" Angie asked.

Preston had pulled into the driveway of a Victorian mansion in Pacific Heights, high atop Jackson Street.

"This is my home."

Angie stiffened. "I'm sorry, Mr. Preston, but—"

"Relax, Angie. I'll just take a minute. I want to give you the spare keys to the *Shopper* offices. Now that you're my editor, I can get away for a couple of days on my yacht. I plan to start first thing in the morning, as a matter of fact. That is, if you'll allow me to give you the keys."

"Surely, others have keys."

"Who's in charge, Angie? You are."

His voice was smooth and reasonable. She felt quite foolish arguing with him.

His eyes widened. "Oh, dear! You aren't thinking I intend any untoward behavior, I hope."

Embarrassed at those exact thoughts, her face reddened as she shook her head.

"My dear, I hadn't thought . . . I mean, I never condone any fraternizing . . . I thought you knew. Well, I'd hoped to show off my antiques to someone who could appreciate them, but if you'd like, you can stay here in the car while I run inside. I didn't mean to discomfort you, Angie."

She felt like a first-class ninny. "It's all right. I'd love to come in."

"You trust me, then?"

"Of course."

"I'm gratified." He got out of the car, hurried to her side, and opened the door for her.

The house looked like a large, brown shingle-home from the outside, but the inside was breathtaking, filled with American antiques of a quality usually found only in museums, bright Oriental carpets, glistening hardwood floors, and primitive American artwork. Everything was perfectly placed and shining, as if on display. Angie stood in the doorway of what Preston called his parlor, hesitant to disturb the quiet ambience.

"Please, enter," he said.

"It's beautiful." She walked into the room and sat on a high-backed, thinly padded chesterfield. "I have a few antiques, too, but mine are English," she added. She thought of Paavo trying to sit in her little Hepplewhite armchair, and a feeling of disquiet filled her. She had to get away soon.

Preston talked about the pieces he owned,

clearly proud of them, as he poured them each a drink. He handed a Benedictine and brandy to Angie.

"My most treasured piece," he said, "is an eighteenth-century desk from Bavaria. It's absolutely exquisite."

Her curiosity was piqued.

"Would you like to see it?"

She nodded.

He smiled. "This way." He took her hand and led her to a narrow staircase.

"Up there?" Her gaze went to the dark upper hall.

"Two flights."

Angie bit her bottom lip and then followed him up the stairs. There's no reason to be afraid of Jon Preston, she told herself. Look at this house. He's obviously a paragon of civility.

At the top of the second landing was a long hallway with only two doors. He walked to the far one, opened it, then switched on the light. True to his word, in the center of the room, facing the grilled windows with a spectacular view of the bay and the Golden Gate Bridge, stood the massive desk.

Angie forgot her fears as she hurried to it and ran her fingers over the smooth, hand-rubbed wood. It was warm to the touch, with a dark patina of age. The top of the desk was slightly rippled near the front, where centuries of elbows and forearms had worn away the wood. Angie sat in the straight-backed chair and placed her own forearms on the desk top, smiling at the way they fit in the bowed areas.

"It's marvelous," she said, smiling at her boss. "Thank you for showing me."

"Thank you for your enjoyment," he replied. Then, as she moved to get up, he added, "Stay there. It's a good place to talk about work. You're a writer, after all." He walked to the leather sofa against the wall and sat down.

"I'm sorry, but I really don't have time—"

"But I was so curious, you see," Preston continued, "about your announcement this afternoon—about meeting your best fan."

Angie felt the room sway. She forced her face to remain immobile. "Yes, my fan, Mr. Crane. Do you know him?"

He laughed. "Not really. Tell me about him."

She hesitated. It can't be Jon Preston, she assured herself. He's just making conversation. "There's nothing to tell," she replied cheerily.

"But you will meet him?"

"I thought I would."

"And when will this 'date' take place?"

She sipped on her liqueur, buying time while she tried to figure out Preston's interest. "I'm waiting for him to contact me."

Preston stood. "I'm a patient man, Angie, but after all, you told the whole office you were meeting Crane. The only reason to proclaim it as loudly as you did was so I might hear you. And I did. Now I want to know when and where this meeting will take place."

"You!" Her voice was hushed, but her heart

pounded. She kept her eye on Preston as he walked around the desk.

He frowned, then shrugged as if throwing off all pretense. "Who else? I need to see Crane, but the man has gone into hiding, it seems. Actually, you've given me an idea, with all your talk about a meeting. I'd like you to write a recipe that will set up a meeting with Crane—one that I'll also attend. I know quite a bit of the code, but not all of it. I want to meet Crane tomorrow night about three A.M. in the Broadway tunnel. Lemon."

"Lemon?"

"Don't play coy! I know Lemon is the Broadway tunnel drop! What I don't know is how to write tomorrow night at three A.M."

"Neither do I!" She looked at him as if he were quite mad.

"Hah!" he snorted. "You expect me to believe that? You have managed to discern a certain relationship among Crane, Sammy Blade, and the mysterious someone who directs the entire operation at the *Shopper*. A neat piece of work, as they say. And you outdo yourself by knowing that the code is encased in some rather dreadful recipes. After all, you are a food columnist, surely competent enough to recognize the woeful deficiencies in a fake recipe when you read it."

Her face burned with anger and embarrassment. Did he think she had been derelict in her job in allowing these obviously imperfect recipes? But her readers had loved them! Or so, George had always told her.

"Write it!"

"I can't!" She shut her eyes as her mind raced, trying desperately to remember the pieces of the strange code she and Paavo had worked on.

He studied her, his eyes narrowing. "You're not a good liar, Angelina. You figured it out, all right."

He opened a drawer in the end table beside the sofa and removed a gun. He pointed it at her. "I'm tired of games, Angelina. Write your recipe, now. I've stopped the presses for tomorrow's *Shopper.* Right now, they're waiting for me to give them a last-minute change and the okay to finish tomorrow's paper. That means there's still time to get it printed in tomorrow's *Shopper,* time for Crane to see it and meet us. Do you understand?"

Holding the gun in his right hand, he pulled open a desk drawer and took out pen and paper with his left. "I want a recipe. Three A.M., tomorrow night."

She looked at the blank sheet with dread. "I don't know if I can."

"Do it."

It must have been the barrel of the gun that inspired her, for her mind had never been so quick. Tomorrow was the twenty-third of the month, and dates, Paavo had said, were indicated by quantity of milk. He'd said something odd about fractions. . . . Oh, hell, 23 cups should do it. The location was *lemon.* The only other ingredient with numbers attached was eggs, so that must be the time: three in the morning. Now all she had to figure out was the kind of recipe: waffle, omelet, blintz, or pancake. She had no idea. Her panic grew. Finally, she hit on one recipe that would at least catch Crane's attention. She wrote:

Stork Waffles
    23 cups milk
    3 *morning* fresh eggs
    splash lemon juice
    lots of flour
Mix and spoon onto waffle iron.

She handed the paper to Preston. As his gaze swept over the sheet, he lay his hand heavily on her shoulder, keeping her in place.

"Very simple, isn't it?" he said with a smirk. "By the way, you're not leaving."

She remained motionless as he walked toward the door. "Have a good sleep now," he said, nodding at her glass, and then left the room, locking the door behind him.

"What?" She looked at the glass and tried to stand. Her legs felt like rubber.

She stumbled toward the door. Numbness worked its way rapidly up her body. The door was locked and very solid. Her head felt light, and her breathing was labored. She slowly crossed the room to the windows. There was a sheer drop of at least four stories, as the house was built on a hill that sloped downward from the front to the back, with the backyard far below street level.

She put her face in her hands as she slipped to the floor. The lethargy coming over her dulled, at least a little bit, the fear of where she was . . . and what would happen to her . . . and when. . . .

30

Angie gasped, squeezed her eyes shut, and sat up, her hands flinging wildly about as she tried to ward off another drenching of the icy liquid on her face.

"Relax, it's only water." The arch tones of Jon Preston broke through her haze.

She opened her eyes and saw her publisher standing over her, an empty glass in his hand.

Wiping the water from her face, she tried to stand, but her legs were too weak to support her. She squinted from the throbbing in her head and the lights in the room. "What have you done?" she whispered.

"You'll be all right. Stop being so dramatic. It's time to get up. We've got a date with a bird."

She stared at him blankly.

"Crane, Angelina, you're going to meet Crane."

"Crane? That's tomorrow night."

"This is tomorrow night. Two A.M., in fact. You've been sleeping like a zombie for over twenty-four hours."

He's mad, she thought, quite mad.

"Look." He handed her the *Bay Area Shopper,* then flipped it quickly to page eight. There, in print, was her column with her recipe—"Stork Waffles." Preston wasn't lying. Slowly, she raised herself off the floor and onto the chair by the desk.

He pushed a mug in front of her. "I made you some strong coffee. You'll need to be alert to-night."

As she drank it, the cloudiness of her mind slowly cleared, and the memory of yesterday's insanity came back to her.

Preston was planning to take her to meet Crane, of that she was sure. Paavo would be fol-lowing Crane, she hoped, so he, too, would arrive at the rendezvous. If, however, Paavo had tried to reach her and hadn't been able to, he might have left Crane to go looking for her. Then, all would be lost.

She rubbed her hand over her face, trying to wipe away the fogginess.

"Let's go." Preston stood.

She blinked hard and rose, gripping the edge of the desk. Her legs felt weak and ready to buckle. "Let me freshen up, at least."

"There's a bathroom on this floor. You've got five minutes."

No escape, she thought, there was nothing she could do now but go with him—and pray.

Steps and banisters, large oil paintings, and antiques flashed before Angie's eyes as Preston dragged her through his house. She stopped, face to face with a massive grandfather clock. It was two forty-five.

She heard the mellow sound of a foghorn on the bay as he led her at gunpoint out of the house to his car. Shivering, she sat quietly as he drove the few blocks to the entrance to the Broadway tunnel, a long cavern traversing Russian Hill from Polk Gulch to North Beach. The streets of the city were empty, and the fog was still heavy in the dark, moonless night. The dull drowsiness which had bothered Angie before was gone now. Every one of her nerves was alive and tense.

As Preston parked at the North Beach side of the tunnel entrance, Angie strained toward the nightclub sector of Broadway, hoping to see someone, anyone, who might help her. Only a couple of cold neon signs still blinked. The rest were darkened, as even Broadway seemed to slumber at this hour.

He got out of the car, hurried around to Angie's side, and pulled her out. "Come this way," he ordered.

"Where are we going?" She tried to free her arm.

"Inside. We wouldn't want any curious souls to be hurt by mistake, now, would we?"

She followed him to the narrow walkway lining one side of the tunnel. As they went deeper into it, the tunnel curved slightly, and the night sky soon disappeared, leaving no light but a few dingy, yellow bulbs casting a jaundiced pall against the dirty tile walls. It seemed she had been here before, but her head still ached, and she couldn't quite remember. . . .

"Isn't this far enough?" she asked. She felt like they had been walking forever.

Preston smiled, his too-perfect teeth throwing off a skeletal glow in the strange lighting. "I'm going to snare him, harpoon him like Ahab did the white whale. But I will be victorious!"

He held her arm, nearly dragging her as they continued deeper into the tunnel. With every step, her conviction that Paavo and the police would not be able to stop this madness grew.

Finally, Preston patted her arm and chuckled. "Our destination awaits you. The door straight ahead is a service entrance. This tunnel is lined with them. They provide easy access, and escape. We wouldn't want to be trapped here, now would we?"

"No," she whispered, a sinking feeling striking her, "no, of course not."

He pulled out his gun again. "On the other hand, you really need not be concerned with how to leave. You won't, you see."

She felt cold, hopeless. "You killed George, didn't you?"

He shrugged. "Curiosity killed George Meyers. I just pulled the trigger. He was curious as to why I took an interest in some putrid little recipes in a rather pitiful food column. Then, after your bomb blast and your telling him that Sam would no longer give you recipes, he began putting bits of information together—and questioning me, of all things! Well, that was that."

Angie blanched.

Preston unlocked the small door tucked unobtrusively in the side of the tunnel, and Angie peered inside. A metal ladder went straight up to a manhole cover in the street high above. "It's amazing what a few dollars can buy," Preston said, fingering the key he had just used before dropping it in his jacket pocket. "Face the North Beach entrance. I want Crane to recognize you."

He stepped into the service area and pulled her arm back, pinning her against the outside of the door. He hid behind the door, out of danger, but still able to see what was happening. She was held securely by him, and his gun wasn't far away. Even though a couple of cars drove by, she knew they could give her no assistance.

"Why am I here?" she pleaded. "Why couldn't you wait for Crane alone?"

"You know too much. I can't have any loose ends. Crane now knows you figured out his code, so he'll be coming to get rid of you. I'll let him. I wouldn't want to have to hurt you myself, Angelina. I've always been quite fond of you, you see. I even tried to save you.

"The gunman I hired knew you saw him in the park when he killed Sammy Blade. When I heard he sent you the bomb, I forced him to stop. I persuaded him to scare you away with the car chase and dead pigeon. He wasn't satisfied, though. I told him about your cousin's big society wedding so that he'd go to your apartment and remove Edward Crane's recipes, but it seems he also used it as an opportunity to send you some poison champagne. You were lucky, but smart enough to run. Next thing I knew, I was so surprised to get your column from Bodega. I must have mentioned it to him . . . inadvertently, of course."

Of course! The sound of his voice made her flesh clammy.

"Once Crane is through with you," Preston continued, "he, too, will die. I'll simply walk up the stairs and go home, finally free of him!"

"Free? What do you mean?"

"What I mean is, he's a greedy little bastard! I told him we had to stop, but he refused. No one defies me."

"Stop what?"

"The automatics, the AK-47's, the Uzis, of course."

"Guns?"

"What else? At first, it was all so simple, you see. I've got a yacht. In a way, it's too bad you'll never see it, you would have appreciated it. Well, naturally, the Coast Guard wouldn't dream of searching a Preston yacht, so it was child's play to bring the guns into the country. Crane had connections with four groups with unlimited needs and money. A bizarre twist of fate actually made Crane and me a rather perfect team."

"And then?"

"Well, then I guess you'd say Crane's luck began to run out. You see, I was quite clever. I set this up so Crane and I both had people we could hide behind while I pulled all the strings. Mine was George Meyers and Crane's was Sammy Blade. Blade was just a go-between, to bring you recipes that were codes to announce a 'sales' meeting with one of Crane's four groups. Unfortunately, Blade had a police record and ties with one of the less savory groups to whom Crane sold the guns. The police started looking at him far too closely, and, even though he didn't know much about the meaning of the packages he delivered, he became increasingly nervous. I could not depend on the arrangement to last forever."

Preston sighed wearily before continuing. "It all became so very messy I decided to simply rid myself of Blade and Crane. I hired a supposedly reputable assassin to do it." Preston snorted. "He wasn't very good, as it turned out."

Angie felt sickened by everything she had heard. The man talked about murder as dispassionately as if he were discussing having his suits dry-cleaned. Still, she needed to know more. "So you wanted Crane dead because you were afraid Blade would lead the police to Crane, and Crane would lead them to you?"

"Exactly. And it almost happened. A homicide detective came across a connection between Blade and Crane in the Tenderloin."

"You killed Matt!" She spat out the words, anguish filling every one of them.

"The assassin pulled the trigger. At least he didn't botch that job! Ah, it's three o'clock. Crane is always meticulously punctual. Face the entrance. He should be here any moment."

They waited in silence. Before long, a car entered the tunnel. The roar of the engine grew louder and louder as it approached. Preston's grip tightened on her arm as she tried to step back into the service area, but he held her in place. The headlights came closer. Her body slumped, and her breathing practically stopped. When the car reached her, she put her hand to her face and cried out. The car sped by, not slowing its pace in the slightest.

She lowered her hands. Her body was quaking so much she could barely stand. Spots danced before her eys.

Another car approached. She was numb, unable to feel or react as she stood, mesmerized by the headlights that neared her. At the last moment, again, she cried out, but that car didn't stop either.

Tears rolled down her face. "Don't do this, Mr. Preston, please."

She heard her voice as if from a great distance, hysteria close to the surface, her tears falling as she stood there, trapped.

The sound of a car engine caught her attention. It revved high and fast, then slowed. That was when she knew it was Crane. The other cars had come through at an even clip, but this one hesitated and then sped up, as if searching for something, or someone. Her body tensed to a snapping point, as Preston's grip tightened, holding her in front of him.

The car stopped, the headlights went off, and the car door swung open. Then, slowly, Crane stepped out and began walking toward her. In the yellowed dimness of the tunnel's light she could see his ashen face as he approached. "Miss Amalfi." His high whining voice pierced the night air. "You called?"

She saw the revolver in his hand.

"Don't!" she screamed, panic overtaking her as she raised her free arm over her face, while trying desperately to break Preston's hold. The roar of another car speeding into the tunnel filled the cavern. Crane's eyes flickered with confusion, and he hesitated, unsure what was happening.

The Austin Healey screeched to a halt beside Crane, and Paavo was out of the car in a moment, his gun pointed. "Drop it, Crane. Police."

Crane let his gun fall to the ground as soon as he heard the word *police*. "This must be a mistake, Officer, I haven't done a thing," he said, ready to say more until he recognized Paavo. Then he stopped talking.

Paavo took a step toward him, glancing at Angie. "I hope you know what you're doing," he said to her. Then his eyes narrowed slightly as he looked again at her pale face and the unnatural way she was standing.

Preston held her so tightly, she couldn't move. Her eyes smarted from the pain. She prayed he'd run up the stairs away from here to escape and leave her and the rest of them alone. She waited, her every nerve attuned to Preston's slightest move. She was afraid to cry out, afraid any sound might cause Preston to start shooting. Instead, she tried to give Paavo a warning with her eyes.

Paavo was backing up, having recognized that something was very wrong, when Angie felt Preston make his move. As he opened the service door a crack wider, she realized the unarmed Crane was no threat to him, that it was Paavo he would be after.

"Run!" she screamed, wrenching herself free from Preston's grasp and stumbling, falling, as she ran toward Paavo. Preston's shot rang out. Paavo dived to the floor—too late.

Angie screamed as she saw the bullet hit him. She stood, unbelieving, the scream and the gunshot blast reverberated, through the tunnel, over and over.

The force of the bullet spun Paavo so that he lay on his back, his eyes shut and his face deathly white as his shirt and jacket turned blood red.

"No!" The anguished cry tore from her as she ran blindly to his side, dropped to her knees, and flung herself across him, her arms spread wide, desperately trying to shelter his body with her own, expecting, fearing, more shots from Preston's gun.

Behind her, she heard the sound of running footsteps, the revving of a car engine, the squeal of tires, and then more gunshots, shouts, and cries. She turned her head to see Preston shooting at Crane's departing car, and the car swerving wildly as it made its way to the exit.

Paavo's gun was inches away, where it had dropped as he'd fallen. Her eyes darted from Preston to the gun. She crawled to it, picked it up, and then backed up so that her body was between Paavo and Jon Preston. She raised the gun, holding it firmly with both hands straight out in front of her.

As Crane's car disappeared from the tunnel, Preston turned around slowly, his compressed lips thin and white, his eyes red with insane fury. He sneered at her holding the gun, kneeling on the ground beside the fallen policeman. Then a smile spread across his face. "You wouldn't have the nerve." He smirked as he raised his gun to take careful aim at Angie.

Angie hesitated but a moment and then squeezed the trigger. The recoil snapped through her body as a deafening roar sounded and the smell of gunpowder filled the air. Preston staggered, looking shocked. Time stopped. She watched his expression.

He fell forward, his gun clanging loudly against the pavement. Angie sank back on her heels, unable to move. She was vaguely aware of the screech of car tires, of white, garish lights from headlamps filling the tunnel, of drivers huddled on the ground out of the lines of fire. Those people had cried out and screamed as the bullets flew, but now they fell silent.

She dropped the gun and turned again to Paavo. She felt more scared than ever before in her life. He was still breathing; he was alive. Slipping one arm under his head, she cradled it as tears fell from her eyes. "Get an ambulance, somebody, please!" she cried. No one moved.

The flow of blood was incredible. Her free hand went to Paavo's chest, trying to stop it, but she couldn't. "Help me! Somebody!" Her cries echoed.

His eyelids flickered open briefly at her touch. "Angie," he whispered, "couldn't find you . . . couldn't. . . ."

"Don't talk," she said, her words forced past the lump in her throat as police sirens filled the tunnel.

"Go," he said. "I don't want you to . . . to remember this. . . ."

"No," she replied. He had shut his eyes again. She felt as if her heart had stopped. "Paavo!" she sobbed as two policemen hurried to him.

They worked quickly, letting her remain at his side as they applied what aid they could.

She looked at his blood on her hands. The spiraling red lights of the police car flashed every second at her and turned the entire tunnel a garish, blood-red color. It was a nightmare, but this one she could not awaken from. . . .

Desperation filled her, and her own helplessness made her frantic. "Help him!" she cried to the other policemen. "Please, help him."

After what seemed an eternity, an ambulance arrived and he was lifted into it. Angie climbed in beside him.

31

Paavo was rushed into the operating room. Angie ran by his side until the nurses stopped her from going farther.

They showed her to the waiting room, where she remained alone, no one approaching her until Chief Hollins arrived. He was followed by Inspector Calderon, who took her statement.

An hour later, Officer Crossen entered the hospital with Aulis Kokkonen, who looked dazed. When he saw Angie, recognition and gratitude filled his face. He walked to her side and took both her hands in his. "I heard you helped my boy," he said.

"He helped me." She choked on the words as she spoke, tears falling. "He saved my life."

Kokkonen only nodded.

A lifetime seemed to pass before a doctor entered the room to tell Kokkonen and Hollins that

Inspector Smith was out of surgery and in intensive care. The bullet had missed his heart, but it had done some damage to one lung, and a considerable amount of damage to the area below his left shoulder. He had lost a lot of blood. His condition was critical.

The group breathed a collective sigh of relief that he had survived the surgery. Angie looked at the faces of the men who had come to wait and realized that Paavo was more than a fellow officer to them.

Inspector Calderon was actually rather gentle as he told her that Preston was dead and Crane mildly wounded in the arm. The gunshot had caused Crane to lose control of his car just outside the tunnel, where he had been quickly apprehended.

Angie and Calderon spoke a long time about Preston. Calderon seemed worried about her reaction to the news of his death, and she understood why—but Calderon hadn't been in that tunnel. She had no regrets over what she did, only regrets that she had had no other choice. If she had not stopped Preston, he would have killed her and Paavo. Someone else would have had to go after him, and possibly that life would have been lost. She had never understood Paavo, Matt, and all the others as well as she had at that moment in the tunnel when she picked up the gun.

Calderon left, and Chief Hollins sat beside her. He complained that his men never listened to him anymore. He had told Paavo to take a vacation, and instead he had nearly gotten himself killed. Hollins declared he should go in and finish the job, and then he had a little trouble with his nose and eyes, and fumbled with his handkerchief a bit before walking away.

The two officers who had retrieved Angie's car from the *Shopper*'s parking lot talked with her awhile, and then they, too, left her to join the other policemen in the room.

Finally Angie sat alone, waiting.

The hospital slowly filled with the light of morning, but no word was forthcoming from the doctors.

Aulis Kokkonen took her arm, slowly leading her into the corridor, away from the others.

"Young lady." He patted one of her hands, his bright turquoise eyes looking at her deeply, as if searching her heart. "I must speak with you. My boy told me the two of you are planning to go your separate ways."

She was surprised that Paavo would have spoken to Aulis about her.

He continued. "If this is what you want, then do it now. Don't see Paavo again. If . . . if he survives, then the break will have been made cleanly. That will be best for Paavo's sake. He expects it. . . . Now, go home and rest. You are exhausted. We will telephone you when there is news."

He patted her hand again and walked away.

She stood there, watching him go, the words he had spoken echoing in her ears.

She walked blindly through the hospital corridors. Paavo thought she was going back to her old way of life, back to her old friends, her family, Stanfield, and the others. He expected it of her, just as she expected he'd be glad to be rid of her.

Aulis was telling her to decide. If she wanted to leave, then do it now. Aulis said for Paavo's sake, it would be the best time. For Paavo's sake. . . .

Angie reached her car, not quite sure how she found it. A chilling breeze swept the air, and she shielded her eyes as she looked at the bright morning sky. It was a typical November morning. Pulling her jacket close about her, she got into the car and drove to Mission Dolores.

As she entered the nave of the church, all was quiet. The comforting smell of incense filled the air. A couple of old women dressed in black were sitting in the pews, softly praying. Angie placed her fingertips in the holy water to cross herself, then walked to the statue of Mary.

"I promised I'd be back," she whispered. She put some money into the collection box and lit five candles for Paavo, then looked up at the serene face of the statue.

She shut her eyes a moment, swaying slightly, and then sank to her knees on the step, tightly gripping the railing as she bowed her head in prayer.

After the church, she stopped by his house to see if everything was all right and to feed Hercules. She left as soon as she could, unable to bear the desolation she felt as she looked around the house at Paavo's things.

When she returned to her apartment, the quiet seemed abnormal. No Joey or Rico to clutter up her life. The sofa looked strangely empty. It's funny, the things one can become accustomed to, she thought.

A telephone call to the hospital told her Paavo was still unconscious. She knew gunshot wounds of this type were a terrible blow to the body and could bring death from shock or infection as well as from the bodily damage done by the bullet. It frightened her.

She wandered into the den, determined to get her mind off the hospital. She couldn't. There was nowhere she could go to forget Paavo . . . nowhere far enough away. . . .

In the bedroom, it was worse. On the night-stand, in a small vase, was the rose Paavo had given her the night of Matt's death. She remembered his tears for his friend, and now . . . The petals had withered, and all but a few lay on the tabletop. She picked them up and placed them, one by one, in the palm of her hand. She sat down on the bed, and her gaze fell to her dress, red with blood.

About an hour later, the telephone rang. Her heart nearly stopped, afraid of what she might hear. She picked up the receiver.

"Miss Amalfi? Calderon."

"Yes?"

"I thought you'd want to know. He regained

consciousness a little while ago. The doctors say the prognosis is good."

"Thank God," she whispered.

Exhausted, unable to do or feel anything more, she lay back on the bed covers and in a short time was granted the forgetfulness of sleep.

32

It was evening when she returned to the hospital. The waiting room was empty, except for Officer Crossen, who rose and approached her as she entered.

"Looks like he's going to be okay. He awoke a few hours ago. Mr. Kokkonen is sitting with him now."

"You're sure?"

"That's what the doctor said."

Heaving a sigh of relief, she sat on a lounge chair.

"Say, Crane's singing like a bird," Crossen said. "He wants to get out of this by laying the whole thing on Preston."

Angie looked up at Crossen. She had almost forgotten about Crane.

"Crane said Preston had connections with a gun supplier, and Crane knew some groups wanting to buy them. He used your recipes to contact them and set up the drop. Trouble was, Preston got nervous and decided to do away with anyone who could trace the gun smuggling to him—Crane, you, and Sammy Blade. After Blade's murder and the bomb attack on you, Crane went into hiding."

Angie didn't want to hear about it any more. "Are you sure Paavo, I mean, Inspector Smith, will be all right?" she asked again.

Crossen smiled at her insistent question. "He won't be running up and down dark tunnels for a while. And he'll probably get another commendation. These gun smugglers have been wanted by the Feds for some time now. Finding them is a real coup. But other than that, and a stiff shoulder on foggy San Francisco nights, it seems he'll be okay."

Angie sighed with relief and ran her fingers through her hair in what she immediately recognized as a very Paavo kind of gesture.

Crossen coughed self-consciously. "The Inspector was awake for a while. A few of us stuck our heads in to say hello."

"You mean he can have visitors?" She hadn't even asked, not expecting to be allowed to see him.

"Only for a minute. Except Mr. Kokkonen—he's been there for hours."

"I see." Her gaze drifted to the hallway that led to Paavo's room.

"When Mr. Kokkonen comes out, I'll take him home. He's been here all day."

She sat, unsure what to do. She didn't want to interrupt Aulis, and had no idea how he'd react to seeing her here—or Paavo's reaction, for that matter. She had never been one to feel intimidated by any other person, but then again, she had never cared so much about another person either. She was intimidated now. Maybe she should just go home.

Crossen caught her eye. He seemed about to say something, but he turned away and began to pace the floor.

Finally, Crossen turned toward her.

"Miss Amalfi, I've been in there with the inspector a few times this afternoon, sort of keeping an eye on the old man, you know. I've watched people go in that room to visit. Each time the door opened the inspector would perk up, see who it was, then sort of sink back into the bed. It was as if whoever he was hoping to see never showed up."

Her brows knitted as he spoke. "I hope I'm not being presumptions, ma'am," he continued, "but I think seeing you will do him a lot more good than seeing all the rest of us put together."

She felt her heart do handsprings. "Do you, Officer Crossen?"

"I do, ma'am."

She stood, biting her bottom lip as she smoothed her jacket. She felt as if a thousand butterflies had taken flight in the pit of her stomach.

She walked down the long hallway to the door and then stopped. What if Crossen was wrong? What if she was wrong and misunderstood the whole situation? What if Paavo really didn't want to see her again?

There was only one way to find out.

She pushed the door open. The first one she saw

was Aulis, his face sad and worried. When he saw her, he looked puzzled, and then he smiled and nodded, slowly standing and walking toward the door. As he passed her, he placed a hand on her shoulder and gave it a squeeze, his eyes sparkling. Quietly, he left the room.

Paavo's eyes were shut. His skin was colorless, except for the dark areas below his eyes. His arm, shoulder, and chest were covered with bandages, and he was hooked up to a tangle of tubes. She gasped, foolishly not expecting what she saw. They lied! she thought. They told me he was all right, but he isn't.

She slowly approached the bed. Paavo opened his eyes. He blinked in confusion for a moment and then seemed to remember all too well where he was and why he felt so bad. He winced and turned his head. His eyes caught hers.

His wide, blue, translucent eyes had the same effect on her as ever. Her emotions were so full she thought she'd burst. Unsure as to what she should do, she stood staring into them, thinking she'd never seen anything so beautiful. Until he smiled.

The smile washed over her, flooding her with relief. In his gaze she saw love, desire, anticipation, and perhaps, a little admiration. Her own eyes grew misty as she took a step toward him, wanting to speak—but, somehow, no words seemed adequate. She, who always had so much to say, stood mute, overwhelmed by her love for him and her relief that he would really be all right.

"Little Angel," he whispered. "I thought you'd gone."

"Never." She blinked hard, trying to keep back the tears that threatened.

"Never. . . . That's a long time, Angie."

"And still not long enough," she said softly.

He looked at her as if he couldn't believe what he was hearing. "It's all wrong for us."

"I can't leave you, Paavo. I tried to listen to you—but I can't go. I love you." Her voice caught.

He remained silent a moment. "Angie," he said finally, "come over here."

She moved to his side.

A grin played on his lips and he cocked one eyebrow. "That's the first time you've done what I've asked without an argument."

She smiled. She had to put her hands to her eyes to wipe her tears. "That's only because you've always asked the wrong thing."

"Maybe," he whispered, "maybe when I get out of here I'll be able to ask the right questions. . . ."

Her heart pounded. His words were spoken as if they were a joke, but his eyes were deadly serious as he studied her reaction. Her fingers intertwined with his. "I'll be waiting, Inspector Smith."

His features relaxed into a smile as he let out the breath he had been holding, and then his hand tightened on hers. "Miss Amalfi, I do love you."

Angie reached for the chair at the foot of the bed, pulled it up beside him, and sat, wrapping his hand in both of hers. Their eyes met, and no more words were needed.